主编/何　烨　何江胜　刘长江

这样说

——新视角大学英语口语突破（下）

Speak This Way

—Oral English from a New Perspective (II)

科学出版社

北京

图书在版编目（CIP）数据

这样说：新视角大学英语口语突破（下）/ 何烨，何江胜，刘长江主编. —北京：科学出版社，2011.5

ISBN 978-7-03-030897-9

Ⅰ. 这… Ⅱ. ①何…②何…③刘… Ⅲ. 英语－口语－高等学校－教学参考资料 Ⅳ. H319.9

中国版本图书馆CIP数据核字（2011）第073569号

责任编辑：阎　莉　张　迪 / 责任校对：郭瑞芝
责任印制：赵德静 / 封面设计：无极书装

联系电话：010-6401 9007 / 电子邮箱：zhangdi@mail.sciencep.com

科学出版社出版
北京东黄城根北街 16 号
邮政编码：100717
http://www.sciencep.com

源海印刷有限责任公司 印刷

科学出版社发行　各地新华书店经销

*

2011年5月第 一 版　　开本：787×1092　1/16
2011年5月第一次印刷　　印张：12
印数：1—6 000　　　　　字数：370 000

定价：32.00元
（含1张MP3光盘）
（如有印装质量问题，我社负责调换）

前　言

　　非英语专业大学生英语口头表达能力不强是当今外语教育中的一大关切。对此，教育部已明确指出"大学英语教学的目标是培养学生的英语综合应用能力，尤其是听说能力，使他们在今后的工作和社会交往中能用英语进行有效的口头和书面的信息交流，……"（《大学英语课程教学要求》试行，2004年）。大学生英语口头表达能力是英语综合应用能力的一个重要方面，怎样提高，是一个值得研究的大课题。

　　早期的结构主义教学理论提倡学习者学习语言规则，尤其语法规则，认为学习者学会了语言规则，就可以生成无限的句子。英语口语中的句型教学就是一个典型体现。后来的功能语言学教学理论则强调人际功能和语篇功能的作用，教学重点由语言规则和理想的话语转向语境和情景。英语口语中的情景教学、功能意念教学是其集中表现。以上两种教学理论和实践有其合理性，能取得一定的教学效果，但各有其不足。结构主义理论中的口语教学易忽略语言的实际交际，难以完成理想的交际任务；功能语言学理论中的口语教学涉及的语境和情景，大多与人们最基本的生活需求，诸如谈天气、打电话、去机场、上邮局、下餐馆等有关。两者对语言所载的文化知识的教学都不够，学生所掌握的谈话内容显得不足。学生只能学会一些固定的句型和简单场景下的生存会话，而在超越一些简单的生活场景，进入文化话题交流时，他们往往话语不多、甚至无话可说。这才是真正意义上的言时少物、甚至无物的"哑巴英语"。

　　本书是一本以文化话题为主线的口语教材，力求传授日常生活中、社会热点话题下的语言知识和文化知识，培养学习者在交际中能较丰富地表达思想，谈论观点，阐述见解的能力。本书的话题在我校三级起点的部分大学英语口语教学班上用过，学生通过一个学期（32学时）的课程学习，明显感到对有关话题的表达有话可说了，表达的内容丰富了，表达的思想深刻了。

　　本书有15个文化话题，涉及英语学习、兴趣爱好、友谊、父母与子女、宠物、食品、能源、广告、妇女、旅游、艺术、社会问题、经济、信息技术、文化。编写体例有：

　　1. 对话：有两篇对话，反映单元话题的相关话语；

　　2. 问题与回答：有15个与话题相关的问题和简要回答，它们与大学英语四、六级口语考试（Spoken English Test）中的话题有关；

3. 看图说话：给出与话题相关的3张图片和简短描述，它们与大学英语四、六级口语中的话题有关；

4. 相关段落：列出5篇与话题相关的段落，提供更多话题范围内的知识。

本书适合英语爱好者学习语言知识和文化知识，扩大文化视野，丰富思想表达；同时还有助于在校大学生准备国家大学英语四、六级口语考试，提高口语考试成绩。

编 者

2011年2月

Contents

Topic One   English Study

Part One: Dialogues

 Dialogue 1   Paper Dictionary vs Electronic Dictionary

(Jack is on his way to the university library carrying his dictionary.)

Jack: Why do you always carry such a thick dictionary with you, a walking dictionary?

Mike: It's my friend.

Jack: Why not get an electronic one? It's lighter.

Mike: You're right. Compared with paper dictionary, an electronic one is portable. But I'm used to finding words in a paper dictionary.

Jack: What's the difference between a paper dictionary and an electronic one? I don't have a paper dictionary.

Mike: You get the word definition from the electronic one. That's all.

Jack: That's what we want.

Mike: No, actually what we need is far more than a list of meanings. In different contexts, or different collocations, the meaning of a word varies, although slightly. A paper dictionary usually provides us with a complete list of meanings and corresponding examples. We read these examples and find out how the word is used in different contexts. With a simple list of meanings in an electronic dictionary, the usage of a word is not clear. Let's take the word "adapt" as an example. What does your electronic dictionary tell you for the meaning?

Jack: (Takes out his electronic dictionary, and punches the keys). Here we go, it means "改编和适用".

Mike: Does it tell you how "adapt" is used in different collocations?

Jack: No.

Mike: That's the difference. "Adapt" means "modify" when it is used in the collocation "adapt sth." (for sth.), whereas in the collocation "adapt to sth.", it means "become adjusted to new conditions."

Jack: You've got your point across. I see the reason why you always have a good mastery of vocabulary.

Mike: Besides, the paper dictionary offers other things such as English meanings, word classes, synonyms and antonyms.

Jack: The electronic dictionary has an obvious advantage. It can "talk". Every word is pronounced. And it's useful for learners to know how to pronounce every word. Learners can learn to pronounce difficult words such as bourgeois, fiancée and psychologist.

Mike: (Smiling) That is why your pronunciation is so good.

◆ Dialogue 2　Making a Speech

(Alice has taken part in the university's speech contest. She is asking Natalie, last year's champion, for advice.)

Alice: Hi, Natalie, I am a sophomore at the college of computer science.

Natalie: Hey, nice to meet you. What can I do for you?

Alice: This year, I've entered the university's speech contest. But I have no experience in making speeches. Last year, you gave a wonderful speech in the speech contest and everyone was impressed. So, I am wondering if you could give me some advice and suggestions.

Natalie: Oh, you are flattering me. Thank you. I think, first of all, you have to be fully prepared.

Alice: And how do I go about this?

Natalie: Do some research on the topic you are going to make a speech about and write a clear, concise and convincing draft.

Alice: I have read some famous speeches, like the ones made by Winston Churchill, Abraham Lincoln and Martin Luther King. I was impressed by Martin Luther King's "I Have A Dream".

Natalie: The parallel structure of "I Have A Dream" highlights his message. People take it as an excellent model. But you should be cautious if you try to use it.

Alice: Why?

Natalie: Speakers use it a lot and it has become a cliché rather than a provocative expression.

Alice: Ok, now what do you mean by doing research?

Natalie: Reading speeches by famous speakers is definitely helpful. At the same time, you should read widely and get useful, insightful and original ideas and then form strong arguments for your speeches. It is important for you to base your opinions on convincing arguments. In this way, your speech will be stronger and more effective.

Alice: Good. Besides, there are some technical things I'd like to ask you about. For example, what kind of gestures should I use? How important is body language? Where should I look when I'm addressing a large group?

Natalie: That's a good question. Usually, speakers behave awkwardly on stage the first few times. I think the first thing you are going to do is to calm down after you step on stage. Then maintain eye contact with your audience. Don't stare at the ceiling or look at your notes. As for gestures, just make them fit the occasion. Don't overdo it.

Alice: Should I put my hands on the table?

Natalie: You could. But don't grip the lectern. Once I saw a speaker gripping the desk so tightly that it shook. Just have confidence in yourself and behave naturally.

Alice: That's easier said than done, but thanks a lot.

Natalie: You're welcome. Good luck.

Words and Expressions

walking dictionary		活字典	
portable	*adj.*	方便携带的	
corresponding	*adj.*	对应的	
collocation	*n.*	搭配	
synonym	*n.*	同义词	
antonym	*n.*	反义词	
bourgeois	*adj.*	资产阶级的	
fiancée	*n.*	未婚妻	
psychologist	*n.*	心理学家	
sophomore	*n.*	大学二年级	
flatter	*v.*	吹捧	
Winston Churchil		温斯顿·丘吉尔，英国传记作家、历史学家、政治家。	

Abraham Lincoln	亚伯拉罕·林肯，美国第16任总统，首位共和党总统。
Martin Luther King	马丁·路德·金著名的美国民权运动领袖，1964年度诺贝尔和平奖获得者，有"金牧师"之称。

provocative	*adj.*	煽动性的
insightful	*adj.*	有洞察力的

Part Two: Related Questions with Suggested Answers

1. Why do you think we should learn English nowadays?

English is a global language and it's a channel to communicate with the outside world. To scholars, international conferences are mainly conducted in the English language and most of the latest scientific research results are published in English. To business people, without

English, will run into communication blocks and therefore trade can't be conducted globally. To travelers, the literacy of English guarantees their oversea journey smoother and more meaningful. You need English when you want to book tickets and hotels, to consult travel agencies, to plan your itinerary and even to ask your way. To Chinese students, English becomes a prerequisite to success. Firstly, English is a compulsory course set by the State Ministry of Education. Secondly, no companies will be pleased to hire potential employees who are poor at English. Thirdly, if you want to go abroad to pursue your further studies, you need to take either A TOEFL or GRE. All these tests challenge candidates to do better in English.

2. What are some of the important language skills for English learners? Why are they important?

Learning any language involves four basic skills: speaking, listening, reading and writing. If you want to understand a foreign language and make yourself understood, you must master the four basic skills. In my opinion, listening and speaking are the most basic skills for English learners. It's said that in learning English well listening and speaking should be given first priority to and reading and writing come next. Let's first think about our first language study. Long before we can read and write, we are able to understand what our parents, family members say. So it's the same with second language learning. For English learners, it's essential to improve their listening and speaking ability before they are able to achieve high English proficiency.

3. How do your English teachers use multi-media technique to teach English in your university or school?

Firstly, my English teachers use PPT as a teaching aid in classroom teaching. In class, my teachers give us background information, teach language points and analyze structures of texts with the PPT they created. Let me take the background information part as an example, my teachers not only provide written description of background information, but also show us some video clips containing background information. In this way, we get both audio and visual stimulation. The use of PPT in classrooms gives us more information and makes learning more interesting. Also my teachers recommend us a lot of useful English study websites for after-class studying.

4. Do you do online learning in learning English? How does online learning help you improve your English?

Online learning, first of all, motives me. Before the computer entered the realm of language study, we were forced to learn English through battling with ponderous textbooks. Online learning, however, gives us visual, audio stimulus and authentic materials. I read, listen and watch both for recreation and language learning. Secondly, I can set my own speed and arrange my own schedule. In a classroom, we have to follow the teacher's paces. In online learning, however, I make my own schedules. Lastly, I feel relaxed when I learn English online. When I am surrounded by my peers and face my English teacher in a classroom, I feel rather anxious because my English is poor. If I can't answer teacher's questions, I feel more upset. However, in online learning I don't have the pressure. The learning atmosphere is relaxing. When I face difficulties and could not answer certain questions, I may consult reference books and ask for help from the learning forum where there are always good English learners online. Since we don't face each other, I don't need to think much about my "face". Online learning is really a good way for students who get nervous and anxious to keep face.

5. Which is a more effective way for students to learn English, classroom learning or autonomous learning?

Well, it's hard to say one is more effective than the other. In autonomous learning, learners need to have self-discipline. They manage their studies by adjusting their learning strategies to facilitate learning. Learning is done according to learners' time, interests and capability. Then what is the focus of classroom learning? These teachers tend to take more initiative and play their authoritative roles. As a result, students take passive roles and are more likely to be spoon-fed. Generally speaking, autonomous learning combined with classroom learning is good for learners to achieve high language proficiency.

6. Students nowadays are encouraged to pay more attention to listening and speaking in English learning. Why are the skills of listening and speaking more important than other skills?

It is said that listening and speaking go first, reading and writing follow. Listening and speaking are the most basic language skills in language learning. With listening and speaking it is possible for language learners to achieve basic communication. For many years, our Chinese students focus on only reading, neglecting listening and speaking. The result is that we are tongue-tied when we meet a foreign guest. We can't understand each other or communicate effectively.

7. Every year there is a "CCTV Cup" English Speaking Contest for college students. Why is it good for students to improve their English?

The "CCTV Cup" English Speaking Contest is held annually and draws quite a lot of attentions from our college students. Eagerness to enter this contest is on the rise among my friends and classmates in these years as more and more college students realize that speaking skill is very important. Last year, I joined the preliminary contest (the first round) held on campus. The topic was Beijing, Olympics 2008. Before the contest, I did a lot of research about Olympic Games, focused my topic on Green Olympics and then wrote my own speech draft. After that, I discussed my draft with my foreign teacher, Amy. Besides, I learned to express my ideas on the importance of hosting a Green Olympics in simple but provocative language. During the process of writing and revising the draft and rehearsing my speech, I learned how to write out a speech and how to express myself and at the same time I realized my weakness in language learning. Now I try to improve my pronunciation as I come from the west part of China with a strong accent even when I speak in English. This year I am going to enter the contest again. The "CCTV Cup" English Speaking Contest provides us with a great opportunity to boost our learning interests and enhance our English skills.

8. In English learning, students are supposed to take some exams. How do you usually prepare for English exams?

Exams are a necessary but excruciating form of torture. In the past years, we experienced a lot of exams. In the process, we learned how to take them. Now let me share my experience of taking CET-4 with you. First of all, remember as many new words and phrases as possible. By that I don't mean that we remember them mechanically. I mean that you can remember more than 4,000 new words by reading. Learning new words in context is the first step. The next step is to practice our listening in our spare time. Now, the CET-4 exams have a high standard of listening for candidates and the listening part accounts for almost 40% of the total scores. If we fail in this part, we have few chances to pass the exam, let alone getting a high score. Lastly, I want to say that practicing our speaking skill is also important for candidates. The qualification scores for Spoken English Test is 550 for CET-4 and 520 for CET-6. That kind of tests is very demanding. If you don't want to disappoint yourself, work hard to improve your speaking skills.

9. You have had English teachers who taught you English with different methods. Tell us one of the teachers whose teaching method impressed you most.

I like my reading teacher very much. I think she is an innovative teacher who always puts our benefits in the first place. Firstly, she tells us about the course curriculum. With her clear instructions, we know what we are supposed to do at the beginning of a new semester. Secondly, she doesn't confine her teaching in the textbook but prepares a lot of authentic reading materials for us. These reading materials, from classical literature to current news, from excerpts from Jane Eyre to reports about Yi Jianlian, highly stimulate our reading interest. Lastly, she encourages us to read extensively outside of class. In order to keep track of our after-class reading, she buys each student a notebook and asks every student to keep reading notes while doing autonomous reading after class. Besides, she would check our reading notes and make some detailed comments bi-weekly.

10. Do you believe in the saying "practice makes perfect" in learning English? Why or why not?

Yeah, of course, absolutely! First of all, "practice makes perfect" is my motto in learning experience, especially in learning English. From the learning experiences of English experts and masters, we know that practice is essential to any language learners. Secondly, no skills can be grasped naturally. As we say no pains no gains. Without hard work and practice, pianists can't play well, singers can't sing beautifully and athletes can't win gold medals. The same is true with English learning. Without practice, no one is able to express himself fluently in English.

Words and Expressions

itinerary	*n.*	旅行计划	autonomous	*adj.*	自动的
compulsory course		必修课	self-discipline	*n.*	自我约束
State Ministry of Education		教育部	strategy	*n.*	策略
potential	*adj.*	可能的	facilitate	*v.*	促进
video clips		视频剪辑	initiative	*n.*	主动性
stimulation	*n.*	刺激	authoritative	*adj.*	权威的
stimulus	*n.*	刺激（物）	demanding	*adj.*	要求多的，
peer	*n.*	同龄人			要求高的
reference book		参考书	motto	*n.*	座右铭

Part Three: Related Pictures with Suggested Descriptions

Picture One   Reading Is the Most Important Way to Learn English

Before you can start speaking and writing in English, your brain must get enough correct English sentences. You can't speak English if you have never seen an English sentence in your life. This is obvious. And you can't speak English well if you have not seen a large number of English sentences.

There are two ways to get correct English sentences: listening and reading. Both are good, but reading is usually much easier than listening. With the help of a good dictionary, you will be able to understand English texts much more easily than, for example, English televisions and movies.

If you read just one book in English, you will see that your English has become much better. You will start using lots of new vocabulary and grammar in your school compositions and email messages. You will be surprised, but English phrases will just come to you when you are writing or speaking! Things like the past simple tense and how to use the word "since" will become part of you. You will use them automatically, without thinking. Correct phrases will just appear in your head.

It will be easy to use English, because your brain will only be repeating the things that it has seen many times. By reading a book in English, you have given your brain thousands of English sentences. They are part of you now. How can you make a mistake and say "I feeled bad", if you have seen the correct phrase ("I felt bad") 250 times in the last book you've read? You simply cannot make that mistake anymore.

This is true for hundreds of words and grammar structures. If you read in English, you can forget about grammar rules. Throw away your grammar book! You don't need to know the rules for the present perfect tense. You don't even have to know the name "present perfect". Instead, read a few books in English and soon you will feel that "I have seen Paul yesterday" is wrong and "I saw Paul yesterday" is correct. How? Simple. Your brain has seen the second kind of sentence 192 times, and the first kind 0 times. This is what we call grammar intuition. This is how native speakers know what is correct. It's no magic. You can do it, too. The only difference between you and native speakers is that they have heard and read more English sentences than you have. Many learners have improved their English grammar and vocabulary in an amazing way because of intensive reading.

Picture Two   How to Read and What to Read?

These great results come especially quickly if you do three things when reading. Pay attention to interesting things: new words, phrases, and grammar structures. Use your dictionary to learn about these interesting things. The more you use your dictionary, the faster you progress.

If you don't like to stop reading (to look up a word in your dictionary), you can write down all the interesting sentences, or you can underline them in the book with a pencil. You can learn the words and grammar in these sentences later.

Add these interesting things to a memo or notebook. This will give you everyday contact with correct English sentences. With such a memo, you will not forget useful words and grammar. Because of this, you can build your knowledge very quickly.

You should always read English texts which are at the "right level". What does it mean? There should be some words that you don't know, because you want to learn something. However, there shouldn't be too many difficult words, because you don't want to use your dictionary 10 times in one sentence.

Here are the kinds of texts that you can read in English:

Literature. If normal books are too difficult for you, we recommend graded readers. These are usually famous books, written in simple language. There are many levels of difficulty—from "easy starts" (which use only 200 basic English words) to "advanced".

Science books. If you are interested in science, you can get great science books written in English. There are many famous English-speaking authors in many subjects, such as psychology, biology, physics or economics.

Text books. If you're studying at a college and you use textbooks written by English-speaking authors, you can get the original English versions. If you are learning a new computer language, you can use a book in English. You will learn your subject and English at the same time.

The web. On the World Wide Web you are completely free. You can read about every subject in the world—whatever interests you. Because you will often spend many hours surfing the web, you can also learn a lot of English.

There are also some small things to do. For example, you can start using English versions of our computer operating system, and other applications. You can also find people who write email in English to you. You should simply read in English as much as possible.

Picture Three　Active Listening and Note-taking

Good listening is the key to good note-taking. How can you be an active listener? Remember the three A's of good listening.

Have a good attitude: give the lecturer a chance. Do not be turned off by dress or remarks. Listen for the underlying message. You are there to learn.

Give the speaker your attention. You can hear, condense, and write so much faster than a speaker can talk. Take advantage of that time difference to evaluate what you hear.

Anticipate what will be said next and recap what has

already been said. Remember the acronym EAR to remind you of this three-step technique to help you concentrate and maintain your attention.

Listen and look for the instructor's vocal, visual and postural clues (for example, material written on the board, handouts, repetition, emphasis words, gestures) to help you identify what is important.

As you use your active listening skills, pay attention to how the lecturer organizes the material. Does the lecturer give a main idea first and then details leading to a main idea? Stay alert for organizational tools such as listing, chronological order, comparison-contrast, problem-solution as ways material may be organized. Be a detective.

You need to take notes while listening. Why take notes? Notes provide a record to study for exams, help you remember the materials for a longer period of time, and force you to be an active learner in the classroom. Good note-taking can be thought of in three steps: what you do before the lecture, during the lecture, and after the lecture.

Before The Lecture: Always be prepared for class. You can check your syllabus for topics and requirements; thoroughly read the text chapter or do a survey/overview of the chapter; review notes from the previous lecture; and write an outline of the chapter to take to class for comparison with lecture material.

During The Lecture: Once you prepare, be there! Go to class! Sit close to show you are interested and help you stay that focused. Have an organized method of taking notes. Be sure to include examples. Note questions from the class, digressions, added information, a change in format and so forth. Use abbreviation to help you quickly take notes.

After The Lecture: Once you have taken notes, be sure to look at them within 24 hours to fill in gaps or edit them. Write cues (words, phrases, or questions) in the left margin to summarize key points and help you test yourself later on your notes. Give visual emphasis (underline and mark your notes) to make key points stand out. Write personal notes/questions to yourself in the right margin (for example, reminders to check gaps or tips from the professor). Study your notes within 24 hours, before your next class, and at the end of the week. These initial reviews will give you a strong start in exam preparation.

All this active learning is hard work, but it will pay off!

Words and Expressions

automatically	*adv.*	自动地	postural	*adj.*	肢体的
memo	*n.*	备忘录	chronological	*adj.*	按时间顺序的
psychology	*n.*	心理学	pay off		产生回报
visual	*adj.*	视力的			

Part Four: Related Passages

1. Why English?

The English language is used by more people in the world than any other living language today. This may seem surprising at first. After all, the population of the United kingdom is one of the smallest in the world. But of course the UK is not the only country whose native language is English; the majority of people in the United States, Canada, Australia and New Zealand are also native English-speakers. However, even if you add up the populations of these countries the total only comes to about 400 million, which is less than one-tenth of the population of the world.

Who else speaks English? Well, if we count all the English-speakers in India, Singapore and some other countries, that adds another 700 million to the total. Add all those people who speak English elsewhere and the total English-speaking population of the world comes to an impressive one and a half million.

This figure shows that there are more non-native speakers of English than there are native speakers. Why is this? There is one important historical reason: the influence of the British Empire—the Empire that stretched across the globe. Although the Empire no longer exists, the English language is firmly rooted in its former colonies—in Africa, India, Pakistan, Bangladesh, the Far East, Australia, New Zealand, the Caribbean and North America.

Other important reasons for the spread of English language are economic. English is the language of international business and commerce. It is also the native language of the United States. So, any country wanting, for example, to trade with the United States, or to take advantage of its technology, must be able to operate in English. Also, most scientific and technological developments have been made by English-speaking societies. To keep up with the such developments, to talk about them in international conferences, or write and read about them in scientific journals and books, scientists, scholars and students must be able to understand English.

These are obvious reasons for the spread and interest in the English language. But there is a rather less obvious reason. English is also the language of a popular culture. All over the globe millions of young people listen to pop music and watch pop videos. The stars who perform in English are by far the most famous. The songs of Paul McCartney, John Lennon, Bob Dylan, The Rolling Stones, Police, Sting, Michael Jackson, and hundreds of other American and British singers can be heard all over the world. English has become an international language.

2. *I Have a Dream* (Extract)

I say to you today, my friends, so even though we face the difficulties of today and tomorrow, I still have a dream. It is a dream deeply rooted in the American dream.

I have a dream that one day this nation will rise up, live up to the true meaning of its creed:

"We hold these truths to be self-evident; that all men are created equal."

I have a dream that one day on the red hills of Georgia the sons of former slaves and the sons of former slave-owners will be able to sit down together at the table of brotherhood.

I have a dream that one day even the state of Mississippi, a state sweltering with the heat of injustice, sweltering with the heat of oppression, will be transformed into an oasis of freedom and justice.

I have a dream that my four children will one day live in a nation where they will not be judged by the color if their skin but by the content of their character.

I have a dream today.

I have a dream that one day down in Alabama with its governor having his lips dripping with the words of interposition and nullification, one day right down in Alabama little black boys and black girls will be able to join hands with little white boys and white girls as sisters and brothers.

I have a dream today.

I have a dream that one day every valley shall be exalted, every hill and mountain shall be made low, the rough places will be made plain, and the crooked places will be made straight, and the glory of the Lord shall be revealed, and all flesh shall see it together.

This is our hope. This is the faith that I go back to the South with. With this faith we will be able to hew out of the mountain of despair a stone of hope. With this faith we will be able to transform the jangling discords of our nation into a beautiful symphony of brotherhood. With this faith we will be able to work together, to pray together, to struggle together, to go to jail together, to stand up for freedom together, knowing that we will be free one day.

This will be the day when all of God's children will be able to sing with new meaning.

3. *Oxford English Dictionary*

The *Oxford English Dictionary* is the accepted authority on the evolution of the English language over the last millennium. It is an unsurpassed guide to the meaning, history, and pronunciation of over half a million words, both present and past. It traces the usage of words through 2.5 million quotations from a wide range of international English language sources, from classic literature and specialist periodicals to film scripts and cookery books.

The *OED* covers words from across the English-speaking world, from North America to South Africa, from Australia and New Zealand to the Caribbean. It also offers the best in etymological analysis and in listing of variant spellings, and it shows pronunciation using the International Phonetic Alphabet.

As the *OED* is a historical dictionary, its entry structure is very different from that of a dictionary of current English, in which only present-day senses are covered, and in which the most common meanings or senses are described first. For each word in the *OED*, the various groupings of senses are dealt with in chronological order according to the quotation evidence, i.e. the senses with the earliest quotations appear first, and the senses which have developed more recently appear further down the entry. In a complex entry with many strands, the development over time can be seen in a structure with several "branches".

The Second Edition of the *OED* is currently available as a 20-volume print edition, on CD-ROM, and now also online. Updated quarterly with between one and two thousand new and revised entries, *OED Online* offers unparalleled access to the "greatest continuing work of scholarship that this century has produced" (*Newsweek*). To find out more about the *OED Online*, why not follow our free tour?

"About the *Oxford English Dictionary*" invites you to explore the intriguing background and distinctive character of the *OED*. Here, you will find in-depth articles about the history of the *OED*, an inside look at the programmes used to enlarge and update the *OED* entries, little-known facts about its content, and much more.

4. Japan Learns English from Obama Speech Textbook

President Barack Obama's speeches are proving a best-seller in Japan—as an aid to learning English. An English-language textbook, *The Speeches of Barack Obama*, has sold more than 400,000 copies in two months, a big hit in a country where few hit novels sell more than a million copies a year.

Japanese have a fervor for learning English and many bookstores have a corner dedicated to dozens of journals in the language, many of them now featuring the new U.S. leader's face. "Speeches by presidents and presidential candidates are excellent as listening tools to learn English, because their contents are good and their words are easy to catch," said Yuzo Yamamoto of Asahi Press, which produced the best-selling text book. "Obama's is especially so. His speeches are so moving, and he also uses words such as 'yes, we can', 'change' and 'hope' that even Japanese people can memorize," he said.

Speeches by George W. Bush and former nominee John Kerry's four years ago did not have the same appeal, however, and nor do those made by Japanese politicians, Yamamoto said. "In Japan, we don't have politicians who have such a positive influence. That's why we have to turn to a foreign president for someone in whom to place our hopes."

The 95-page paperback features Obama's speeches in English from the 2004 Democratic National Convention and during the Democratic Party primaries, in which he defeated Hillary Clinton. They are accompanied by Japanese translations. The 1,050 yen ($12) book, which includes a CD of the speeches, tops the bestseller list on bookseller Amazon's Japanese Website, "Readers have sent in postcards saying that when they heard the speeches, they were so moved and cried even though they don't understand English very well," Yamamoto said.

He said lawmakers from Japan's main opposition Democratic Party had bought the book to study Obama's speeches. Following Obama's inauguration on Tuesday, Asahi Press plans to issue a sequel that includes his inaugural address, as well as President John F. Kennedy's 1961 inaugural speech. It will also feature a reading of President Abraham Lincoln's Gettysburg address of 1863.

5. American English

Most people around the world who learn English as a second language learn either American English or British English. The worldwide use of English began when Britain created a worldwide empire. Today, most people who learn English as a foreign language still learn British English. This happens because Britain has had a long-standing interest in teaching English and has publishers and institutions in place to promote it. The English vocabulary is more extensive than that of any other language in the world, although some other languages—Chinese, for example—have a world-building capacity equal to that of English.

American English is taught more and more, however, because of the worldwide success of American business and technology. This success also leads speakers of British English—even in England—to adopt many Americanisms. English has truly become a world language in science and business, and over time it will come to have more of an American English sound.

Languages are changing all the time, of course, and the English language is no exception. Some people welcome change as healthy; other people regard it as inevitable, but do not welcome it; still other people welcome certain changes but not all; and still other people regard all changes as bad. Today, American English has a lot of influence on the development of the English language.

English language, chief medium of communication of people in the United Kingdom, the Untied States, Canada, Australia, New Zealand, South Africa, and numerous other countries. It is the official language of many nations in the Commonwealth of Nations and is widely understood and used in all of them. It is spoken in more parts of the world than any other language and by more people than any other tongue except Chinese.

All learners of English share a common linguistic system and a basic set of words. But American English differs from British English, Australian English, and other national varieties in many of its pronunciations, words, spellings, and grammatical constructions.

American English, variety of the English language spoken in the United States. Although all Americans do not speak the same way, their speech has enough in common that American English can be recognized as a variety of English distinct from British English, Australian English, and other national varieties. American English has grown up with the country.

Topic Two   Hobbies

Part One: Dialogues

Dialogue 1   What Is Your Hobby?

(James, an overseas student, and Wang, a Chinese student, bump into each other on campus.)

James: Hi, Xiao Wang. Fancy meeting you here. How are you doing?

Wang: Hi, James. Can't complain. I'm busy with my lab experiment. But after work I often play some sports.

James: Like what?

Wang: Like swimming, running and basketball.

James: Basketball? That's my favorite game. Say, what're you doing this weekend? Some of us are going to play basketball. Would you like to join us?

Wang: Marvelous, I really need to relax. By the way I've heard that you're a good dribbler and shooter.

James: Thanks, I know you are a good swimmer. I really admire people who can swim well.

Wang: Practice makes perfect. After you learn how to swim you try to practice as often as you can. Actually I've been swimming regularly for 10 years since high school.

James: Now I can only do the butterfly. What is your favorite style?

Wang: The side stroke is my favorite, but I can do the butterfly and side stroke as well.

James: That is why you have such strong arms.

Wang: Swimming builds my body and my character as well. Now in winter I keep swimming twice a week.

James: Wow, swimming in winter. It makes me shiver even to think of it.

Wang: It would not be so frightening if you have gotten used to it.

James: How far can you go at one time?

Wang: Not much, perhaps 400 meters.

James: Wow. That's something. I'm out of breath after a mere 20 meters.

Wang: I need to run now, I have a meeting at 2. See you later; don't forget to call me this weekend.

James: Sure! See you.

◆ Dialogue 2　So Many Hobbies

(Susan, the American teacher, is chatting with her Chinese colleague, Wu.)

Susan: Have you finished your embroidery yet? It is so beautiful. I can't wait to see it finished. Do you plan to display it in the campus arts exhibition?

Wu: I hope I can have it finished by then. It takes such a long time when we embroider one stitch after another by hand. My mother makes beautiful embroideries. Maybe she will come over and help me finish. Are you entering something in the exhibition?

Susan: You know, I really enjoy taking photography. Maybe I could enter one or two of the pictures I took when I was traveling around China last year.

Wu: You really have a lot of hobbies, Susan. Painting, photographing, collecting coins and traveling. How do you find time to keep up with all of them?

Susan: That's the nice thing about being a teacher. I have a plenty of time available after I finish my job. I have always had a desire to do more in the field of art.

Wu: I know you took a Chinese traditional painting class at the community college last semester. What are you doing this semester?

Susan: I think I'll sign up for a Beijing opera class. It is so much fun to try my hand at all these things I've always wanted to do. You have a lot of hobbies yourself, Wu. What about all that sewing and knitting you do?

Wu: Yeah, I enjoy that sort of thing. I find it very relaxing to sit down with my knitting in the evening.

Susan: I think everyone needs at least one hobby, something that is enjoyable and relaxing after a hard day's work. After work, I enjoy coming home and spend a little time with my hobbies.

Wu: I agree. Everyone should have a hobby.

Words and Expressions

bump into		偶遇	shiver	v.	发抖
dribbler	n.	运球的人	embroidery	n.	刺绣
shooter	n.	投篮的人	photograph	n.	照片
butterfly	n.	蝶泳	sew	v.	缝纫
side stroke		侧游	knit	v.	编织

Part Two: Related Questions with Suggested Answers

1. Can you tell us one of your hobbies? Why do you keep this hobby?

My hobby is cooking. Cooking brings me a lot of fun. Cooking is creative. I try to combine different ingredients together to make a new dish. Or I use new recipes to make exotic cuisines for my family and friends. I am credited to be the best cook among my friends and so everyone loves to come to my parties. And sometimes I would exchange my own recipes with people who also love cooking on the Internet. In this way, I gain not only cooking skills but also make new friends. In one word, cooking can boost my self-esteem, release my creativity, and bring me pleasure and a sense of accomplishment.

2. Why is it important to have a hobby in our life?

Getting into a hobby has a lot of benefits. Firstly, in our lifetime we have lots of free time. Interesting hobbies can help us spend that time meaningfully. Secondly, hobbies can help us deal with the stress and frustrations we often have in our daily lives. Stress is a major symptom of competitive societies. Hobbies bring us relief and comfort. After working in the office all day long, dealing with daily traffic jams, we need the comfort, relief and relaxation that hobbies bring. Last but not least, hobbies make our lives interesting. Individuals who have hobbies are happier people. Hobbies can do wonders to our minds, bodies and souls. So have a hobby and have fun.

3. Reading can be a hobby for some people. What could they get out of it?

It is said that book-lovers never know lonely hours as long as they have books around them, and the better books people have, the more delightful company they find. Reading is a great pastime, in this sense. Besides, good books enrich minds. We "watch" plays, "listen" to poems and enjoy stories. Good books give our vision, increase our knowledge, widen our horizon, improve our personality, and moreover, teach us the truth of life.

4. Stamp-collecting can also be a hobby for some people. What could they learn from it?

Firstly, little stamps are windows to the world and they give a lot of information to stamp-collectors. From stamps, we know what is happening in the world and in our country. We know important scientific or literary figures and important dates in history. We know the significance of a revolution to a certain country and the beautiful and exotic historical spots in the west. Secondly, stamp-collectors can make money from their hobbies of stamp-collecting. They learn what kinds of stamps are good for investment. Some of stamp-collectors are great investors who make a great fortune in their life.

5. What kind of hobbies is not suitable for college students nowadays? Why?

In my opinion, playing computer games is not suitable for college students because it is not only a waste of time but also harmful to their physical and mental health. Nowadays, more and more college students are indulged in online games and spend day and night playing these games. What do they get from these games? Nothing valuable except the rush of temporary excitement! Like cigarettes and alcohol, computer games are addictive. The more you play, the more you become hooked on them. Some students even skip meals and lose precious sleep in order to become so-called "game masters". And some of computer games are poorly designed and contain violence and pornographic scenes, which are harmful to students' mental health.

6. Are there any factors that could influence our choice of hobbies?

There are numerous factors that may influence our choice. Personality, environment and economy, for example. As the saying goes: different strokes for different folks. Personality does play an important role in determining people's choice of hobbies. Quiet people may find pleasure in fishing; others may think fishing is far too boring and they put their vitality to better use, such as dancing and climbing. Classical music like Mozart and Beethoven's symphonies has its fans. Pop music, too. Furthermore, environment plays a role in choosing a hobby. If you grow in a family that loves gardening you'll probably be a plant lover. If your parents think a good weekly dose of exercise and fresh air is vital to their existence you will too. Say, Langlang, the young Chinese piano player. He was brought up in a district where most of inhabitants are musicians. Lastly, economy also influences our choice of hobbies. Some hobbies are expensive, like traveling, baseball and golf.

7. How do you develop a hobby?

Firstly, you discover you have an interest in something. You find it esthetic, exciting, calming and maybe educational. It is said that interest is the best teacher. Only interest motivates us to overcome all kinds of difficulties and enjoy life. Secondly, developing a hobby requires devotion which involves time and energy. Workaholics are unable to develop hobbies because their schedule is always overbooked. Only those people who are willing to devote their time to a hobby will experience the happiness that a hobby can bring. Lastly, developing a hobby needs socializing. No matter what hobbies one develops, making friends and changing ideas are important parts of the experience.

8. In what way does fishing help people?

Fishing is a good hobby for those who want to have patience. Fishing demands great patience. Sitting at the bank of a river, holding a fishing rod and staring at the end of the pole, a fisherman may wait for a long time before getting the first catch. Even for a professional fisherman, not every day is a lucky day.

9. In what way does gardening help old people keep a healthy life?

First of all, gardening is a good form of physical exercise. Sowing, weeding and watering are good ways for the elderly to keep moving around and stretching their muscles. Secondly, gardening brings them fulfillment. Seeing vegetables grow, flowers blossom and fruit ripen are rewards of their hard work. Most of senior citizens suffer from loneliness and isolation. Gardening can be a good way for them to keep both their hands and minds busy and happy.

10. What do we learn from loving music?

Music can affect our physical, mental and emotional state of being. Soft and sweet music soothes the wearied, the sad, the restless, while grand music fills strong men with great ambition. Furthermore, music is a universal language and sometimes it can communicate more clearly than words. Music helps people express love, longing, happiness, anger and frustration. Music can make us laugh, cry and feel happy or sad.

Words and Expressions

recipe	*n.*	菜谱	workaholic	*n.*	工作狂
boost	*v.*	提升	socialize	*v.*	社交
symptom	*n.*	症状	sow	*v.*	播种
exotic	*adj.*	有异域风情的	weed	*v.*	锄草
temporary	*adj.*	暂时的	soothe	*v.*	安抚，安慰
pornographic	*adj.*	色情的			

Part Three: Related Pictures with Suggested Descriptions

Picture One   Hobby

A hobby can be almost anything a person likes to do in his spare time. Hobbyists raise pets, build model ships, weave baskets, or carve soap figures. They watch birds, hunt animals, climb mountains, raise flowers, fish, ski, skate and swim. Hobbyists also paint pictures, attend concerts and plays, and perform on musical instruments. They collect everything from books to butterflies, and from shells to stamps.

People take up hobbies because these activities offer enjoyment, friendship, knowledge and relaxation. Sometimes they even bring about financial profit. Hobbies help people relax after periods of hard work, and provide a balance between work and play. Hobbies also offer interesting activities for persons who have retired. Anyone, rich or poor, old or young, sick or well, can follow a satisfying hobby, regardless of his age, position, or income. A hobby can help a person's mental and physical health. Doctors have found that hobbies are valuable in helping patients recover from physical or mental illness. Hobbies give bedridden or wheel-chair patients something to do, and provide interests that keep them from thinking about themselves. Many hospitals treat patients by having them take up interesting hobbies or pastimes.

Sir William Osler, a famous Canadian doctor, expressed the value of hobbies by saying, "No man is really happy or safe without a hobby." Therefore, it's necessary for people to have as many hobbies as they can to make life more interesting.

Picture Two   Yoga

Have you ever tried to hold our breath for a long time and then let it out slowly? This is one of the techniques of an ancient Indian discipline known as Yoga. For thousands of years, people have used Yoga to help search for happiness and contentment.

Students of Yoga often study for as long as 20 years before becoming masters, or Yogis. They learn many different physical exercises. These exercises are designed to put the students in good physical condition. They can concentrate on deep religious thoughts without worrying about physical discomforts.

Many Yoga exercises involve putting the body into difficult positions. Some of them are very hard to learn. Have you ever tried to fold your legs over one another? This is one of the basic Yoga positions. It is called the lotus position. Most people find it difficult to stay in that position for even a few minutes. But Yogis train themselves to remain in the lotus position for hours or even days. They are taught to overcome the physical discomforts of holding these positions. Other exercises and rules teach concentration. Yogis feel this is the key to finding inner peace. This kind of concentration is called meditation.

Yogis and many other people practice mediation. They claim that it makes them feel relaxed and peaceful. Some people say that it makes them feel better—just as good exercise does. But other people claim that it is a way of achieving a strong religious feeling. These people say that meditation helps them feel much closer to God.

The word Yoga itself comes from an ancient Sanskirt word meaning "union". Many people in the Western word are practicing Yoga and they believe Yoga would bring healthy and spiritual benefits to their life.

Picture Three　Skin Diving

Skin diving is a new sport today. Many people are interested in this sport. Some go under water to catch fish. Some go under water to see beautiful scenes. Others go down into deep water to take pictures of swimming fish. It is not very dark under water. This sport takes you away into a wonderful new world. It is like a visit to the moon. When you are under water, it is easy for you to climb big rocks, because  you are no longer heavy. Here under water, everything is blue and green. During the day, there is plenty of light. Sometimes, people taking pictures under water do not have to use a flash. When fish swim near by, you can catch them with your hands.

There are two ways of skin diving. When you do not go down deep, you put on a mask with a snorkel and a pair of flippers. For diving in deep water, you need another thing—a tank of air for breathing. You can put two or three tanks of air on your back. They will let you go down very deep into the sea.

When you have tanks of air on your back, you can stay in deep water for a long time. But you must be careful about diving in deep water.

Some years ago, a young man went down too deep and got sick, because he was not a trained diver. Then he did a very foolish thing. He took off his mask in the water! He was nearly drowned. Many skin divers do not try to go down very deep. They just swim with masks and snorkels, and try to catch fish. Catching fish is one of the most interesting parts of this sport.

Some years ago, pearl divers worked under water without breathing. So they were in great danger.

Now, tanks, masks and snorkels are changing their work. Divers trained in using them can gather many pears with little danger.

There are more uses for skin diving. You can clean skips without taking them out of the water. Skin divers get many things from the deep sea.

Now you can see that skin diving is both very useful and interesting.

Words and Expressions

bedridden	*adj.*	卧床的	skin diving		轻装潜水（只带简单的呼吸器具而不穿潜水服）
wheel-chair	*n.*	轮椅			
discipline	*n.*	磨炼；强身法			
yogi	*n.*	瑜伽功师			
the lotus position		（瑜伽功）盘腿打坐	snorkel	*n.*	氧气面罩上的呼吸管
meditation	*n.*	默想；冥思	flipper	*n.*	拖鞋
Sanskirt	*adj.*	梵文的	pearl diver		潜水采珍珠的人
union	*n.*	结合；和谐			

Part Four: Related Passages

1. The Benefit of Music

Music to your ears can be music for your heart, too. Songs that make our hearts soar can make them stronger too, US researchers reported on Tuesday. They found that when people listened to their favorite music, their blood vessels dilated in much the same way as when laughing, or taking blood medications. "We have a pretty impressive effect," said Dr. Michael Miller, director of preventive cardiology at the University of Maryland Medical Center in Baltimore. "Blood vessel diameter improved," he said. "The vessel opened up pretty significantly. You can see the vessels opening up with other activities such as exercise." A similar effect is seen with drugs such as statins and ACE inhibitors. When blood vessels open more, blood flows more smoothly and is less likely to form the blood clots that cause heart attacks and strokes. Elastic vessels also resist the hardening activity of atherosclerosis.

"We are not saying to stop your statins or not to exercise but to add this to an overall program of heart health," said Miller, who presented his findings to a meeting of the American Heart Association in New Orleans. Miller's team tested 10 healthy, non-smoking men and women, who were told to bring their favorite music. They spent half an hour listening to the recordings and half an hour listening to music they said made them feel anxious while the researchers did ultrasound tests designed to show blood vessel function. Compared to their normal baseline measurements, blood vessel diameter increased 26 percent on average when the volunteers heard their joyful music. Listening to music they disliked—in most cases in this group heavy metal—narrowed blood vessels by six percent, Miller said.

2. Companionship of Books

A man may usually be known by the books he reads as well as by the company he keeps; for there is a companionship of books as well as of men; and one should always lived in the best company, whether it be of books or of men.

A good book may be among the best of friends. It is the same today that it always was, and it will never change. It is the most patient and cheerful of companions. It does not turn its back upon us in times of adversity or distress. It always receives us with the same kindness, amusing and instructing us in youth, and comforting and consoling us in age.

Men often discover their affinity to each other by the love they have each for a book. The book is a truer and higher bond of union. Men can think, feel, and sympathize with each other through their favorite author. They live in them together and him, in them.

A good book is often the best urn of a life enshrining the best that life could think out; for the world of a man's life is, for the most part, but the world of his thoughts. Thus the best books are treasuries of good words, the golden thoughts, which, remembered and cherished, become our constant companions and comforters.

Books possess an essence of immorality. They are by far the most lasting products of human effort. Temples and statues decay, but books survive. Time is of no account with great thoughts, which are as fresh today as they first passed through their authors' minds, age ago. What was then said and thought still speaks to us as vividly as ever from the printed page. The only effect of time has been to sift out the bad products; for nothing in literature can long survive but what is really good.

Books introduce us into the best society, they bring us into the presence of the greatest minds that have ever live. We hear what they said and did; we see them as if they were really alive; we sympathize with them, enjoy with them, grieve with them; their experience becomes ours, and we feel as if we were in measure actors with them in the scenes which they describe.

3. Golf—an Expensive Hobby

If you have the money and nothing better to spend it on, golf can be an expensive game. By insisting on the best that modern technology can devise out of carbon graphite, beryllium copper and laminated hardwood, it is quite possible to spend more than £ 1,000 on a set of clubs. You then need a bag trolley to put them in, so add at least another £ 100. A trolley to move the whole lot round the golf course costs about £ 30, but why stop here when about £ 400 will get you an electrically-powered version with a little seat attached to take away all the tiresome effort of walking between shots?

You now need to dress for the occasion. So add about £ 80 for a pair of really good golf shoes with metal spikes in the soles, the best part of £ 30 for one of those sweaters with the little lion on the breast and, if you live anywhere that rain is likely to fall, about £ 70 for a set of up-market waterproofs. Come to think of it, you'd better spend another £ 15 on one of those multi-colored umbrellas, just in case people think you can't afford it. A special golfing shirt is not essential, neither is a pair of golfing trousers, but you can get both for about £ 50. You will need a glove. Just one, for the left hand, but you had better buy a set of three because they wear out—at a cost of about £ 20 for real leather ones though you can probably spend more if you look around a bit.

You really should get a few balls as well. Without them the game can be a little pointless. These tend to come fairly cheap but don't let that put you off. What you save here can be spent on the small stuff: fur-lined leather covers to protect the heads of the wooden clubs, a leather score-card holder with personal monogram, a thing that looks like half an orange with foam lining to clean your golf balls, tees to rest the ball on before driving off. You could spend about £ 25 on this lot and you're now more or less ready to step on to a golf course.

4. Sports Around the World

Not all people like to work but everyone likes to play. All over the world men and women and boys and girls enjoy sports. Since the days of long ago, adults and children have called their friends together to spend hours, even days, playing games.

Sports help people to live happily. They help to keep people healthy and feeling good. When they are playing games, people move a lot. This is good for their health. Having fun with their friends makes them happy.

Many people enjoy sports by watching others play. In small towns, crowds meet to watch the bicycle races or the soccer game. In the big cities, thousands buy tickets to see an ice-skating show or a baseball game.

What are your favorite sports? Is the climate hot where you live? Then swimming is probably one of our sports. Boys and girls in China love to swim. There are wonderful beaches along the seashore and there are beautiful rivers and lakes across the country.

Or do you live in a cold climate? Then you would like to ski. There are many skiers in Austria where there are big mountains and cold winters. Does it rain often where you live? Then kite flying would not be one of your sports. It is one of the favorite sports of Thailand.

Surfing is an important sport in Hawaii. The Pacific Ocean sends huge waves up on the beaches, waves that are just right for surfing. But you need to live near an ocean to ride the waves and enjoy surfing.

People in Switzerland love to climb the wonderful mountains of their country. Mountain climbing and hiking are favorite sports there. But there can be no mountain climbing where there are no mountains.

Sports change with the season. People often do not play the same games in winter as in summer. Sailing is fun in warm weather, but when it gets cold it's time to change to other sports. People talk about sports' seasons. Baseball is only played for a few months of the year. This is called "the baseball season".

5. The World Cup

One of the first things that people studying English learn is that the game they call football is called soccer in North America. Soccer has been popular for more than 100 years, and today it is probably the most popular sport in the world.

Every four years, teams from all over the world compete in the famous World Cup. The Cup is a series of games in which teams form many countries play to see which is the best. By one estimate, almost one billion people watched the 1982 championship game on television. People in Asia had to get up in the middle of the night to see Italy beat West Germany on TV in a game played in Spain.

The World Cup began in Montevideo, Uruguay, in 1930. At the times, it did not seem like a true world competition since only 13 teams decided to play, and eight of them were from South America. The team from Uruguay won.

In 1934 and 1938, the Cup was held in Europe. More than 30 teams played in each of these competitions, and Italy won both of them. The larger number of teams meant that some rules had to be changed. There were too many teams playing, so they had to have elimination matches first. Some of the games were played in countries other than host countries. This system is still used today, and only the sixteen teams left after elimination actually compete for the Cup.

There were no World Cup championships in 1942 or 1946 because of World War II. When the Cup play started again in 1950, there was little enthusiasm. It was like 1928 all over again: Only 13 teams competed, the games were in Brazil, and Uruguay won. In 1958, when the games were held in Sweden, interest was once again very high. 53 teams wanted to compete. This was the first time that the world saw Pele. His team, from Brazil, won the Cup for the first time that year, and Pele became the greatest soccer player of all time.

In the past thirty years, soccer has become the sport of the world. Each World Cup is more successful than the last. Since 1966, probably one-quarter of the world has listened to or watched the championship game.

In the 1970s, Pele retired from the national team of Brazil and became a professional player for a team in New York. Soccer wasn't very popular in the United States at that time. Few North Americans knew about his fast moving sport. There was no money to pay professional players, and there was little interest in soccer in the high schools and colleges. When Pele and other international stars began playing in various US cities, people saw how interesting the game was and began to go to the matches. Today there is a professional league called the North American Soccer League. It is common for important game to have 50,000 to 60,000 fans.

Topic Three   Friendship

Part One: Dialogues

◆ Dialogue 1   Help Needed

(At noon, Jack is at the front of the university canteen.)

S1: Let's put the donation box here by the canteen door.

S2: And I'll tape this poster on the wall beside it.

(A student is approaching the post.)

James: Hi, what's going on here? Selling movie tickets?

S2: No, nothing of that sort. Look at the poster over there.

James: (Reads the poster) Help needed to save life. Wu Xiaoming aged 19, a sophomore of the Civil Engineering Department is suffering from bone cancer. An immediate surgery and blood transfusion is critical to save his life, but the fees and related expenses far exceed what his family can afford. The Student Union therefore calls on every student to give him help and support. A donation will be highly appreciated. Oh, My God! He is so young. How could he get cancer? (He puts a ten Yuan note into the box.)

S1: Thank you very much.

James: Well, I don't have much money. I am an editor of campus newspaper. Maybe we can write an article asking for help.

S2: A great idea.

James: Give me some detailed information about Wu Xiaoming. Besides we may mail the article to the *Evening Newspaper* of our city to get some help from the society.

S1: That is terrific. Thanks a lot.

James: My pleasure. I will come this evening to get the information.

S2: No problem.

◆ Dialogue 2   Bumping into an Old Pal

(Michael and James are old classmates and James comes across Michael in the street.)

James: Hi, Michael, haven't seen you for ages. More than three years, I think. How time flies!

Michael: Yes, I remember we met at the birthday party at John's a couple of years ago. And then, wasn't there some other party afterwards?

James: Yeah, it was Sunny's going-away party. If I'm not mistaken, that was the last time we saw each other.

Michael: How is everything going with you?

James: Oh, I'm still pursuing my Ph.D. It's a long and torturing process.

Michael: You're the top student in our class and you're born to be a professor.

James: Don't flatter me! You are the smartest girl in our class. How is life?

Michael: No complaints! How about Tom? I wonder how he's getting along.

James: He quitted his teaching job and now he is working in an American corporation. We called each other several days ago and he was promoted to manager of his office. Remember Paul, the basketball player in our class? He is now running a company selling athletic equipments and he makes a fortune.

Michael: Hey, he is not interested in studying but he has a great brain for business. Have you heard from the only three girls in our class?

James: No. As far as I know, Susan is now studying at Cambridge in UK. I bet you want to know about her.

Michael: To tell you the truth, I didn't have a chance to contact her after we graduated. I guess she's quite well-off now.

James: Yeah. She writes blogs in a website, so we can chat with each other via the Internet from time to time.

Michael: Maintaining friendships over time and distance is not easy. After we graduate and settle down in different cities, old friendships often suffer.

James: Yeah, hey, Michael, next year is the 5th anniversary of our graduation. Why don't we organize a class reunion?

Michael: Sounds great. Let's work out the details together. I am looking forward to seeing my old classmates.

James: I can't wait either.

Words and Expressions

donation	*n.*	捐款	exceed	*v.*	超过
sophomore	*n.*	大学二年级	have a crush on *sb.*		暗恋某人
surgery	*n.*	手术	blog	*n.*	博客

Part Two: Related Questions with Suggested Answers

1. Do you like making friends? Why or why not?

Yes, I do. I like making friends because I believe that a person who has many friends will not feel lonely. Ever when I was a child, I always tried to make friends with others so I always had someone to play with them. What's more, I could tell them about stories I read. Later, at school, I was eager to introduce myself to new classmates. I loved to talk with them about our studies. I loved to discuss problems we encountered in everyday life. As a result, I always had many friends around me and seldom felt lonely. It's the same today. I'm always on the lookout for a new face. Moreover, the process of making friends with others may help me develop better interpersonal communicative skills. These skills will be very important when I get a job, I think.

2. Who is your best friend? Tell us something about him or her, please.

Well, I should say my best friend is Alice. I met her on the first day of my university life. She impressed me as a friendly and easy-going girl. She looks like a school teacher with a pair of black frame glasses. Actually, her dream is to become an English teacher in the future. She studies very diligently in order to realize her dream. And whenever there is a chance, she will strive to jump at it and practice as a teacher. For example, during the last summer holiday, she joined in an English Summer Camp and worked there as an English teacher for nearly two months. She thinks such kind of practice is helpful to her. I sincerely hope that she can attain her goal after graduation.

3. What do you think of the saying that "A life without a friend is a life without a sun"?

Well, I quite agree with this saying as my personal experience tells me that friends are very important in our daily life just as the sun is. I believe that friendship is the key to happiness. I mean that true and lasting happiness depends to a large extent on the friends we keep. Without friends around our life there will be lack of companions. That means we will be alone and have to do all the things by ourselves. But things will be different if we have many friends around because they can help out when we are in trouble. We can share our joys and sorrows with them. In our life, there will certainly be some rainy days. But good friends are like a sun. They will make our life sunny and colorful. I think only with good friends around can we enjoy our life better.

4. How do you choose friends?

Well, I think that is a very complicated question. But generally I choose friends who share my interests and hobbies. You know, when two persons share interests and hobbies, they will have a variety of topics available to talk about. On the contrary, it is difficult to communicate with a person whose interests and hobbies are different from yours. For example, one of my major hobbies is playing badminton. If my friends are not interested in it, we will not be able to share these experiences together. Without being able to have the same experiences, it is difficult for us to strengthen our friendship. What's more, choosing friends who are quite similar to me in interests and hobbies can help me to come up with new ideas about things we are interested in. If I am particularly interested in a project, but cannot advance the thought to my satisfaction, it is quite likely that one of my friends will be able to offer insight into the subject that I have not previously thought of. That's why I like to make friends with those who share with me the same interests and hobbies.

5. What do you think of the saying "A friend in need is a friend indeed"?

Well, personally, I agree with this saying. And I believe that this time-tested saying shows us an important quality of true friends, namely, to offer his/her help timely. We may have many friends in our life. However, there are only a few friends who can stand by us, no matter whether we are rich or poor, healthy or sick. These friends will always give us a hand when we are in need of help. To my mind, only these friends can be called true friends. In our life, we may also make many more fair-weather friends who run away as soon as we are in trouble. They choose to stay with us only when we are successful. These friends are not true friends. They are not qualified to be our true friends. Only a friend in need can be a friend indeed. Only a friend who stays around when you are in need is a friend indeed.

6. What should friends do to keep the friendship going?

I think there are many things we should do to keep the friendship. First, we should apologize when we're wrong. Everyone makes mistakes in his life. When we realize our mistakes or faults, it doesn't matter who is to blame. What matters is we should learn to apologize. Say we're sorry. Be sincere in our apology. Mean what we say. Chances are that our friend will forgive us. He may apologize to us, too.

Second, remain calm. Never lose our temper. Never say or do anything rash. Take time out and calm down. Count to ten. Take a deep breath. Then talk about the problem. If we're calm, our friends will listen.

Third, don't avoid our friend. Don't isolate ourselves. Try to communicate with them. The last is that we should be ready to compromise. Be open to suggestions. See things from our friends' point of view. Don't always insist on our opinions. Our friends may know things better. Be tolerant and understanding. Walk a mile in their shoes. That's the secret to keep friendship, I think.

7. Some people can be fair-weather friends. What do you think of this kind of friends?

We know that some people will stand by us when our conditions are good, but they will leave us alone when things get difficult. This kind of friends is called a fair-weather friend. Fair-weather friends, in my opinion, are not true friends at all, because as the old saying goes, a friend in need is a friend indeed. But fair-weather friends will not be in the same boat with us in difficult times. Chances are they will abandon us when we are in trouble. If we manage to overcome the difficulties, they may choose to come back to us in order to enjoy the sunshine and happiness with us. To tell the truth, I hate this kind of friends because they are not sincere. They are shameful. They don't know what true friendship really means. They are self-centered. When something happens, they may immediately think how to defend their own interests instead of helping out. So, if I find fair-weather friends around me, I'll break up my friendship with them without a moment's hesitation.

8. How do you respond to a friend who betrays you?

If a friend of mine betrays me, I would be very angry. But at the same time, I know that anger cannot solve the problem. I know that I must respond to his betrayal rationally. So in most cases, I will first try my utmost to calm down. Then I should consider why my friend betrays me. What mistakes did I make? Or what did I do to irritate him or hurt him? After taking these questions into consideration, I try to seek a chance to talk with him directly. In this way, some possible misunderstandings can be cleared up and we can become good friends again.

9. If you have to compete with your friend, what do you choose first, friendship or competition? Why?

As far as I'm concerned, true friendship means a lot. Although the society is becoming more and more competitive, people need friends to exchange ideas and share happiness and sorrow with. I do have to admit that competition is a source of progress. Without competition we would become lazy. So competition is also important for our students. But, friendship or competition, which one to choose, that's a really tough question. If I had to choose one, I think I would choose competition. But the competition should be based on some moral codes. In this way, my friend and I can both benefit from the competition. We can advance our career by helping each other. What I mean is that competition doesn't necessarily mean hostility. Competition can also lead to friendship. To compete fairly, we learn to respect our rivals and acquire greater motivation to work harder. Take university life for example. Competition between students exists everywhere like academics, athletics, romance, and popularity. If we want to win the scholarship, for instance, we have to be competitive in our studies. Competition among students helps us keep get ahead. If we take a good attitude to this competition, we can keep our friends no matter whether we win or lose. What we should do is to find a balance between competition and friendship.

10. Why does friendship sometimes evolve into romantic love?

As we look around we can see some good friends later become lovers of different sexes. And some of them will step into the church and become husband and wife. Why? In my opinion, there are at least three reasons. The first is that they may have a lot in common since they are already good friends. According to researches, we like to make friends with people who share our hobbies and interests. In this sense, friendship has laid a sound foundation for their later marriage. The second reason is that friends know each other very well. They often take part in activities together because they are friends. For example, they may go traveling together. They may enjoy the same film. They may read the same books. After staying together for certain time, they learn more about each other and grow closer to each other. The third reason is that friendship is an important source of love. If you make friends with someone of the opposite sex, you feel more comfortable and enjoyable when you stay together. That's because a person will be naturally attached to the other sex. And in order to be attractive, you will pay more attention to your words and behavior. You will like each other better. A nodding acquaintance will grow into a real friendship and later then passionate love.

Words and Expressions

interpersonal	adj.	人际的		code	n.	（道德）规范
easy-going	adj.	随和的		hostility	n.	敌意；敌对态度
frame	n.	边框		rival	n.	对手
diligently	adv.	勤奋地、勤勉地		academics	n.	学术
jump at		热切地抓住（机会）		scholarship	n.	奖学金
badminton	n.	羽毛球		nodding acquaintance	n.	点头之交
fair-weather friends		不能共患难的朋友				

Part Three: Related Pictures with Suggested Descriptions

Picture One   A True Friend

In ancient Greece, Socrates was reputed to hold knowledge in high esteem. One day one fellow met the great philosopher and said, "Do you know what I've just heard about your friend?" "Hold on a moment," Socrates replied. "Before telling me anything I'd like you to pass a little test. It's called the Triple Filter Test." "Triple Filter Test?" "That's right," Socrates continued. "Before you talk to me about my friend, it might be a good idea to take a moment and filter what you're going to say. That's why I call it the Triple Filter Test. The first filter is Truth. Have you made absolutely sure that what you are about to tell me is true?" "No," the man said, "Actually I just heard about it and..." "All right," said Socrates. "So you don't know if it's true or not. Now let's try the second filter, the filter of Goodness. Is what you are about to tell me about my friend something good?". "No, on the contrary..." "So," Socrates continued, "you want to tell me something bad about him, but you're not certain whether it's true. You may still pass the test though, because there's one filter left: the filter of Usefulness. Is what you want to tell me about my friend going to be useful to me?" "No, not really." "Well," concluded Socrates, "if what you want to tell me is neither true nor good nor even useful, why tell it to me at all?"

From this story we can see the Triple Filter Test is an important way to sustain friendship. Always avoid talking behind the back about your near and dear friends. Whatever we do, we should remember to do something true, good and useful to our friends.

Picture Two   Friendship Forever

Two inseparable friends, Sam and Jason, met with an accident on their way to Boston City. The following morning, Jason woke up blind and Sam was still unconscious. Dr. Berkeley was standing at his bedside looking at his health chart and medications with a thoughtful expression on his face. When he saw Sam awake, he beamed at him and asked. "How are you feeling today, Sam?" Sam tried to put up a brave face and smiled back saying, "Absolutely wonderful, Doctor. I am very grateful for all that you have done for me." Dr. Berkeley was moved at Sam's deed. All that he could say was, "You are a very brave man, Sam, and God will make it up to you in one way or another". While he was moving on to his next patient, Sam called back at him almost pleading, "Promise me you won't tell Jason anything".

"You know I won't do that. Trust me." and he walked away.

"Thank you", whispered Sam. He smiled and looked up in prayer: "I hope I live up to your ideas...please give me strength to be able to go through this. Amen!"

Months later when Jason had recovered considerably, he stopped hanging around with Sam. He felt discouraged and embarrassed to spend time with a disabled person like Sam.

Sam was lonely and disheartened, since he didn't have anybody else other than Jason to count on. Things went from bad to worse. And one day Sam died in despair. When Jason was called on his burial, he found a letter waiting for him. Dr. Berkeley gave it to him with an expressionless face and said: "This is for you, Jason. Sam had asked me to give it to you when he was gone".

In the letter he had said: "Dear Jason, I have kept my promise in the end to lend you my eyes if anything had happened to them. Now there is nothing more that I can ask from God, than the fact that you will see the world through my eyes. You will always be my best friend...Sam".

When he had finished reading, Dr. Berkeley said: "I had promised Sam to keep his sacrifice a secret from you. But now I wish I hadn't stuck to it because I don't think it was worthy of it".

All that left for Jason while he stood there was tears of regret and memories of Sam for the rest of his life.

This story tells us no matter what happens to our friends, we should stand by them till the end. Life is meaningless without friends.

Picture Three   On Making Friends

As a human being, one can hardly do without a friend, for life without friends will be a lonely voyage in the vast dark sea or one in the barren desert. Truly, a friend gives out light and warmth like a lamp. For this reason, I have always felt it a blessing if a friend comes to console me in my sadness, cheer me up in my low spirits, or heartedly share with me my happiness. It is wonderful, too, to feel that someone is standing by me and ready to provide help and encouragement in my pursuit of a noble and

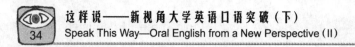

glorious cause.

For millions of years, people heaped beautiful verses and essays upon friendship. Yet, they, too, mercilessly accused false friendship, for there are always some mean characters that approach you and act as dear friends when you are wealthy or influential, but desert or even betray you the instant you come down in the world or are entrapped by unfortunate things. Therefore, people all attach great importance to the recognition of true friendship. And a faithful friend is considered even more precious than a priceless pearl or a precious stone. The old saying "A friend in need is a friend indeed" has become the standard for true friends.

Still, it is natural that different people observe different principles in making friends. Some view it important to make friends with whom they may share similar interests or hobbies. Others are liable to befriend VIPs so as to gain some favors or privileges. And I am of those who think very little of similarity or position or power. So long as a person has a heart of gold, being warm-hearted, selfless, honest, open-minded, but not brutal, cold, shortsighted nor narrow-minded, I am willing to make friends with him or her, give my due support and help, and remain faithful to him or her all my life.

Words and Expressions

Socrates		苏格拉底（古希腊哲学家）	barren	*adj.*	贫瘠的
esteem	*n.*	尊敬；敬重	blessing	*n.*	幸事；幸运
Triple Filter Test		三重过滤测试	console	*v.*	安慰；慰藉；安抚
sustain	*v.*	维持	verse	*n.*	诗句
medication	*n.*	药物	mercilessly	*adv.*	无情地
plead	*v.*	哀求；恳求	mean	*adj.*	卑鄙的
whisper	*v.*	低语；悄声说	entrap	*v.*	被（不好的事情）缠身
live up to		不辜负			
sacrifice	*n.*	牺牲	pearl	*n.*	珍珠

Part Four: Related Passages

1. Only Friendship Can Be Everlasting

Friendship is a kind of relationship that many accompany you all your life. The relationship with your wife or husband occurs only after you are married and runs the risks of being cut down by divorce. The relationship with your parents will be put to an end with their passing away. The relationship with your children begins late in the middle of your life. You have an association with your colleagues, but it is always changing, because one day, one or another colleague may disappear suddenly out of your routine by changing jobs and you may similarly jump out of your colleagues' lives. You have connection with your neighbors only for the sake of living in the same neighborhood and it will break down when you or one of your neighbors moves. Only friendship can be everlasting.

You may have friends as early as infancy. No matter whether you are married or not, no matter where you live and work, your friends are your friends. It is not based on bloodline. It is not absolutely an objective social relationship which befalls you. It is rooted in the desires and feelings derived from social experiences. It relies on your intention. In my opinion, that is the social nature of friendship. Making friends is to meet people's varying needs. People have all kinds of desires. To achieve progress, you make friends with those who surpass you. To enjoy freedom, equality and mutual respect, you make friends with those who are of equal stature with you. On behalf of your vanity and relaxation you make friends with the inferior. To you, some friends are fun-loving, some give encouragement, some offer knowledge, and others help you to find your own identity. You expose your worries and weakness to some friends, while you show only your merits, your bright side, in the face of other friends. Before your friends, you may act as a supervisor, a learned brother, a lovely child, a gentleman or a playmate. In a word, friendship helps you to be a full person. So friendship can benefit every individual and thus complete society which is composed of numerous individuals. That is the very social function of friendship.

2. Friendship and Love in College

In college, we meet many students from different places and some of them like to make friends with one another. With the help of friends, we can share many things in our daily life, such as sorrows and joys. We can also live in a friend's house when we visit a strange place. I once heard of a song which says "it is hard to look for a friend from a distant place and we pass smoothly when we have enough friends". There is also a well-known saying that a friend in need is a friend indeed. Since we gather from different places, why not develop friendship and help with each other? As for me, I honestly like to make friends with all of you and I wish that all of you could find true friendship and enjoy the school life.

Love, which is a hot topic among us, inevitably takes place in the school life. Love can produce a strong power in one person. It can make one to fight with another person and even kill him. But it can also make one to study hard to get great achievement so as to get her heart. If we want our college life to become wonderful, I suggest that we should look for love. For one thing, we can have a long time to know each other. When we have a job, it will be hard for us to look for love and can not know him or her clearly. For another thing, lovers can encourage each other to do many things. For example, lovers make each other study hard to fight for the future. Finally, marriage is not like a child game. It is related to one person's whole-life happiness. So we should look for lover carefully.

In a word, achievement, friendship and love can make our college life wonderful. Only when we study hard, find true friendship and love can we realize how much we enjoy the college life!

3. A True Friend

Everyone wants a true friend, and many of us believe that we have a friend who can be called a true friend. What kind of relations do friends share? When can we call a friend a true friend, and when can our friends take us as their true friend. After a romantic relationship, friendships are the most important relationships we can have. Though all of us have family and distant family, most of us rely on friends for advice, comfort and inspiration. How do we define a relation that can be called as one of true friendship?

The very first sign of a very good friend, not necessarily a true friend is that we are not worried about courtesies. You will call your friend at any hour and talk without any thought of time in your mind. Similarly, whenever you need support, you will call a very good friend and ask him/her to help you out. They expect the same from you. Another important trait of such relations is that we are not much worried about exposing ourselves. We speak about everything in our mind without worrying about what our friends will think. We are sure that they will take our talk in the spirit it was made. We are unguarded and open with friends in our talk.

A true friend is a little more than a very good friend. A true friend will support you even if it hurts his/her own interest. A true friend will understand your motives and needs and will be with you without any analysis or criticism. A true friend will come forward to help without any request and be with us in need without showing it or expecting anything in return. With a true friend, you can be sure that you will get help to the extent possible by him/her. Nothing will remain unturned. A mother is a true friend of her children. If we share such relations with an adult we can say that we are true friends.

A true friend makes no excuses of having work or appointments or anything but will be with you whenever you need him/her. In your hour of desperation, a true friend will support you even if the whole world opposes you. A true friend is not an opportunist. A true friend means to have someone who is like mother, as I said earlier. Instead of having hundreds of good friends, if you have a true friend, treat yourself lucky. If you can also become a true friend of someone, you will be blessed, because it is much easier for all of us to expect but very difficult to give. Be a true friend yourself first.

4. True Friendship

How can we find true friendship in this often phony, temporary world? Friendship involves recognition or familiarity with another's personality. Friends often share likes and dislikes, interests, pursuits, and passion.

How can we recognize potential friendship? Signs include a mutual desire for companionship and perhaps a common bond of some kind. Beyond that, genuine friendship involves a shared sense of caring and concern, a desire to see one another grow and develop, and a hope for each other to succeed in all aspects of life. True friendship involves action: doing something for someone else while expecting nothing in return; sharing thoughts and feelings without fear of judgment or negative criticism.

True friendship involves relationship. Those mutual attributes we mentioned above become the foundation in which recognition transpires into relationship. Many people say, "Oh, he's a good friend of mine," yet they never take time to spend time with that "good friend". Friendship takes time: time to get to know each other, time to build shared memories, time to invest in each other's growth.

Trust is essential to true friendship. We all need someone with whom we can share our lives, thoughts, feelings, and frustrations. We need to be able to share our deepest secrets with someone, without worrying that those secrets will end up on the Internet the next day! Failing to be trustworthy with those intimate secrets can destroy a friendship in a hurry. Faithfulness and loyalty are keys to true friendship. Without them, we often feel betrayed, left out, and lonely. In true friendship, there is no backbiting, no negative thoughts, no turning away.

True friendship requires certain accountability factors. Real friends encourage one another and forgive one another where there has been an offense. Genuine friendship supports during times of struggle. Friends are dependable. In true friendship, unconditional love develops. We love our friends no matter what and we always want the best for our friends.

5. Friends Are of Like Mind

The Lord Jesus Christ gave us the definition of a true friend: "Greater love has no one than this that he lay down his life for his friends. You are my friends if you do what I command. I no longer call you servants, because a servant does not know his master's business. Instead, I have called you friends, for everything that I learned from my Father I have made known to you". Jesus is the pure example of a true friend, for He laid down His life for His "friends". What is more, anyone may become His friend by trusting in Him as his personal savior, being born again and receiving new life in Him.

Proverbs is a good source of wisdom regarding friends. "A friend loves at all times, and a brother is born for adversity". "A man of many companions may come to ruin, but there is a friend who sticks closer than a brother". The issue here is that in order to have a friend, one must be a friend. "Wounds from a friend can be trusted, but an enemy multiplies kisses". "As iron sharpens iron, so one man sharpens another".

The principle of friendship is also found in Amos. "Can two walk together, except they be agreed?" Friends are of like mind. The truth that comes from all of this is a friendship is a relationship that is entered into by individuals, and it is only as good or as close as those individuals choose to make it. Someone has said that if you can count your true friends on the

fingers of one hand, you are blessed. A friend is one whom you can be yourself with and never fear that he or she will judge you. A friend is someone that you can confide in with complete trust. A friend is someone you respect and that respects you, not based upon worthiness but based upon a likeness of mind.

Finally, the real definition of a true friend comes from the Apostle Paul: "For scarcely for a righteous man will one die; yet perhaps for a good man someone would even dare to die. But God demonstrates His own love toward us, in that while we were still sinners, Christ died for us". "Greater love has no one than this, than to lay down one's life for his friends." Now, that is true friendship!

Topic Four   Relations Between the Young and Their Parents

Part One: Dialogues

Dialogue 1   Different Ages Have Different Tastes

(Jenny, a college student, is discussing music with her father Mr. Smith)

Jenny: Good news!

Mr. Smith: What's up?

Jenny: Eason Cheng is going to have his live performance in our city next month. I can't wait!

Mr. Smith: Who is Eason Cheng?

Jenny: Dad, he is my favorite. I'm surprised you do not know who he is. Listen. (Jenny turns on her MP3 and hands it to her father.) This is his new album.

Mr. Smith: What on earth is it anyway! I don't like pop songs very much, especially the rock and roll. Most of the pop songs are too loud and wild for me.

Jenny: But dad, it makes us feel powerful and energetic and Eason is one of the most famous singers from Hong Kong.

Mr. Smith: I don't care. It just sounds like noise to me. I simply can't take it.

Jenny: Listen to his songs for a while and you'll like them. (Jenny plugs the loudspeaker and plays the songs at full blast. She moves her body to the accompaniment of the songs.) Oh, it is the right feel.

Mr. Smith: Turn down the volume, please! That only hurts my eardrums and drives me crazy.

Jenny: (Showing disappointment) I love him, but if you really hate it that much, I'll put on something else. What do you want to hear now?

Mr. Smith: What about some easy-listening music? Maybe something by Celine Dion?

Jenny: Not from her again! Her music isn't very hip any more. I think she is a bore.

Dialogue 2   Saving for the Rainy Day

(Jenny comes into the room while her parents are reading the newspaper in the living room.)

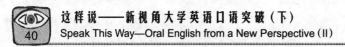

Jenny's Father: Look, just look at this! It's really unbelievable. A guy won 5 million Yuan in the lotto!

Jenny's Mother: What luck!

Jenny: (To her mom) What would you do if you won 5 million Yuan, mom?

Jenny's Mother: Me? You know I'm not crazy about buying lotto tickets. They say 100% of the winners brought tickets. But they don't tell you 100% of the losers did too. And there are a lot more losers.

Jenny: Just image what if…?

Jenny's Mother: Well, I know what I wouldn't do! I wouldn't throw it all away on junk. If I won so much money, I would for sure donate some to poor kids in the developing regions of our country.

Jenny: What a noble idea! But if I won, I make spend the first two million having a good time and buying things I've always wanted.

Jenny's Mother: What would you buy?

Jenny: A Poche or A Farrari, and I'd definitely spend the rest of money traveling around. You know, there's nothing I enjoy more than traveling.

Jenny's Mother: Hey, you'd spend your winnings like that? Wouldn't you think of keeping some for the rainy day? I'd keep most of my winnings in the bank.

Jenny: Come on, Mom. How stingy can you be!

Jenny's Mother: Maybe I am stingy from your perspective. I'll make sure that I'd be very careful to make that amount of money last me for the rest of my life. There are always times we need money.

Jenny: What use would that be, if you didn't have any fun?

Jenny's Mother: Oh, I'd have fun. I'd just be careful about how much fun I had. You'd end up penniless if you spent your winnings like that.

Words and Expressions

Eason Cheng		陈奕迅，香港著名歌手	Celine Dion		席琳·迪翁被认为是有史以来最伟大的歌手之一
album	*n.*	唱片	hip	*adj.*	新潮的
at full blast		最大音量	lotto	*n.*	乐透（一种赌博游戏）
to the accom-paniment of		在……伴奏下	Porsche		保时捷轿车
eardrum	*n.*	耳膜	Farrari		法拉利轿车
easy-listening music		悠扬悦耳的音乐	from the perspective		从……角度
			end up		以……结束

Part Two: Related Questions with Suggested Answers

1. Is there really a generation gap among the young and their parents? Why or why not?

Yes, I think so. The generation gap is a real problem we face nowadays. Children often complain that their parents do not understand them while parents worry about their children's behaviors and ideas. The generation gap between children and parents does exist for several reasons. Firstly, people who live in different times have different viewpoints towards social customs and tradition. For example, parents who were born in the 1950s are very surprised at the fashion in the 1990s. Secondly, the parents and children seldom sit down together to talk or communicate with each other equally. Thirdly, the children want to be more independent, but parents still want to keep their children under their wing.

To solve the problem and bridge the generation gap, parents should treat their children as friends and try to understand the feelings and thoughts of the young. Meanwhile, children should respect their parents and look at problems from their parents' point of view. Furthermore, parents should keep studying and keep up with the latest trends in fashion. In this way, they can better understand their children. Work together and the problem will be solved.

2. Would you like to live together with your parents when you get married? Why or why not?

Well, it depends. If they want to come and live with us, that's OK. In this case, we can look after each other. I can take care of my parents and they can take care of me and my child. Of course, that's a very ideal situation. But if I work in a faraway city, my parents do not want to leave their old home, and then they will continue to live there. In that case, I will try to go and see them when I have time. They can enjoy harmonious relationships with the people all around them and they will live happily.

3. Why do young people and their parents often see things differently?

I think, first of all, young people and elderly people live in different times and have different ideas about many things they do. For example, elderly people who were born in the 1950s are very surprised at the fashions in shops today. Secondly, the education young people and their parents have received is not the same with each generation emphasizing on the values and life styles that prevail in their own times. Take television remotes, for example. People in their 1950s learned very little about television remotes when they were young. So they don't know how to switch from one television channel to another. Some of them even think that they might break something if they hit a button they have never touched before. Using mobile phones is another case in point. Many of them are clumsy in using mobile phones, especially when they want to

compose messages. They see mobile phones as useless or even monstrous.

4. What are some of the main differences concerning work, consumption, clothing, behavior and family life between the young people and their parents?

Older people think that once a man takes a job, he should do it until he gets retired, while the young believe that people should change their jobs if they are unhappy about it. Parents believe that people should save the money in case some unexpected things happen; while young people insist that they should enjoy life first before trying to save money. Parents wear clothes just out of necessity, while young people never stop chasing fashion. Some of them even wear weird clothes to be fashionable. Parents tend to be more conservative in behavior while young people are often aggressive and risk-taking. Parents think family life is very important and their whole concern, while young people think the family life is only part of their life.

5. Who do you prefer the classroom instruction, young teachers or elderly professors? Why?

Well, it is really difficult to say which better teachers are. For me, in university, I would rather be taught by older professors. Generally speaking, older professors are more knowledgeable because of the more years they have spent on learning and research. Also they are more experienced because they've been teaching for so long. Knowledge and experience are the most important things for teachers to make their teaching effective. Students like to attend classes that are informative and well organized. In addition, older professors are more patient. They spare no efforts in making important yet difficult points clear to students. I think in middle school, pupils usually like to be taught by young teachers because young teachers are more energetic and friendly. Young teachers tend to have more passion in the classroom and have more in common with students. They can talk to the students and argue with them in order to make points clear.

6. Do you think parents are always conservative? Why or why not?

Well, we can't say that all parents are conservative. But there is a tendency to become more conservative as you grow older. This is because as you grow old you see more and experience more. As a result, you are not as radical and aggressive as you once were. You see the world as it is and you don't try to do something about it. Secondly, you are not as ambitious as before. You don't try to learn something new. You don't want to argue with others. And you don't want them to argue with you.

7. What should young people learn from their parents?

Some people say that the best classroom in the world is at the feet of an older person. Young people can learn a lot from older people. Older people are wise. Having lived many years elderly people have a lot of experience and they've learned from it. They know first-hand what it's like to live through tragedies and triumphs, times of war and peace, both personally and as a member of society. For example, a baby who suddenly gets sick calls her mom because she knows her mother knows how to care for sick children. The mother knows when it's time to consult a doctor about children's illnesses because of the experience she's acquired raising her family.

Also parents exhibit a sense of calm because they have lived through so many events. They know that life goes on despite adversity. For many of them, fears about what could happen have been replaced with a sense of acceptance, and, with acceptance comes peace.

8. If you sometimes disagree with your parents on certain things, how do you deal with the situation?

When I disagree with my patents I don't try to argue with them or challenge with them right now. If the disagreement is not of a big deal I let them voice their opinions on the matter. Even if the disagreement matters a lot I try not to argue. Instead, I let them know why I disagree with them. I avoid pointing out that the generation gap. Saying that we cannot communicate because of the generation gap would offend them and make matters worse. Sometimes I listen to them patiently, smiling and making jokes. I listen to them taking about their old stories and their young days. Then I figure out the problem on my own.

9. Why do people say that young people are the hope of tomorrow?

As we know, people are mortal. When old people die, young people replace them. Young people have to live, to contribute and to keep the world going. They have to work as world-builders. They can do that because, first of all, young people are vigorous and energetic. They have enough energy for work and life. Without energy you can't contribute so much and you can't work more efficiently. Secondly, young people are more curious to learn. They want to know and learn more about the world. Out of curiosity, they get the knowledge and skills that are needed in creating more wealth. Thirdly, they are confident. They know what they can do to shape a better world. For all these reasons young people are the hope of tomorrow.

10. How do you understand the Chinese virtue "Respect the elderly and take care of the young"?

The elderly and the young are two indispensable parts in our society and we should treat them nicely. On the one hand, the elderly should be given enough respect and care. We should always bear in mind that what we have and enjoy now was earned by the elderly when they are young. Those people who don't think that way can't deny that they are bound to become old one day. Therefore, any kind of maltreatment of old people should be prohibited. On the other hand, we should take good care of the young, too. It is in the young that we see future, for they are the future builders. Taking care of them and protecting them from being hurt has become our

duty. We are supposed to provide them with a good environment to grow up in and give them educational opportunities for their development. However, we should be careful not to spoil them. Instead, we should tell them to work hard and be independent.

Words and Expressions

harmonious	*adj.*	和睦的	tendency	*n.*	趋势
prevail	*v.*	流行，盛行	ambitious	*adj.*	雄心勃勃的
switch	*v.*	转换，换台	adversity	*n.*	困境，逆境
monster	*n.*	猛兽	figure *sth.* out		将某事弄清楚
conservative	*adj.*	保守的	offend	*v.*	冒犯
aggressive	*adj.*	激进的	maltreatment	*n.*	虐待
energetic	*adj.*	精力充沛的			

Part Three: Related Pictures with Suggested Descriptions

Picture One   China's Population

China, with about over 1.3 billion people, is the world's largest and most populous country. As the world's population is approximately 6.7 billion, China represents a full 20% of the world's population. So one in every five people on the planet is a resident of China.

China's population growth has been somewhat slowed by the one child policy, in effect since 1979. As recently as 1950, China's population was a mere 563 million. The population grew dramatically through the following decades to one billion in the 1980s.

China's total fertility rate is 1.7, which means that, on average, every woman gives birth to 1.7 children throughout her life. The necessary total fertility rate for a stable population is 2.1; nonetheless, China's population is expected to grow over the next few decades. This can be attributed to immigration and a decrease in infant mortality and a decrease in death rate as national health improves.

By the late 2010s, China's population is expected to reach 1.4 billion. Around 2030, China's population is anticipated to peak and then slowly start dropping.

In the next few decades, India, the world's second most populous country is expected to surpass China in population. By 2040, India's population is expected to be 1.52 billion; that same year, China's will be 1.45 billion and India will become the world's most populous country.

Picture Two   Not All Younger Generation Problems Are Negative

There is no denying fact that younger generation problem is frequently referred to as "negative sign" for the simple reason that the problem often does harm to the younger to some extent. In fact, some problems can help young persons to broaden their minds, strengthen their characters and increase their necessary experiences.

What is younger generation problem? No one can collect all the younger generation problems together. It is believed that you can define the "problem" in broad sense and narrow sense. This can give rise to curious situation: in its broad sense you will find it inevitable the "problem" involved almost every young person; in its narrow sense you will get the answer in an opposed way. There is no doubt that every generation has had their own problems. But human race is developing without a stop from then on. The development is always based on resolving problems. It certainly does in young generation as well. History has proved that it is true again and again.

According to a national poll last year, eighteen to twenty-nine-year-olds agreed by large percentages that young people today are "less idealistic" and "more selfish", and that they are less concerned with the problems of society than with their own personal future. And few things seem to stir up more fear among today's young people than the prospect of a military draft. Feelings of patriotism are articulated much more freely now, but there seems little enthusiasm for military conscription, and no one wants to spend several years in the armed forces engaged in activities which have nothing to do with their future work.

One of the great early writers once said that human character is formed by society. As we all know, younger generation will be always the owner in the future. It is true that they will lead our society to forward by overcoming their shortcomings caused by present society.

Picture Three　China's One-child Policy Burdens Younger Generation

China's one child policy, which has heavily skewed the ratio of young people to retirees, is placing an increasingly heavy burden on the next generation of workers.

In the State's "ideal" family, the only son will have to support six people in his adult years: his own parents, his mother's parents and his father's parents. As the traditional family structure begins to suffer, the number of people in the work force is decreasing. It's getting more and more difficult. Now there are a lot more factories and fewer workers because of the one-child policy. Costs are going up. It's not looking good.

The ranks of elderly people are steadily increasing, however, and within the next few decades, China will be taking care of 400 million elderly people. As a result, elderly care businesses and senior homes are having a steady influx of clients. Because of the one-child policy there are fewer children in China. So, many schools are changing into old people's homes. It's very common now.

According to the Guardian Unlimited, the State claimed that its population control policies have prevented 400 million births since the 1979 when the restrictions were first introduced into the country. The government's one-child policy, oftentimes implemented through forced sterilization and abortion, has created an unprecedented problem in the work force that is causing more and more concern in society.

In 2004, Zhang Weiqing, National Population and Family Planning Commission Minister, predicted that the increasing disproportion between seniors and working people would eventually have serious effects on China's retirement system. He noted, "The aging problem is much more severe in the country's rural areas than in urban areas, which challenges the establishment of a health insurance system and social security system for the elderly."

In 1999 there were 10 workers for every senior in China. The number is predicted to drop sharply to six workers per retiree by 2020 and fall again to three workers for every retired person by 2050.

Words and Expressions

approximately	*adv.*	大约地	skew	*v.*	此处指紧密相连
resident	*n.*	居民	ratio	*n.*	比率
fertility	*n.*	生育能力	retiree	*n.*	退休的人
anticipate	*v.*	期待	implement	*v.*	实施；执行
inevitable	*adj.*	不可避免的	sterilization	*n.*	绝育
prospect	*n.*	可能性	abortion	*n.*	流产
military draft		征兵	unprecedented	*adj.*	前所未有的
articulate	*v.*	清楚地表达	disproportion	*n.*	不成比例
conscription	*n.*	征兵			

Part Four: Related Passages

1. Bringing Up Children

One reason why the family unit is crumbling is that parents have relinquished their authority over children. The permissive school of thought says, "Let the child do what he wants to when he wants to, no matter what it is, don't warp his personality, don't thwart him, you'll ruin him for life. Because of this we've got a generation of spoilt self-centered brats with no respect for their elders. Children always push to see how much they can get away with; if you give them nothing to push against, there are no moral limits, and no moral convictions will develop in the children. We have this in the schools-children have much less respect for their teachers nowadays."

How do you define respect? "Realizing that someone else might have desires also. Respect doesn't mean that when someone in authority says 'jump' you jump—that's the military approach—but young people today, if they have an opinion that's different from yours, then you are the fool and they are right, even if they don't have enough experience to judge."

How do you feel about children using swearword?

"I never hear them swear, but I saw one of my daughter's diaries and it was full of a word that I'd have spanked her for if she'd said it aloud. Swearing goes against my sensibilities. It's mental laziness. If people aren't allowed to swear they use their brains to find a better word."

Do you think it's just a matter of convention or do you think there's a deeper moral objection to swearing?

"I think it's not done. It's taboo in nice society. We've been taught not to swear, and I think well-brought-up people should avoid it. If I ever hear a woman use 's-h-i-t' I think a lot less of her."

2. Generation Gap

One of the most popular topics many people talk about now is generation gap. "It's like being bitten to death by ducks." That's how one mother described her constant squabbles with her fourteen-year-old daughter. And she is hardly alone in the experience. According to a poll, the relations between parents and teenagers are frequently marked by squabbling, nagging and arguing despite considerable love between them. What causes this verbal behavior and which party is at fault: the adolescent or the adult?

One of the major causes for the misunderstandings between them is that parents and children see almost everything in different perspectives. While children always complain that their parents are out of touch with modern ways, the parents criticize their children for the radical ways to deal with things. The gap seems unbridgeable.

Accounts of conflict between adolescents and their parents can also date back virtually as far as recorded history. But our predecessors enjoyed an important advantage over today's parents: adolescents rarely lived at home much beyond puberty. Poverty drove high-school-aged youngsters out of home to learn their trade as apprentice. But now the higher standard of living has brought extended schooling, which has prolonged youngsters' economic dependence on their parents and delayed their entrance into full-time work roles. The net result has been a dramatic increase in the amount of time that physically mature youngsters and their parents must live in close contact, and hence in the conflict between parents and their adolescents.

Beyond these obvious reasons, however, lies a deeper cause: the changing attitude of the youth. For years, offspring, especially sons had been expected to remain at home permanently, bring their spouses home to the big, extended family when they got married. But that's changing now. With growing demand for independence and the improved living standard, more and more young people seek to leave the parental family to establish their own households. Young people want to be independent. They have their own philosophy of life, their own way of filling leisure, and their own method of raising and educating children. To leave their parents and live independently is to avoid disagreement and quarrels brought about by the generation gap, and to enjoy the freedom from constrains of a big family.

As young people, we should know what the differences are between the two generations; otherwise, we cannot understand why we can't get along well with the older generation.

3. Old People and Young People

Old people are always saying that the young are not what they were. The same comment is made from generation to generation and it is always true. It has never been truer than it is today. The young are better educated; they have a lot more money to spend and enjoy more freedom. They grow up more quickly and are not so dependent on their parents. They think more for themselves and do not blindly accept the ideals of their elders. Events which the older generation remembers vividly are nothing more than past history. This is as it should be. Every new generation is different from the one that preceded it. Today the difference is very marked indeed. The old always assume that they know best for the simple reason that they have been around a bit longer. They don't like to feel that their values are being questioned or threatened. And this is precisely what the young are doing. They are questioning the assumptions of their elders and disturbing their sense of feeling contended. They doubt that the older generation has created the best of all possible worlds.

These are not questions the older generation can shrug off lightly. Their record over the past forty years or so hasn't been exactly spotless. Traditionally, the young have turned to the older for guidance. Today, the situation might be reversed. The old—if they are prepared to admit it— could learn a thing or two from their children. One of the biggest lessons they could learn is that enjoyment is not sinful. Enjoyment is a principle one could apply to all aspects of life. It is surely not wrong to enjoy your work and enjoy your leisure; to shed restricting inhibitions. It is surely not wrong to live in the present rather than in the past or future. The world is full of uncertainty and tension. This is their glorious heritage. Can we be surprised that they should so often question the sanity of the generation that passed it down?

4. The Old Age of Young Age

Did you ever experience the desire to be older than you were as a young man/woman? Did you ever have the unconscious or involuntary urge to say you were older than you were just because you wanted to sound and look more mature, to gain more credibility and support or even an advantageous image in the world of grown-ups, but as time passed by and you grew older, you realized that you had been rushing all along to reach an age you were going to reach anyway and even sooner than you expected? I experienced this feeling (and still do) many times in many ways, in many situations and I'm sure lots of you did (and still do) too. I guess it's only natural to be or feel older than you are because this way one feels more important, maybe more in tune with the world, has the illusion of having more experience, of knowing more things than he/she knows, of dealing with things better, of becoming more of who he/she is. This is basically the consequence of acting on the "oldie but goldie" principle that older is better, and maybe more fulfilling and rewarding from many points of view, since becoming older means one is getting closer to the "grandfather of all knowledge" status. Yet, when we really do reach a certain old age, we realize we were better off when we are kids, and some of us even begin acting like one, so it's probably all a mater of perspective, of perceiving time: it's fast when we are young, because we want it to be, and all too slow when we get old, because we don't want it to be. Humans are truly fast-paced animals; human nature, on the other hand is never satisfied with what is already there, but with what is not and apparently should be.

5. Old People

Compared with the Chinese elderly, why are there apparently more old people in America who pursuit independent life? Although we have the fine tradition of respecting and raising aged people in China, the phenomena that different ages bring about the contradiction of ideas between old people and their children, has to be paid more attention. Likewise, the traditionally independent character in America, I think, is possibly attributed to fill the gap of the thoughts between the old and the young. I conclude there are other reasons as followed:

First of all, living condition is the one of other main reasons. In China, with the increasing number of people, there seldom are the families which can provide spare houses for the elderly. This situation tends to lead them to reluctantly stay with their sons.

Secondly, the elderly Chinese have no belief or religion which can rescue people out of fear of death. They are unwilling to live alone, because no one can help them out of emergency. In spirit, they are discouraged to face death lonely without their relative's cherishing.

Moreover, illiteracy is a problem among the elderly Chinese. Most of the aged people have no ability to acquire the knowledge from books except of some superficial TV programs. On the other hand, the barrier of communication impels them to connect only with a limited few friends. Therefore, they focus either on their family contradictions which are likely to anguish and frustrate them deeply, or on how to negatively avoid illness and death, which, to some extent, take a heavy burden on their mind.

Topic Five   Animals and Pets

Part One: Dialogues

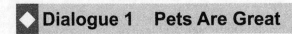
Dialogue 1   Pets Are Great

(Cheng and Nancy are friends and they are exchanging their opinions about pets.)

Nancy: People say dogs are men's best friends.

Cheng: Yeah, my neighbor's husband died a couple of months ago and her daughter bought her a lovely dog to cheer her up. With the little dog, the old lady isn't so lonely and she is gradually recovering from the pain of losing her husband.

Nancy: Westerners often take pets, especially dogs as their friends, even family members. They say westerns treat their pets like they treat their children—sometimes even better.

Cheng: Yeah, I heard that in America a widow left $12 million in a trust for her little dogs. Now, more and more Chinese people are beginning to raise pets. What kind of pets do western people prefer?

Nancy: Dogs, cats, horses, fish, monkeys, crocodile, anything can be a pet.

Cheng: Do you have a pet?

Nancy: I have some tropical fish.

Cheng: Fish is beautiful, but what is fun of having fish?

Nancy: At the end of a tiring day it cheers me up when I just sit and watch them swimming around through weeds and corals.

Cheng: I can understand. After a day's work, I just want to find something to help me relax too.

Nancy: The fish I keep are small and beautiful. They give me peace of mind and hours of entertainment. Actually there are more advantages than that. Watching fish swimming alleviates eye strain and even depression. I highly recommend getting one or two fish yourself.

Cheng: Maybe I should!

Nancy: Well, I need to go back to feed my fish. Talk to you later.

Cheng: Ok, bye.

◆ Dialogue 2　Pandas Are Cute

(Wang and Nancy are chatting.)

Nancy: What is your favorite animal?

Wang: The giant panda, of course!

Nancy: Hey, Chinese people are crazy about pandas.

Wang: Don't you think they're cute?

Nancy: Yeah, I like pandas. I just find out that pandas enjoy high privilege in China, and panda is one of the representative animals of the mascots for 2008 Olympic Games.

Wang: You're right. You know, a pair of pandas, Tuan Tuan and Yuan Yuan, was flown from Wolong Nature Reserve to Taipei last week.

Nancy: As far as I know, the pandas' names, when putting together, mean reunion in Chinese and we hope the move will help thaw the relations between Taiwan and Main-land China.

Wang: Yeah, pandas are an emblem of China and a symbol of cultural exchange between the main-land and Taiwan. Besides, there are more than twenty pandas living in oversea zoos as gifts from Chinese people.

Nancy: Pandas are an endangered species which only inhabit in China.

Wang: Yeah, the panda is a living fossil that has survived the Ice Age. Their natural habitat is the mountains of the southeast part of China. Three decades ago it was threatened by the loss of their habitats, by a very low birthrate and by a shortage of bamboos. Fortunately, with the efforts made by scientists, nature reserves have been established and wild pandas have increased in numbers.

Nancy: You mention bamboo. People say that the couple, Tuan Tuan and Yuan Yuan, are now gradually getting used to the bamboos grown in Taiwan.

Wang: Yeah, though bamboo shoots are pandas' main diet, the panda is classified as a carnivore. With little energy and little protein from bamboo, the panda tends to spend most of its time eating bamboo. So that is also the reason why the panda is usually described as reclining peacefully and eating bamboo, which fosters its image of innocence and baby-like cuteness.

Nancy: Hey, you're almost a panda expert.

Wang: Don't flatter me! I'm just a panda lover. Actually, I have a few videos, magazines and books about pandas. You may borrow them if you're interested.

Nancy: Sure! Thank you for your offer. Let's go to your room to have a look at how many pandas you have in your collection.

Words and Expressions

alleviate	v.	减轻；缓和	fossil	n.	化石
mascot	n.	吉祥物	carnivore	n.	食肉动物
Nature Reserve		自然保护区	protein	n.	蛋白质
thawing	n.	化解	recline	v.	躺；斜倚
emblem	n.	标志	cuteness	n.	可爱
endangered species		濒于灭绝的物种			

Part Two: Related Questions with Suggested Answers

1. Do you like going to the zoo? Why or why not?

Well, I think so. I like to see all kinds of animals and various wonderful animal performances. In the zoo, we can also get a lot of information about the animals and their different living habits and various living conditions. I think going to the zoo is a good way to learn, especially for children. I still remember the first time I saw the pandas. They were so lovely and cute. I just wanted to take them home with me. The lions I saw were so powerful. The tigers were adorable. I like going to the zoo. I always have fun there.

I enjoy going to the zoo because I like to see different kinds of animals and learn a lot about them. The first time I went to the zoo, I was attracted by lovely pandas, naughty monkeys and elegant cranes. Besides domestic animals, we also get a chance to see animals which inhabit different countries or other continents: kangaroos from Australia, giraffes from Africa, even penguins from the South Pole. Thus visiting the zoo is a good way to broaden our horizon. Furthermore, there are a lot to learn when we visit a zoo. Usually, a zoo provides a brief introduction to wildlife. Some zoos even set up exhibitions and shows about certain animals. Through these channels, we can get a lot of information about these animals, their living habits and habitats.

2. Panda is known as a national treasure in China. Why is that so?

Panda is known as a national treasure in China because the number of them is very limited. Panda is one of the scarcest animals in the world. People in the world like panda very much. There used to be many pandas in China long ago. As their habitat was reduced and also due to global warming, the number of pandas dwindled. Great efforts have been made to save pandas from being extinct. In Sichuan, China, a big nature reserve for pandas has been set up to keep pandas free and let them live in the wild again. Still there is no sign of significant increase in their number. Also there is a greater demand from other countries for pandas.

3. What wild animals do you find most interesting? Why?

I think the red-crowned crane is very interesting. Red-crowned cranes are very beautiful and elegant. They are regarded as birds of good luck in China. Cranes have been part of Chinese culture for over 3,000 years. There are a lot of legends and stories about cranes. Red-crowned cranes can live as long as 60 years, making it the longest-living member of a bird species. For centuries, cranes have been revered in China as symbols of longevity because of this. The image of the red-crowned crane can be seen in many places in China. People often draw red-crowned cranes and pine trees together. The lifespan of both pines and cranes are very long. Red-crowned cranes can dance beautifully. While dancing, they keep their wings half-open, jump around and sing for each other. That's why people think the red-crowned crane is the animal of elegance. Red-crowned cranes are one of the world's most endangered species. Despite protective laws, poaching remains a major problem.

4. Why do some people like having dogs as their pets?

People love dogs because dogs, like us, are social animals. That trait accounts for their trainability, playfulness, interaction and ability to fit in to household situations. Dog packs mimic human behavior. They see us as members, hopefully the leaders of their pack. Dogs meet a variety of human needs, such as service dogs for the handicapped and as companions. The dog has the nickname of "man's best friend". People love dogs also because no matter whether poor or rich, ugly or pretty you are; dogs are loyal to you and still love you. Think about it. A dog will never turn its back on you if you don't make a lot of money. It will never ignore you. Some people don't have children and treat dogs as children. Dogs can bring their owners joy because they can make them feel loved and needed.

5. Why do some people like to have cats as their pets?

Some people simply love cats. People love cats for a variety of reasons. Cats are playful, they are mysterious, and they have attitude. These are all welcome traits from one human to the next. We can relate to these types of behaviors because we display many of them ourselves. Cats clearly provide a sense of love and communication. They bring joy with their purring and their cuddling, and the way they rub their faces along our hands or legs ignites a sense of warmth and soulful comfort. Cats also possess great intelligence which involves a keen sense of survival, a playful wit, and also a more profound knowledge that enables them to relate to us without language. Do you ever notice a cat as it stares intently at the door handle, quietly but directly telling you its wishes to go outside? What about a hungry cat looking for her food bowl, intermittently glancing at the bowl and her owner, demanding to be fed? There is no doubt that their intelligence makes taking care of them much easier.

6. What do you think of some medical experiments performed on animals?

Well, this is really a difficult question to answer. Scientists who work in medical labs know from experience that there is a very high chance that drugs that work on animals also work with people. Sometimes mice are used in the first stage of research, then later dogs and monkeys. So far, medical testing on animals has produced some of the most useful drugs known to mankind, saving countless lives. This somewhat mitigates sacrificing animals for potentially huge benefit for the people who will be taking the drugs. Without these drugs some patients will suffer horribly before dying.

However, testing medicines on animals should be minimized. It is cruel, unjust, unethical and inhumane to carry out medical experiments on animals. Animals have the same rights as humans. Their lives should be protected from danger inflicted by humans. Humans can find alternatives to replace drug testing on animals.

7. Why do we have to be friends with animals?

Cats, dogs, pigs, birds and even sheep are all our friends. We get to love them, protect them and give them a safer and healthier place to live in. If an animal becomes rare or endangered in an area, then any other animals or plants in that environment are also affected, due to the disruption of the food chain. For instance, if a small animal dies becomes extinct, then all its predators will suffer from starvation. Also, if all the predators are wiped out, the prey will become overpopulated, and use all of their food. If one animal becomes extinct it will inevitably lead to the extinction of other animals connected to the original in the food chain. The more animals that become extinct, the worse the world's situation will become.

Animals are our future, so if we kill all the cuddly and different creatures, we will live in a very boring world. Animals help us and animals are our friends.

8. Why do vegetarians decide not to eat meat?

Today, some people choose not to eat meat. They are called vegetarians. Those who eat nothing associated with animals or fish are called vegans. They believe that animals and fish, like us, have lives too. They even believe that animals feel pain when we kill them. They think that killing animals is immoral. To them, if we eat meat, it is just like killing animas ourselves. Some people don't eat meat because of their religious beliefs. They believe God made animals and they are not to be killed and eaten.

Vegetarians believe that there is a great variety of foods other than meat for people to eat. They eat the kinds of vegetables that can also give them nourishment and even make them live longer.

9. Animals are in danger nowadays. What are some of the causes of that?

One of the causes is that man kills animals. Throughout history man has been a hunter. He still is. Many modern hunters don't just kill for food. Some fill for pleasure, others for profit. Hunters like these are called poachers. As a result many rare animals are dying out. For example, in the 1970s, there were 1.3 million African elephants. Today, because of poaching, there are fewer than 85,000.

Also, people keep cutting down trees, which destroy animals' habitats. Some of the animals and birds such as monkeys and woodpeckers live in the treetops in the rainforest. They are always swinging and flying from one tree to another looking for food among the leaves and branches. With trees disappearing, these animals are losing their homes.

Thirdly, worldwide pollution has destroyed so many animals' habitats. Industrial pollution has changed the balance of nature. Each species in a habitat, for example, wood, jungle, marsh or forest, needs and helps the rest. If one animal, bird or insect disappears, all the others suffer, too.

10. How do we protect animals?

First, find what the root of the situation is. People are damaging the environment. People have hunted animals for meat. Actually, wild animals are endangered by man's behavior. What can we do? First, we have to pass laws to protect endangered species. We have to create protective areas. This will create a safe environment for animals to live in. Sending animals to zoos is not the best choice, but better than continuing to kill or harm them. Basically, we must be aware of the importance of protecting animals, and be ready to share the earth with them.

Words and Expressions

red-crowned cranes		丹顶鹤	guarantee	v.	保证
longevity	n.	长寿	predator	n.	食肉动物
poach	v.	盗猎；偷捕	extinct	v.	灭绝
the handicapped		残疾人	cuddly	adj.	可爱的；逗人
intermittently	adv.	断断续续地			爱的
sacrifice	v.	牺牲	vegetarian	n.	素食主义者
potentially	adj.	潜在的	poacher	n.	盗猎者；偷捕者
minimize	v.	减少到最低程度	woodpecker	n.	啄木鸟
unethical	adj.	没有伦理道德的	habitat	n.	栖居地

Part Three: Related Pictures with Suggested Descriptions

▶ Picture One   Pets Are Good for You ◀

The basic meaning of "pet" is an animal we keep for emotional rather than economic reasons. A pet animal is kept as a companion, and we all need companions to keep us feeling happy. But pets offer us more than mere companionship; they invite us to love and be loved. Many owners feel their pets understand them, for animals are quick to sense anger and sorrow. Often a cat or dog can comfort us at times when human words don't help. We feel loved, too, by the way pets depend on us for a home, for food and drink. Dogs especially, look up to their owners, which make them feel important and needed.

A pet can be something different to each member of the family, another baby to the mother, a sister or brother to an only child, a grandchild to the elderly, but for all of us pets provide pleasure and companionship. It has even been suggested that tiny pets should be sent as companions to astronauts on space ships, to help reduce the stress and loneliness of space flights.

In this Plastic Age, when most of us live in large cities, pets are particularly important for children. A pet in the family keeps people in touch with the more natural, animal world. Seeing an animal give birth brings understanding of the naturalness of childbirth, and seeing a pet die helps a child to cope with sorrow. Learning to care for a pet helps a child to grow up into a loving adult who feels responsible towards those dependent on him. Rightly we teach children to be good to their pets. They should learn, too, that pets are good for us human beings.

▶ Picture Two   Do Animals Communicate? ◀

When we think of communication, we normally think of using words—talking face-to-face, writing messages and so on. But in fact we communicate far more in other ways. Our eyes and facial expressions usually tell the truth even when our words do not.

Then there are gestures, often unconscious: raising the eyebrows, rubbing the nose, shrugging the shoulders, tapping the fingers, nodding and shaking the head.

There is also the even more subtle "body language"—language of posture: Are you sitting or

standing—with arms or legs crossed? Is that person standing with hands in pockets, held in front of the body or hidden behind? Even the way we dress and the colors we wear communicate things to others.

So, do animals communicate? Not in words, although a parrot might be trained to repeat words and phrases which it doesn't understand. But, as we have learnt, there is more to communication than words.

Take dogs for example. They bare their teeth to warn, wag their tails to welcome and stand firm, with hair erect, to challenge. These signals are surely the equivalent of the human body-language of facial expression, gesture and posture.

Colors can be an important means of communication for animals. Many birds and fish change color, for example, to attract partners during the mating season. And mating itself is commonly preceded by a special dance in which both partners participate.

Picture Three   Animal Rights VS Human Health

Thanks to modern science and technology, great progress has been made in the field of medicine during the last few decades. However, when enjoying the comfort and security that modern medicine brings us, very few people come to realize that animals help us a lot in the whole process of developing certain kinds of medicines, which even means deadly body experiments to the animals in most cases. As a result, a heated discussion concerning whether animal rights are ignored for human health has been initiated around the world.

It is true that as life forms just like human beings in the earth, animals have the same rights for survival and safety. Therefore, many zoophiles believe that it is definitely species discrimination that researchers do drug or bacteria experiments on animals without regard to their safety and lives. In spite of all these arguments, I prefer to support medical experiments on certain kinds of animals.

On one hand, carrying out animal experiments is still the only way for researchers to find the safest and most effective treatment to some diseases today. Although animal experiments are quite cruel sometimes, the science must develop. Mankind still faces a great many problems, especially the deadly diseases people cannot deal with today; and usually we have to solve the problems at the sacrifice of some animals to achieve the universal happiness of the entire humanity. However, compared to the development of the society and the happiness of the members living in it, the sacrifice is quite worthwhile.

On the other hand, the earth we live in is a competitive world according to the famous law of the evolution put by Darwin, which demonstrates that the strong always defeat the weak and eventually become the master of the world. If we don't try to find out the way to defeat and cure all kinds of diseases, what will be waiting for us is perhaps the extinction of the whole human race. When "birds and beast flu" bursts out all over the world, human beings capture and kill millions of chickens and ducks. That probably means it is an obvious law that people protect themselves first when there exists the conflict of survival rights between human beings and animals.

In fact, human beings and animals can live and develop together in harmony. As long as we don't break the ecology balance, no one can blame it.

Words and Expressions

companionship	n.	陪伴	equivalent	adj.	对应的，同等的
astronaut	n.	宇航员	mating season		交配季节
unconscious	adj.	无意识的	precede	v.	位于……之前
shrug	v.	耸肩	zoophiles	n.	爱护动物者
tap	v.	轻敲 轻扣	Darwin		达尔文
posture	n.	姿势	extinction	n.	灭绝
parrot	n.	鹦鹉	ecology balance		生态平衡
erect	v.	直立			

Part Four: Related Passages

1. An Unmatchable Cat

I was sick that winter. It was inconvenient because my big room was due to be whitewashed. I was put in the little room at the end of the house. The house, nearly but not quite on the top of the hill, always seemed as if it might slide off into the corn fields below. This tiny room had a door, always open, and windows, always open, in spite of the windy cold of a July whose skies were an unending light clear blue. The sky, full of sunshine, the fields and sunlit.

But cold, very cold. The cat, a bluish grey Persian, arrived purring on my bed, and settled down to share my sickness, my food, my pillow, my sleep. When I woke in the mornings my face turned to half-frozen sheets; the outside of the fur blanket on the bed was cold; the smell of fresh whitewash from next door was cold and clean; the wind lifting and laying the dust outside the door was cold—but in the curve of my arm, a light purring warmth, the cat, my friend.

At the back of the house a wooden tub was set into the earth, outside the bathroom, to catch the bathwater. No pipes carrying water to taps on that farm; water was fetched by ox-drawn cart when it was needed, from the well about two miles away. Through the months of the dry season the only water for the garden was the dirty bathwater. The cat fell into this tub when it was full of hot water.

She screamed, was pulled out into a cold wind, washed in permanganate, for the tub was filthy, and held leaves and dust as well as soapy water, was dried and put into my bed to warm. But she grew burning hot with fever. She had pneumonia. We gave her what medicine we had in the house, but that was before antibiotics, and so she died. For a week she lay in my arm purring, purring, in a rough, trembling little voice that became weaker, then was silent; licked my hand, opened huge green eyes when I called her name and begged her to live; closed them, died, and was thrown into the deep old well—over a hundred feet deep it was—which had gone dry, because the underground water streams had changed their course one year.

That was it. Never again. And for years I matched cats in friends' houses, cats in shops, cats on farms, cats in the street, cats on walls, cats in memory, with that gentle, blue-grey purring creature which for me was the cat, the Cat, never to be replaced.

And besides, for some years my life did not include extras, unnecessaries, and ornaments. Cats had no place in an existence spent always moving from place to place, room to room. A cat needs a place as much as it needs a person to make its own.

And so it was not until twenty-five years later my life had room for a cat.

2. Dogs Have a Sense of Humor

The question of whether dogs have a sense of humor is often fiercely argued. My own opinion is that some have and some haven't. Dachshunds have, but not St Bernards or Great Danes. Apparently a dog has to be small to be fond of joke. You never find a Great Dane trying to be a comedian.

But it is fatal to let any dog know that he is funny, for he immediately loses his head and starts overdoing it. As an example of this I would point to Rudolph, a dachshund I once owned, whose slogan was "Anything for a Laugh". Dachshunds are always the worst offenders in this respect because of their peculiar shape. It is only natural that when a dog finds that his mere appearance makes the viewing public laugh, he should imagine that Nature intended him to be a comedian.

I had a cottage at the time outside an English village, not far from a farm, where they kept ducks, and one day the farmer called on me to say his ducks were disappearing and suspicion had fallen on my Rudolph. Why? I asked, and he said because mine was the only dog in the neighborhood except his own Towser, and Towser had been so carefully trained that he would not touch a duck if you brought it to him with orange sauce over it.

I was very annoyed. I said he only had to gaze into Rudolph's truthful brown eyes to see how baseless his suspicions were. Had he not, I asked, heard of foxes? How much more likely that a fox was the Bad Guy in the story. He was beginning to look doubtful and seemed about to make an apology, when Rudolph, who had been listening with the greatest interest and at a certain point, had left the room, came trotting in with a duck in his mouth.

Yes, dachshunds overplay their sense of humor, and I suppose other dogs have their faults, but they seem unimportant compared with their virtues.

3. She's All for the Birds

Twice a week, 58-year-old Mrs. Winifred Cass shops in the market for her main supplies, "topping up" daily by calling at local shops on her way home from work. But she's not buying family groceries!

She returns home laden with heavy bags of mixed hen corn, pigeon corn, peanuts and large packets of bird food to feed her larger "family", the wild birds of Leeds. And she's been doing this for 16 years.

Daily, she feeds the birds which frequent her garden, the area around the shop where she works part-time, and several patches of waste-ground near her home. Then, twice every week, she loads the carrying basket with bags of grain on to her tricycle and sets out to pedal the 20-min late ride up to the city centre.

"In the morning, birds on my own roof at home hang almost upside-down trying to see me through the windows." She laughed. "In severe conditions last winter, I had as many as four robins in my garden at the same time, though they're well known to be territorial birds."

"It's amazing how many different kinds of birds I see in the city itself. In Park Square, as well as the usual starlings, pigeons and sparrows, there are blue tits, great tits, thrushes, doves, and sometimes even seagulls."

It all started when Winifred was working at a cafe. She used to throw out stale bread and buns, and developed such an interest in the wild birds which accepted her offerings that she started taking food along to those in City Square as well.

On one occasion, an old lady sitting in the square remarked that the birds could do with a more nutritious diet. So Winifred began buying corn for them.

"In the end, I was carrying so much weight and tramping so far that my feet and arms really ached," she said, "I tried using wheeled shoppers, but with the weight of all that corn they were breaking within weeks. So I splashed out and bought this tricycle."

Winifred has come across other wild-life on her travels, too. "I stop to feed families of hedgehogs which I found at the side of the railway near the park." she said.

Despite her love of birds, she'd never want to keep one because she can't bear seeing them caged.

Disaster struck recently when a car reversed into her parked truck, damaging its wheels. But two local business men, hearing of her activities, decided kindly to help by replacing the wheels for her.

So now the "Bird Woman of Leeds" is back in action again, doing the job she loves best-caring for the host of feathered friends who have come to rely on her.

4. Too Many Pets in France

In France a campaign has been launched to warn against the danger of a threatening over-population…of pets. The country is the second most densely populated country in the world as far as domestic animals are concerned. At the moment it is inhabited by more than 8% million dogs and almost as many cats. Every second family in Paris owns one or more pets, which cause problems of hygiene that cannot be solved. In the year 2000 France will have more than 15 million dogs if no drastic measures are taken to stop this increase.

The French organization for the protection of animals has appealed to the owners to have their dogs and cats of both sexes sterilized, because the animals themselves are in danger of becoming the first victims. Every summer, when the holiday-exodus begins, thousands of dogs and cats are abandoned, because their owners, unable to take them along, do not want to or cannot find homes where their pets will be looked after during their absence. Only one of three of these stray animals can be adopted, the other two must be killed.

A great number of pet-owners, however, object to sterilization on grounds of "inadmissible cruelty".

5. Pets in the U.S. A

More than half of all U.S. households have a companion animal. Pets are more common in households with children, yet there are more pets than children in American households. There are more than 51 million dogs, 56 million cats, 45 million birds, 75 million small mammals and reptiles, and uncounted millions of aquarium fish.

It is important at this time to assess whether these populations have any beneficial impact on physical, social, and psychological health.

To this end, the National Institutes of Health convened a Technology Assessment Workshop on the Health Benefits of Pets on September 10-11, 1987. After a day-and-a-half of presentations by experts in relevant fields, a working group drafted the following report to provide the scientific community with a synthesis of the current knowledge and a framework for future research and to provide the public with the information it needs to make informed decisions regarding the health benefits of pets.

Throughout history animals have played a significant role in human customs, legends, and religions. Primitive people found that human-animal relationships were important to their very survival, and pet keeping was common in hunter-gatherer societies. In our own time, the great increase in pet ownership may reflect a largely urban population's often unsatisfied need for intimacy, nurturance, and contact with nature. However, it is impossible to determine when animals first were used specifically to promote physical and psychological health. The use of horseback riding for people with serious disabilities has been reported for centuries. In 1792, animals were incorporated into the treatment for mental patients at the York Retreat, England, as part of an enlightened approach attempting to reduce the use of harsh drugs and restraints. The first suggested use of animals in a therapeutic setting in the United States was in 1919 at St. Elizabeths Hospital in Washington, D. C., when Superintendent Dr. W. A. White received a letter from Secretary of the Interior F. K. Lane suggesting the use of dogs as companions for the psychiatric hospital's resident patients. Following this, the earliest extensive use of companion animals in the United States occurred from 1944 to 1945 at an Army Air Corps Convalescent Hospital at Pawling, New York. Patients recovering from war experiences were encouraged to work at the hospital's farm with hogs, cattle, horses, and poultry. After the war, modest efforts began in using animals in outpatient psychotherapy. During the 1970s, numerous case studies of animals facilitating therapy with children and senior citizens were reported.

Topic Six   Food

Part One: Dialogues

◆ Dialogue 1   What Do You Have for Breakfast and Lunch?

(In a university's canteen, Cheng and Nancy are talking about the differences of Chinese and western breakfast.)

Nancy: Let's go to the cafeteria.

Cheng: Yeah, I was already pretty hungry after the third period. Now, I'm starving to death.

Nancy: What do you usually have for breakfast?

Cheng: Porridge and a mantou, very traditional Chinese breakfast.

Nancy: Do you drink anything, like milk?

Cheng: I know milk is nourishing, but it does not agree with me. It upsets my stomach. I prefer something light.

Nancy: Breakfast is the most important meal of a day. Your breakfast is a way too light when you've got four whole hours of class ahead of you every morning.

Cheng: Then what do you have?

Nancy: Milk, cereal, toast, eggs and fruits.

Cheng: How do you manage to find the time to eat such a full breakfast? Isn't it a luxury for anyone rushing off to class?

Nancy: You bet. It's hard to set my alarm clock 15 or 20 minutes earlier than I'd have to otherwise. But just because we're busy or in a hurry doesn't mean we can skip breakfast. Eat breakfast like a king, lunch like a prince, and dinner like a pauper.

(At noon, they arrive at the dinning hall, choose their food for lunch and find free seats to sit down.)

Cheng: Look at what I got, pork, beef, cabbage, rice and Coca-Cola. Eat lunch like a prince.

Nancy: Hey, a carnivore. (Nancy has ordered bean, potato, and eggs.)

Cheng: Are you on a diet? How could you work with so little food?

Nancy: Well, I used to eat a lot of meat, and my waistline got thicker and thicker and the scale kept inching up. I was so sleepy in class after lunch that I couldn't concentrate on what the teacher was saying. My eyes wouldn't even stay open. Then I started drinking coffee to stay alert. It was a vicious circle. Now that I've turn to vegetables, I feel better. To be frank, it's not healthy to consume a great deal of red meat.

Cheng: I don't care so much about my weight, high blood pressure and high blood fat. We are young and we need nutrition to cope with the pressure here.

Nancy: I see what you mean. You are right that wholesome foods are what we need to have a healthy body. But, red meat is by no means nutritious. Try something different, like white meat, fruits and vegetables. Besides, the caffeine in Coca-Cola is addictive, and drinking Coca-Cola with meals spoils your appetite.

Cheng: That sounds sensible. But it's really hard to exclude red meat from my diet.

◆ Dialogue 2   Western-style Food

(Wang is working in a western-style restaurant as a waiter in his spare time. He introduces his friend Cheng something about his restaurant.)

Wang: Right now I am working in a western-style restaurant as a waiter.

Cheng: A western-style restaurant? Sounds very interesting. Is the food served there different from food in Chinese restaurants?

Wang: Sure. Our restaurant provides customers with western-style meals.

Cheng: What does an American breakfast usually include?

Wang: Toast, eggs, ham, bacon, sausage, milk, tea or coffee.

Cheng: It's a big meal.

Wang: Yeah, western people think breakfast is important. They believe that it not only starts a day off right but also starts them on the road to a healthy lifestyle.

Cheng: Then what about lunch and supper?

Wang: Generally speaking, people don't have a lot of time for lunch, so they prefer a quick lunch. And the supper or dinner in the evening is more formal.

Cheng: What do you usually have for a quick lunch?

Wang: A typical lunch consists of a burger or sandwich, French fries or chips, a dessert and a coke or coffee.

Cheng: I see. Then how many dishes do you have for dinner?

Wang: We don't call them "dishes". We call them "courses". At dinner, the appetizer, soup or salad, entrée or main course, dessert will be served in order. Guests usually have many choices. Beverages, like coffee, tea, soft drinks, will flow freely. My restaurant offers a bottomless cup of coffee.

Cheng: Bottomless?

Wang: It means you can have as many refills as you want.

Cheng: Aha, sound amazing. I love dessert. I have a sweet tooth. I'll visit the restaurant and try some western cuisine another day.

Wang: The deserts are tempting, but look out, that's where the calories are.

Words and Expressions

cafeteria	*n.*	食堂	bacon	*n.*	烤肉
appetite	*n.*	食欲	sausage	*n.*	香肠
luxury	*n.*	奢侈	dessert	*n.*	甜点
pauper	*n.*	乞丐	course	*n.*	一道菜
carnivore	*n.*	食肉动物	appetizer	*n.*	开胃菜
waistline	*n.*	腰围	entrée	*n.*	主菜，正菜
nutritious	*adj.*	营养丰富的	appeal to		吸引某人
caffeine	*n.*	咖啡因	cuisine	*n.*	烹饪；菜肴
addictive	*adj.*	让人上瘾的	calorie	*n.*	卡路里（食物的
toast	*n.*	吐司			热量单位）

Part Two: Related Questions with Suggested Answers

1. What is your favorite food? Why?

I like different kinds of food. Eggs are my favorite. I like eggs because they contain a lot of nutrients essential to the human body. The egg is a source of animal protein. Animal protein has a higher biological value than vegetable protein due to the fact that their amino acid composition is like that in human protein. The hens' eggs are one of the richest foods created by nature. They are rich in protein, poor in sodium, contain minerals and all vitamins except vitamin C because hens can produce it inside their bodies and don't need to get it from the food. Eggs have the highest biological protein quality of all natural foods.

It is also convenient to cook eggs. If you want to fry eggs, you just crack them into a pan, stir them evenly, add some salt and oil and fry them. Your food will be ready in just a couple minutes. If you want boiled eggs, that's even easier. Soldiers used to carry eggs to the frontline as their food. I just like eggs.

2. Do you like fast food? Why or why not?

Fast food can be cheap and quick. Sometimes this quick-and-cheap temptation is hard to resist. I myself don't like fast food. Fast food contains little nutrition and much fat. Eating too much of it not only does no good but also gives us too much calories, sodium and fat to be absorbed by our body. With a steady diet of fast food, the kilos pile on and you lose your figure as fast as you empty your wallet. Thus, growing children should especially keep away from fast food. In addition, eating on the rush can also lead to indigestion of food and even long-term gastric diseases. Trust those who say, they are fast, they taste great and they can kill you.

3. What do you think a healthy diet is?

I think a healthy diet is delicious and varied. Meals are rich in vegetables and fruits, with whole grains, high-fiber foods, lean meats and poultry, fish at least twice a week, and fat-free or 1 percent fat dairy products. Pumpkins, onions, cauliflower, peppers, peas, tomatoes, carrots, and garlic sprouts are particularly recommended. In addition, walnuts, peanuts, pistachios, cashews, pine nuts, almonds, soybeans, and other shellfish are also healthy food. You just learn to make smart choices and you can enjoy a healthy diet.

4. Do you eat out a lot? Why or why not?

Well, I do. I eat out because it's easy, it's quick, and it's funny. Nowadays, you can see people eat out a lot whether it is a business meeting over lunch, or a dinner arranged by friends. Eating out is a part of our life.

But one thing you have to make sure is that the food is healthy. Restaurant food can be unhealthy. You have to plan ahead, choose wisely and make sure that you find foods that fit into your meal plan. Today, many restaurants are trying to meet diners' health needs. You need healthy foods because you have diabetes—and you're not alone. More and more people want healthy food choices. Some are watching calories. Others want to keep their cholesterol under control or eat less fat. Some restaurants offer foods with lower saturated fat, or sodium, and higher fiber. In addition, it's easy to find salads, fish, vegetables, baked or broiled food, and whole-grain breads. Many restaurants offer menu items that are "heart healthy". Ask for calorie and fat information on menu items. If you ask, chefs will often make low-fat entrees using low-cholesterol eggs or lean cuts of meat. Enjoy your food when you eat out. It can be a lot of fun and healthy too.

5. Some people say that cooking can be enjoyable. What do you think?

Well, I agree that "cooking is enjoyable". People who like to cook are the people who like to eat. The foods that people cook at home are usually healthy, with less added fats and maximum nutritional value. Well, of course, it also costs less. This is a very important point for families who have a very limited income. I have an aunt who is a wonderful cook. Her friends and relatives enjoy the food she makes. Since cooking is a really fabulous thing when you can make very delicious food, I have the idea that in future I will cook during my leisure time.

6. What do you think of the food in your university's canteens? What suggestions would you like to give them?

To tell you the truth, the food in our canteens is pretty good. Most students are rather satisfied with the food at our university canteens. I would suggest that they serve higher quality food. Also there's still room for improvement in their services. Recently, the prices have risen considerably high so that they have added financial burden to poorer students. A few of my classmates who come from remote mountainous areas have to eat mainly staple foods. That isn't good for their health and would even affect their studies. I think a university canteen should not aim to make a profit. Instead, they should provide students with a variety of nutritious foods at the most reasonable prices they can offer.

7. What are some of the typical dishes you have at home during the Chinese Spring Festival? Why?

The Chinese people eat a lot during the New Year. Vast amounts of traditional food are prepared for families and friends, as well as for those who have left for the celestial home. Well, in my hometown, a city in the northern part of China, on New Year's Day, families eat a vegetarian dish called jai. The main ingredients in jai are root vegetables or fibrous vegetables. Many people attach various superstitions to them. Other typical foods in my hometown include a whole fish to symbolize unity and abundance, and a chicken to represent prosperity. The chicken must be presented with its head, tail and feet to show wholeness. Noodles must be uncut, as they represent long life. Steamed-wheat bread (mantou) and small meat dumplings are the preferred food. The tremendous amount of food prepared at this time is meant to symbolize abundance and wealth in the household.

8. What are some of the differences in Chinese eating habits and western eating habits?

Chinese and westerners have different eating habits. The main difference is the way the food is served. In the west, every one has his own plate of food, while in China all the dishes are shared and every one eats out of the serving dishes.

A typical Chinese meal starts with cold dishes, like boiled peanuts and cucumber with garlic. Cold dishes are followed by the main courses, hot meat and vegetable dishes. Finally soup is brought out, which is followed by the staple food, which is usually rice or noodles or sometimes dumplings. Westerners like to eat separate dishes. After they have eaten one dish they move on to another. They have several different dishes on the table at one time.

Another difference is that in China, we use bowls to have rice and soup and eat with long, thin chopsticks. Westerners use plates to hold food, and knives and forks to cut food and to get food into their mouths.

9. Do you want to go on diet? Why or why not?

No, I don't want to go on diet. Now, I am really satisfied with my figure. I think good health and happiness are the most important things in the world. Although I don't want to be on a diet, I always watch what I eat. I choose healthy food. I never eat fast food, because I think fired chicken and chips contain too much fat. I eat vegetables, fruits and certain amount of meat every day. I exercise a lot usually three times a week. As long as I can live a happy and healthy life, I don't think there is any need for me to always be thinking about diets.

10. What are some of the causes for the world current food shortage nowadays?

Natural disasters such as floods, tropical storms and long periods of drought are on the increase with calamitous consequences for food security in poor, developing countries. Drought is now the most common cause of food shortages in the world. In many countries, climate change is exacerbating already adverse natural conditions. War is another reason for short and long-term food crises. Fighting displaces millions of people from their homes, leading to some of the world's worst hunger emergencies. Another reason is the poverty trap. In developing countries, farmers often cannot afford seed to plant the crops that would provide for their families. Craftsmen lack the means to pay for the tools to ply their trade. Others have no land or water or education to lay foundations for a secure future. The poverty-stricken do not have enough money to buy or produce enough food for themselves and their families. In turn, they tend to be weaker and cannot produce enough to buy more food. In short, the poor are hungry and their hunger traps them in poverty.

Words and Expressions

protein	n.	蛋白质	carrot	n.	胡萝卜
amino acid		氨基酸	walnut	n.	胡桃
sodium	n.	钠	peanut	n.	花生
vitamin	n.	维生素	pistachio	n.	开心果
crack	v.	（使）开裂	cashew	n.	腰果
temptation	n.	诱惑	pine nut	n.	松子
nutrition	n.	营养	almond	n.	杏仁
calories	n.	卡路里（食物的热量单位）	crustaceans	n.	贝类
			snack	n.	小吃
digestion	n.	消化	diabetes	n.	糖尿病
gastric	adj.	胃的	cholesterol	n.	胆固醇
whole grain		全麦	fiber	n.	纤维
poultry	n.	家禽	salad	n.	色拉
dairy	n.	奶制品	entrée	n.	主菜，正菜
pumpkin	n.	南瓜	maximum	n.	最大量
onion	n.	洋葱	fabulous	adj.	极好的
cauliflower	n.	花菜	canteen	n.	小餐厅

staple food		主食	exacerbate	v.	（使）恶化
fibrous	adj.	含纤维的, 纤维性的	adverse	adj.	恶劣的
dumpling	n.	饺子	displace	v.	（使）离开家园
chip	n.	薯片	ply one's trade		从事（熟练的）
drought	n.	干旱			工作
calamitous	adj.	悲惨的	poverty-stricken	adj.	贫苦的

Part Three: Related Pictures with Suggested Descriptions

Picture One   Food and Health

食品质量安全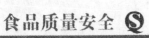

严紧每道工序操作
确保食品安全卫生

QUALITY SAFETY

The food we eat seems to have profound effects on our health. Although science has made enormous steps in making food more fit to eat, it has, at the same time, made many foods unfit to eat. Some research has shown that perhaps eighty percent of all human illnesses are related to diet and forty percent of cancer is related to the diet as well, especially cancer of the colon.

Different cultures are more prone to contract certain illnesses because of the food that is characteristic in these cultures. That food is related to illness is not a new discovery. In 1945, American government researchers realized that nitrates and nitrites, commonly used to preserve color in meats, and other food additives, caused cancer. Yet, these carcinogenic additives remain in our food, and it becomes more difficult all the time to know which things in the packaging labels of processed food are helpful or harmful.

The additives that we eat are not all so direct. Farmers often give penicillin to beef and poultry, and because of this, penicillin has been found in the milk of treated cow. Sometimes similar drugs are administered to animals not for medicinal purposes, but for financial reason. The farmers are simply trying to fatten the animals in order to obtain a higher price on the market. Although the Food and Drug Administration (FDA) has tried repeatedly to control these procedures, the practices continue.

Picture Two　Men and Women Differ in Their Eating Habits

Men and women differ in their eating habits. Men and women have different tastes in food, with men favoring meat and poultry, and women fruits and vegetables, researchers said in what was touted as the most extensive study to date of gender differences in eating habits.

More than 14,000 adult men and women were surveyed from May 2006 to April 2007, for the Foodborne Disease Active Surveillance Network (Food Net), to determine their eating habits, including high risk foods such as undercooked meat and eggs.

"There was such a variety of data, we thought it would be interesting to see whether there were any gender differences," said Beletshachew Shiferaw, a lead researcher on the study.

"To our knowledge, there have been studies in the literature on gender differences in eating habits, but nothing this extensive," the epidemiologist told the 2008 International Conference on Emerging Infectious Diseases in Atlanta, Georgia.

Researchers found that men were more likely to eat meat and poultry, especially duck, veal, and ham, and certain shellfish such as shrimp and oysters. Women instead were more likely to eat vegetables, especially carrots and tomatoes, and fruits, especially strawberries, blueberries, raspberries and apples.

Women also preferred dry foods, such as almonds and walnuts, and were more likely to consume eggs and yogurt when compared with men.

There were also some exceptions to the eating trends of each gender: men were significantly more likely to eat asparagus and brussels sprouts than women, while women were more likely to consume fresh hamburgers as opposed to the frozen kind, which the men preferred. And regarding high risk foods, the researchers found that significantly more men consumed undercooked meat and eggs than women, while more women were more likely to eat alfalfa sprouts.

Picture Three　Western Fast Food Is Popular in China

You seem to be wandering around in the jungle, appreciating the exotic plants, shaking

hands with chimpanzees when all of the sudden a thunder storm hits.

Believe it or not, you are just at a Rainforest Cafe.

The theme restaurant, which is headquartered in the US state of Minnesota, opened its first chain store in Beijing, the third in China. On the menu are roast ribs, salad and macaroni.

Rainforest Cafe has become the newest member in the western fast food market here in China among McDonald's, Kentucky Fried Chicken (KFC) and Pizza Hut, which have won the favor of many Chinese consumers.

Experts pointed out, as the income of Chinese people has increased, fast food has become an important part of their daily life.

The turnover of fast food, worth of 20 million yuan, occupied over 40 percent of the total Food and Beverage income last year in China, according to the latest report from National Bureau of Statistics (NBS).

The survey showed that the urban people are frequent customers of fast food restaurants, especially those in the well-off regions of eastern and southern China.

Western fast food restaurants tend to attract more kids and young people, who have created a big potential market for the food. Most of these people are fond of trendy and new food, putting emphasis on different tastes.

"I really like the soft music, clean environment, good service and seasonal promotions here," a frequent female customer at the Pizza Hut said.

The adaptation of Chinese favors also contributed to the expansion of western fast food in China, such as the red bean pie at McDonald's and KFC's soup.

"We hope to bring exotic culture to Chinese people who never got a chance to travel overseas," said Chen Zhaoguan, director of operations of the Rainforest Cafe.

Experts believe more styles and flavor of western food will come to China, which is expected to bring along with them advanced managing ideas, methods and a standard production process. And this will help stimulate the development of Chinese food, fast food in particular.

Words and Expressions

colon	adj.	结肠	tout	v.	叫嚣
prone	adj.	有……倾向	survey	v.	调查
nitrates	n.	硝酸盐	epidemiologist	n.	流行病学家
nitrites	n.	亚硝酸盐	veal	n.	小牛肉
additive	n.	添加剂	shellfish	n.	有壳的水生动物
carcinogenic	adj.	致癌物（质）的	shrimp	n.	虾
penicillin	n.	青霉素	oysters	n.	牡蛎

strawberry	*n.*	草莓	roast	*v.*	烤
blueberry	*n.*	蓝莓	rib	*n.*	肋骨
raspberry	*n.*	树莓	chain store		连锁店
yogurt	*n.*	酸奶	macaroni	*n.*	通心粉
asparagus	*n.*	芦笋	turnover	*n.*	营业额
brussels sprout		汤菜	beverage	*n.*	饮料
alfalfa	*n.*	苜蓿	trendy	*adj.*	赶时髦的
sprout	*n.*	发出的嫩芽	seasonal promotion		季节性的促销
exotic	*adj.*	异国的	red bean pie		红豆派
chimpanzee	*n.*	黑猩猩			

Part Four: Related Passages

1. I Feel Better with Vegetarian Food

I grew up in Texas on double cheeseburgers with hickory sauce, chili, fried chicken, T-bone steaks, and eggs. Many people report that they lose the taste for animal foods after eating a vegetarian diet for a while, but it hasn't fully happened to me. I still enjoy the way animal foods taste and smell, but I usually don't eat them.

Why not? Because I like the way I feel when I don't eat these foods so much more than the pleasure I used to get from eating them. I have much more energy, I need less sleep, I feel calmer, I can maintain an ideal body weight without worrying about how much I eat, and I can think more clearly (although some might debate the last point).

I began making some dietary and lifestyle changes during my second year of college and have been eating this way ever since. I wasn't worried about coronary heart disease at age nineteen—my cholesterol level then was only 125 (and it still is). I began feeling better after I started eating this way, so I continue to do so. Eating this diet probably will help me to live longer, but it's not my primary motivation. Feeling better is.

In my clinical experience, I often find that fear may be enough motivation for some people to begin a diet, but it's usually not enough to sustain it. As I've said earlier, who wants to live longer if you're not enjoying life?

Since I began making these dietary changes in 1972, eating this way has become increasingly accepted. Beans and grains are becoming, believe it or not, high-status foods.

2. Fast Food Culture

A young man once remarked to me that since there are so many KFC's and other fast food

restaurants in Urumqi, I must feel right at home. This is one of two common misapprehends. The second is that fast food is more suitable to the western lifestyle. According to recent research, the culture of fast food is more popular in Asia than anywhere else.

The AC Nielson Group is an international research organization, which recently conducted an international online consumer survey. It found that 35% of Americans patronize fast food restaurants on a monthly basis. However, 61% of residents of Hong Kong and 41% of residents of mainland China do the same. In fact, according to the survey nine of the world's top ten markets for fast food are in the Asia-Pacific region.

The world's three top fast food brands are McDonald's, KFC and Pizza Hut and they are all from America. However, two out of three Americans avoid these kinds of places. I personally avoid them because they are extremely unhealthy and while it may taste good going down, it fells like a rock in my stomach afterwards. Most Americans who are in the habit of eating at these places do so only for convenience.

Despite the fact that cheese burgers, pizza and fried chicken are part of American cuisine, they do not represent the best on the menu. In my family, a good quality American meal starts with a fresh' green salad with homemade vinaigrette sauce followed by lobster bisque. The main dish will be a small tender loin steak with a side of boiled broccoli covered with melted cheese, and fresh rolls. This is all washed down with a bottle of California red wine.

This kind of fare has yet to be introduced to Urumqi except in its starred hotels. It is cost prohibitive and requires time and patience. It is an experience that is simply foreign in fast food restaurants. The world's first fast food chain McDonalds has grown to over 30,000 stores today. It has not exported the best of American food to other countries but rather a modem lifestyle that craves convenience.

McDonald's has become a symbol of this modem lifestyle. When the first store opened in Kuwait City in 1994, for example, there was a line ten kilometers long. As an American, I cannot under stand this because for me McDonald's is a symbol of the negative side of modernization. I hope I never see it in Urumqi. If it does come, I will certainly not feel more at home.

3. Fast-food Restaurant

Everybody knows that a favorite food of the Americans is the hamburger.

The favorite place to buy a hamburger is a fast-food restaurant. In these restaurants, people order their food, wait just a few minutes, then when the food is ready they carry it to their tables themselves. They can either eat in the restaurant or take the food out in a plastic box and eat it at home, at work, or in a park. At some restaurants people can drive up beside a window. They order the food, and a worker hands it to them through the window. Then they drive off and eat in their cars or wherever they like.

Hamburgers are not the only kind of food that fast-food restaurants serve. Some serve fish or chicken, or sandwiches, and also soft drinks, coffee and so on.

Fast food restaurants are very popular because the service is fast and the food is not too expensive. For many people, this is very important. In the United States, about 50 percent of married women with children work outside the home. They are often too busy or too tired to cook dinner for the family at night, and fast-food restaurants are a great help to them.

Now there are fast-food restaurants in countries all over the world. Usually, we can see many kinds of western fast-food in our lives, so as KFC, McDonalds, Pizza. However, why is western fast-food so popular and successful in Chinese food market, and why do so many people prefer western fast-food to Chinese food?

I think there are many reasons for this dramatic performance. First, many Chinese people are very curious to foreign fast-food. Second, these foods have a good credit in services. Third, a number of new thoughts are applied in fast-food.

As far as I see, these factors also bring Chinese food industry a big challenge and a shock. An the same time we should improve and enhance the fast-food industry in every place.

4. Change Your Eating Habits

Because all of us have been brought up eating junk food, well most of us, it is not easy to change our eating habits. Your eating habits have developed since childhood based on what your mothers or fathers cooked and what your psychological make-up was during that time.

The foods you eat and crave help keep pass trauma and present anxiety in check. Food helps make you feel good when you start to feel bad. Eating is a natural defense mechanism that the brain-body uses to keep you from going crazy.

So, you see, it is very difficult to change our eating habits. When we do, we start to feel bad. We start to feel uncomfortable, we feel pain, we have withdrawal symptoms, and we may feel sick. Is it any wonder that any of us ever succeed in changing our eating habits?

I consider every thing that has been packaged to be junk food. There are a few exception and you need to read ingredient labels carefully. Very few food manufacturers and even restaurants prepare food with your health in mind. Of course, they want to satisfy you, but they don't use foods that are in your best interest.

Most people eat junk food 85% of the time and then eat good food the other 15%. It should be the reverse of this—eat good food 85% and junk food 15% of the time.

To have better health, here are some foods to stop eating. Eliminate these foods over the next two to three weeks. They are milk, bread, sugar and sodas. Most people eat too much salt— over 10,000 milligrams per day. We only need around 200-300 mg per day. Excess salt is also in involved with kidney problems, cardiovascular disease, stomach cancer, and excess sensitive to stress. For the next two weeks try adding the following foods to your eating habits. They are lecithin, chorine flax seed oil, fiber and apple juice and apples.

5. The Main Difference Between Chinese and Western Eating Habits

The main difference between Chinese and western eating habits are that unlike the West, where everyone has their own plate of food, in China the dishes are placed on the table and everybody shares. If you are being treated by a Chinese host, be prepared for a ton of food. Chinese are very proud of their culture of cuisine and will do their best to show their hospitality.

And sometimes the Chinese host uses their chopsticks to put food in your bowl or plate. This is a sign of politeness. The appropriate thing to do would be to eat the whatever-it-is and say how yummy it is. If you feel uncomfortable with this, you can just say a polite thank you and leave the food there.

Don't stick your chopsticks upright in the rice bowl. Instead, lay them on your dish. The reason for this is that when somebody dies, the shrine to them contains a bowl of sand or rice with two sticks of incense stuck upright in it. So if you stick your chopsticks in the rice bowl, it looks like this shrine and is equivalent to wishing death upon a person at the table!

Make sure the spout of the teapot is not facing anyone. It is impolite to set the teapot down where the spout is facing towards somebody. The spout should always be directed to where nobody is sitting, usually just outward from the table.

Don't tap on your bowl with your chopsticks. Beggars tap on their bowls, so this is not polite. Also, when the food is coming too slow in a restaurant, people will tap their bowls. If you are in someone's home, it is like insulting the cook.

Topic Seven　Energy

Part One: Dialogues

◆ Dialogue 1　Solar Energy

(Mary, a foreign teacher, is talking with her students about solar energy in her oral English class.)

Mary: As we all know, the sun is simply our nearest star. Without it, there would have been no life on our planet. We use the sun's energy every day in many different ways. Could you tell us how we use solar energy?

S1: We hang laundry outside to dry in the sun.

All Students: (Laugh) Dry our clothes.

Mary: (Smile) Yeah, a good point. Any more points?

S2: Plants use the sun's light to make food.

Mary: Yes, we call it photosynthesis. Actually, millions of years ago decaying plants produced the coal, oil and natural gas that we use today. So fossil fuel is actually sunlight stored millions and millions of years ago.

S3: In my hometown, almost every household installs solar hot water heaters. They proved to be a big improvement over wood and coal-burning stoves.

Mary: Solar hot water heaters are also used in the states. Do you know why it is so popular?

S3: It is cheap and clean.

S4: Solar energy can also be used to make electricity. As far as I know, there are several solar power plants word-wide.

S1: But I heard that solar energy plants can't create energy on cloudy days or at night.

Mary: That is the disadvantage. The problem with solar energy is that it works only when the sun is shinning.

S2: Oh, there are also solar cells.

S5: I have a calculator with solar cells in it.

Mary: Solar cells can be found on many small appliances, like calculators, and even space spacecraft. Some experimental cars with solar cells are driven by converting sunlight directly into the energy to power electric motors on the car. We have made a list of the usages of solar energy. Now let's read an article about solar energy. (Turn to S1) Please hand out the article to your classmates, thanks.

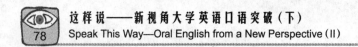

◆ Dialogue 2   Energy Crisis

(Nancy and Alice are talking about the energy crisis.)

Alice: How do you manage during this unusually hot weather?

Nancy: I have my air-conditioners.

Alice: Our human beings are so dependent on electricity that we barely know we are facing energy crisis.

Nancy: Energy crisis is a big issue. Several years ago, the blackout in northern American and Canada caused great panic. Could you believe I was in New York visiting my sister when the light and the gas were out? I was at home with my sister's 2-year-old twins. I had no battery, no candles. Everywhere is dark.

Alice: Oh, that is unimaginable, especially when you were babysitting two little children.

Nancy: Yeah, mostly we use coal to generate power. But few of us have the awareness that there is definite reserve of coal in the earth for us to enjoy our life with the consumption of coal.

Alice: Not only coal, but also wood, petroleum. Wood and coal can't be reproduced easily and petroleum is non-renewable.

Nancy: Yeah, these fuels are being used at a much faster rate than they are produced, and may be unavailable to future generations.

Alice: The waste of these fuels is also harmful. It can contribute to global warming.

Nancy: Hydroelectric power, solar energy and nuclear energy can be great alternatives. They're renewable energy sources.

Words and Expressions

solar energy		太阳能	reserve	*n.*	储备；储备量
laundry	*n.*	洗熨好的衣服	petroleum	*n.*	汽油
photosynthesis	*n.*	光合作用	hydroelectric power		水电力
solar cells		太阳能电池	alternative	*n.*	代替物
blackout	*n.*	停电	renewable	*adj.*	可再生的

Part Two: Related Questions with Suggested Answers

1. What are the main forms of energy? How are they produced?

There are several major forms of energy, namely: heat, light, sound, electrical, chemical, nuclear and mechanical energy. Heat energy is the effect of moving molecules. Heat energy is easily lost. Light is a form of energy from light wave. Sound energy is produced when we talk. Sound energy enables us to hear others. Electrical energy is produced by moving electrical charges from one point to another in a conductor. Electrical charges moving through a conductor is called electricity. Chemical energy is stored in food, biomass, fuel and explosives. It will be lost or gained in the formation of compound. Nuclear energy is stored in the nucleus of an atom. Mechanical energy is produced by mechanical work. Every form of energy is able to change from one form to another.

2. What are some of the energy problems nowadays? How do we solve them?

At present, people all over the world pay much attention to the energy problems for energy has close relationship with the development of the world. Over the past few years, the demand for energy has increased. Nonrenewable energy has been used a lot, especially the coal. The energy-efficiency in most countries is very low. Moreover, energy has caused much pollution to the environment. The excessive use of energy has brought about negative effect on our living surroundings. To solve these problems, we have to work hard to find renewable energy such as solar energy to take the place of the nonrenewable ones. We can make use of science to improve the energy-efficiency. At the same time, we should take measures to protect the environment as we develop economy and science. We have to keep in mind that it is our responsibility to save energy.

3. Why is water shortage becoming a more and more serious problem now?

There are several reasons for this. Firstly, the drinkable water on the earth is limited. Most of the water resource on the earth is sea water. Secondly, the demand for water is increasing. We all know that agricultural production needs a lot of water. The industry has developed so rapidly that it needs more water now. Besides, the increasing growth of population raises the demand for water. In some big cities, water is expensive and is supplied within some limited time. Thirdly, water pollution is becoming more and more serious with the development of the industry. Some chemical factories put waste water into rivers and lakes without any disposal. When the water around a city is polluted, its citizens may have no water to drink. It is very serious and dangerous indeed.

4. Why are we encouraged to use solar energy and wind energy?

Nowadays, energy shortage has become an important issue. People are encouraged to use solar energy and wind energy. It is reasonable because solar energy and wind energy have many advantages. Firstly, they are widely located. Solar energy and wind energy are predictably intermittent energy sources available most of the time. We can predict with a very good degree of accuracy when it will and will not be available. People all over the world can use them. It is a great waste if we do not make a good use of them. Secondly, they are renewable. Energy from sun and wind is unlimited. Now, people are trying to use solar energy and wind energy to take the place of the nonrenewable energy. Thirdly, they are clean. Solar energy and wind energy almost cause no pollution to the environment. Environmental protection is also important to us. I think to use solar energy and wind energy is a good solution to the environmental problem.

5. What effects do you think global warming will bring us? Why?

Global warming is dangerous. It will bring many negative changes to the earth. The increase in global temperature may cause glacial retreat and sea level rise. Some coastal areas may disappear. The production of agriculture will decrease because the weather is changeable and is not suitable for crops to grow. The extreme weather events such as typhoon, destructive storms will become frequent. Most areas will never snow. The desert will expand. In summer, it will be extremely hot. Human beings may have to face more disasters. Global warming also will bring many diseases to some lower countries for the earth will be covered by water. Virus is active in moist condition. Thousands of people would leave their homes.

6. What should people do at home to save energy?

We have much to do to save energy at home. For example, we can use energy-saving bulbs instead of the ordinary ones. We should turn off the screen when we turn off the computer. The TV should be completely closed or it will need electricity as well. In summer, people are used to turning the air-conditioning to a very low temperature. There is no need to do so. It is OK to set it at 27-28 degrees. If the water tap is leaking, we should repair it as soon as possible. We use too much tissue at home. Tissue is made from nonrenewable energy. So we can try our best to decrease the use of tissue. It is everyone's responsibility to save energy. We should begin with small things around us.

7. What measures does the government have to take in your country to save energy?

In our country, the government has put great emphasis on energy saving. Recently Shanghai Municipal Government has taken ten measures to save energy. They are: strictly controlling high energy consumption and polluting enterprises; speeding up the cleansing of enterprises with backward production facilities; closing down small firepower plant and initiating new power plant projects; strengthening the management of key energy consumption enterprises; strengthening the management of key energy saving sectors; pushing forward technological improvement on energy saving; implementing differentiated electricity prices; enlarging the investment on energy saving efforts; consolidating the construction of pollution elimination projects; and strengthening the supervision on pollution emission. These measures are effective in saving energy. They are also good for the whole country.

8. Is it possible for people to turn garbage into energy? How?

Yes, it is possible. As long as there are people on the planet, there will be garbage. The garbage often piles up in landfills that produce a harmful greenhouse gas called methane. Methane contributes significantly to global warming. Yet it is not all bad. If captured correctly, methane can generate electricity. United States, for example, has already established some gas plants that could decompose garbage and pipe methane to electricity plants to generate electricity. These gas plants also produce steam that local dairies use to pasteurize milk and clean equipment.

9. What are some of the renewable energy? How can we get them?

The main forms of renewable energy are geothermal, wind, solar and ocean energy. Geothermal energy is energy obtained by tapping the heat of the earth itself, usually from kilometers deep into the Earth's crust. It is expensive to build a power station but operating costs are low resulting in low energy costs for suitable sites. Ultimately, this energy derives from heat in the Earth's core. Wind energy is produced from wind. It is determined by the speed of the wind, so it is not very stable. Solar energy refers to energy obtained from sunlight. It is huge and widely used. We can get ocean energy from flowing stream of water or sea swell.

10. Why is energy conservation important for us now?

Energy conservation is the practice of decreasing the quantity of energy used while achieving a similar outcome. This practice may result in increase of financial capital, environmental value, national security, personal security, and human comfort. Individuals and organizations are direct consumers of energy. They may want to conserve energy in order to reduce energy costs and promote economic, political and environmental sustainability. Industrial and commercial users may want to increase efficiency and thus maximize profit.

On a larger scale, energy conservation is an important element of energy policy. In general, energy conservation reduces the energy consumption and energy demand per capita, and thus offsets the growth in energy supply needed to keep up with the population growth. This reduces the rise in energy costs, and can reduce the need for new power plants, and energy imports. The reduced energy demand can provide more flexibility in choosing the most preferred methods of energy production.

By reducing emissions, energy conservation is also an important part of lessening climate change. Energy conservation is a more environmentally benign alternative to increased energy production.

Words and Expressions

molecule	n.	分子		facilities	n.	设备
electrical charge		电荷		initiate	v.	发起
conductor	n.	（电或热）的导体		implement	n.	实施；执行
biomass	n.	（用于燃料或提供能量的）生物质		differentiate	v.	区分；区别
				elimination	n.	去除
nucleus	n.	（原子）核		supervision	n.	监管
excessive	adj.	过多的		landfill	n.	废弃物的填埋场
renewable	adj.	可再生的				
disposal	n.	处理；处置		methane	n.	甲烷；沼气
intermittent	adj.	间歇的		decompose	v.	（使）腐烂
glacial	adj.	冰的；冰川的		tap	v.	挖掘；开发
tap	n.	水龙头		crust	n.	地壳
tissue	n.	卷纸		conservation	n.	（动植物、森林等的）保护
municipal	adj.	市政的				
enterprise	n.	企业		offset	v.	补偿；抵消

Part Three: Related Pictures with Suggested Descriptions

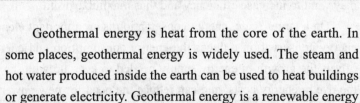

Picture One   Geothermal Energy

Geothermal energy is heat from the core of the earth. In some places, geothermal energy is widely used. The steam and hot water produced inside the earth can be used to heat buildings or generate electricity. Geothermal energy is a renewable energy source because the heat is produced inside the earth when the water is replenished by rainfall. Geothermal energy is generated in the earth's core, about 4,000 miles below the surface. Temperatures there are far hotter than the sun's surface. Some applications of geothermal energy use the earth's temperatures near the surface, while others require drilling miles into the earth.

There are three main uses of geothermal energy. The most ancient one is direct use and district heating systems which use hot water from springs or reservoirs near the surface. The second one is electricity generation. A power plant requires water or steam at very high temperature. Geothermal power plants are generally built where geothermal reservoirs are located within a mile or two of the surface. The third one is geothermal heat pumps. They use stable ground or water temperatures near the earth's surface to control building temperatures above ground. The first one is the direct way to use hot water as an energy source. It has been happening since ancient times. The Romans, Chinese, and Native Americans used hot mineral springs for bathing, cooking and heating. Today, many hot springs are still used for bathing, and many people believe the hot, mineral-rich waters have natural healing powers. After bathing, the most common direct use of geothermal energy is for heating buildings through district heating systems. Hot water near the earth's surface can be piped directly into buildings and industries for heat.

Geothermal energy is renewable, huge and clean. But only a certain areas are suitable to explore geothermal energy.

Picture Two   Nuclear Energy

Nuclear energy is huge and powerful. It is reported that about 16% of the world's electricity is produced by nuclear energy. Nuclear energy is created in a nuclear reaction which refers to the changes in the structure of the nuclei of atoms. There are two kinds of these changes. One is nuclear fission

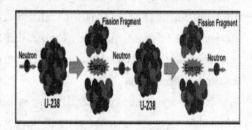

and the other is nuclear fusion. Fission reactor is more dangerous than fusion reactor.

Nuclear energy can be produced naturally. For example, the sun and the other stars make heat and light by nuclear reactions. Nuclear energy can be also produced in man-made way. As we all know, coal and oil on the earth is limited. It is not economical to produce electricity by coal or oil. One ton uranium produces more energy than that is produced by one ton coal. On the other hand, when coal and oil are burning, they pollute the air. Nuclear power plants produce no waste if they are properly operated. They do not harm the environment. However, nuclear is extremely dangerous. The world has enough nuclear bombs to kill all people around the world. Some powerful nations have many nuclear weapons. It will be a disaster if there is a nuclear war. Nuclear explosions produce radiation. The nuclear radiation damages the cells of the body. It makes people sick even years after the nuclear explosion accident. Nuclear reactors also have waste disposal problem. Nuclear waste produced by nuclear reactor has radiation. It should be treated in a specific way or it could kill people who touch it. It is terrible.

Different people have different opinions about nuclear energy. Some people hold that we

should make use of nuclear energy for it is useful. Others say that we should be away from nuclear energy and it is not suitable for us to establish nuclear power plants. Both opinions are acceptable. We should be careful about nuclear energy and say goodbye to nuclear weapons.

▶ Picture Three   Wind Energy ◀

Wind energy is a kind of energy produced by the movement of air. It is generated by the unbalanced heating of the earth surface by the sun. Therefore, different types of lands would produce different rates of wind. Wind energy has been used since ancient times. At the very beginning, people used wind to sail ships. And then people built windmills to raise crops and pump water. In modern time, people use wind turbine to produce electricity using a generator. The turbines are turned by wind. Many wind turbines are relatively small, and large numbers are required to produce appreciable amounts of energy.

Wind energy is not equally distributed. A certain areas of the country are particular suitable for wind turbines. The coast of California, for example, has cliffs that receive high winds on a consistent basis. A number of wind turbines, together referred to as wind farms, have been constructed in the areas that are near the sea. These wind farms provide almost all the electricity for the local residents.

Nowadays, people generally use wind energy to produce electricity. It is considered as a renewable energy source for we will have wind energy as long as the sun shines. It is as huge and powerful as solar energy. Meantime, wind energy is clear. Much pollution would be caused if the electricity was generated from fossil fuels. Wind energy can solve this problem. It produces little pollution.

Words and Expressions

geothermal	*adj.*	地热	reactor	*n.*	反应堆
replenish	*v.*	补充	uranium	*n.*	铀（元素）
rainfall	*n.*	降雨量	disposal	*n.*	处理
reservoir	*n.*	水库	windmill	*n.*	风车
pump	*v.*	抽水	turbine	*n.*	涡轮机
fission	*v.*	（原子）裂变	cliff	*n.*	（海边的）悬崖
fusion	*v.*	（核）聚变			

Part Four: Related Passages

1. We Are Becoming More Dependent on Foreign Oil

In the world, only a few countries can produce all of the energy that they need or use. Most countries depend on other countries. Taking the United States for example, every year it imports or buys a large amount of the oil from other countries. The price of energy is controlled by the economics of supply and demand. Usually as the demand goes up or the supply goes down, the price goes up. The price of energy has great influence on the world's economy and political patterns.

OPEC, the Organization of Oil Exporting Countries is a group formed by the countries that have the largest oil supplies or reserve. OPEC meets regularly and controls the amount of oil that they will export or sell to other countries. In this way, they can influence or set the price they get for the oil that they sell. In the 1970s, during the period called "energy crisis" or "oil crisis", gasoline prices are very high.

A large amount of the world oil reserves are in Arab countries in the Middle East. In the future, if they refuse to sell their oil to us at any price again, another "energy crisis" would appear. And then new political situations could be formed. Cutting off the oil would not only affect our ability to drive our cars, but would have a significant effect on our entire economy, throwing the country into a recession or even a depression. We are becoming more dependent on foreign sources of oil for energy. Every year, we are paying a lot of money for the oil. From the long term, this would have negative effects on our economy.

2. Pollution Is with Us

People now are more and more concerned with the pollution caused by energy using. Almost all energy production and use involve some form of pollution of our environment. Each different source of energy, from fossil fuels to nuclear, pollutes in a different way and to a different degree. Global warming is caused by some gases, like carbon dioxide. It has much negative effect on the world's weather and environment, causing a gradual increase in the average world temperatures, melting of the ice caps, rising ocean levels, and changes in weather patterns. The air is badly polluted, making it difficult for elderly people and people with lung problems to breathe. The fission nuclear power plants put thousands of tons of radioactive waste without disposal. This waste will be dangerous for thousands of years. There has been much argument about where to put it. No one wants this waste anywhere near their own communities, and people have not found a safe way to store it.

Nuclear radiation is terrible. Though radiation leaks are rare, there have been some small leaks and even a few larger ones. Small leaks allow radioactive gases to get into the atmosphere.

If people breathe it, it could help cause cancer. We all know the large leak in the Soviet Union. A lot of areas are polluted by the radioactive material. These areas are still unusable today.

When you drive by a nuclear power plant, you might see the huge cooling towers. They are used to cool the hot reactor. The water from these cooling towers contains excess heat energy and is released into the local rivers or lakes. The water in the rivers or the lakes gets warmer. This will kill the creatures in the rivers or lakes.

3. Use Renewable Energy

In order to solve the problem of energy shortage, people are trying to explore and make the best use of renewable energy. Renewable energy refers to sources of energy that are always there. It can be reproduced immediately after being used. This energy is so huge and powerful that we can not see the end in our or our children's lifetimes. Solar energy is one of the most common examples. The sun comes up every day and it will continue to do so for another 5 billion years or so. That is to say, the sun will provide solar energy for human beings for 5 billions years.

However, we come across a problem when we tap these energy resources. While the energy is there, the cost of getting it is actually greater than using our more popular energy sources of fossil fuels and uranium. So some countries prefer to use the non-renewable energy not wanting to pay the high price for the renewable energy. As we run out of our supply of fossil fuels and uranium or the cost of these fuels rises for economic or political reasons, the cost of renewable energy may become a challenge.

We all know that energy using produces pollution. The other important advantage of renewable energy is that it produces much less pollution. Some people believe that take the costs of pollution into consideration, like the medical costs of cancer, renewable energy is already cost effective and should be used much more often.

Besides, nations should put more funds into the research into the renewable energy. Nations with little non-renewable energy will be dependent on other nations unless they make advantage of their own renewable energy.

4. China Needs More Energy for Its Industrialization

China is now in the middle stage of industrialization phase. Energy-extensive machinery, auto, iron and steel sectors in China develop very fast. Urban residential consumption of energy also rose dramatically due to the country's fast pace of urbanization and improved standard of living. That's all the reasons for the energy shortage.

Another reason is low energy efficiency. It remains a problem for China for a long time as its comprehensive energy efficiency stands at 33 percent. That is 10 percentage points lower than that of developed countries. China's energy consumption for per-unit output value is twice as much as that of developed countries. A survey conducted by China's power sector shows its coal-fired power plants and power transmission companies would save an equivalent of

120 million tons of standard coal if their energy efficiency was raised to the advanced level of developed countries.

In addition, energy consumption of buildings in China is double or triples that of developed countries of comparable climate. Experts estimate that if new buildings and existing buildings in China all conform to advanced energy conservation standards by 2020, their energy consumption would drop by an equivalent of 335 million tons of standard coal per year. That's about one fifth of China's annual energy consumption.

The shortage signals more problems than it appears, such as the country's worsening pollution due to growing consumption of coal, and energy security. It is time for us to focus on these problems.

5. China's Measures to Solve Energy Shortage

As the development of economy and science, China as well as other nations is facing a problem of energy shortage. This situation may worsen before 2020. An industrial report forecasts China will face a more severe power shortage this year than it did in 2003.

In order to ease the present energy shortage, the Chinese government has taken a series of measures to deal with the issue. It has stopped blind investment and wasteful duplications in some industries and cutting irrational demand. It has also improved coal supply for areas suffering from power shortage. At the same time, China has speeded up the construction of energy and transport projects to expand supply and improved efficiency of energy consumption.

It is said that China's power shortage would ease due to increased energy supply, but the balance between the supply and demand would not last long if China failed to increase supplies. It is still a challenger.

The government decided to educate the public about methods to save energy. Among these methods, citizens are advised to unplug their electrical appliances if they would lay idle for a long period, avoiding power consumption from the standby mode. These methods have been carried out in many cities.

A lot of cities have paid attention to energy efficiency in buildings have taken steps in this direction. Shanghai has taken the lead in the reform. Design and construction of new residential buildings and public buildings in the country's biggest industrial city must comply with energy conservation standards made by the government.

Topic Eight　Advertisement

Part One: Dialogues

Dialogue 1　I Want to Play Like Yao Ming

(Jenny's little brother John is demanding a pair of basket ball shoes.)

John: I want to buy a pair of basketball shoes for the match.

Mom (Mrs. Smith): You have several basketball shoes. Why do you need a pair of new shoes?

John: Oh, mom. The old ones look sort of funny.

Mrs. Smith: Funny? It is ridiculous.

John: It is a really important basketball match. I need a pair of new shoes.

Mrs. Smith: There is still a lot of life in the old shoes. Furthermore, none of them is worn. Why do you need a new pair of shoes?

John: Oh, please look at the poster. Yao Ming wore the band of the shoes in the NBA. I want to play like Yao Ming.

Mrs. Smith: Don't be silly. Advertisements are misleading. Yao Ming plays well because he practices hard and he is tall. It has little to do with his shoes.

John: There are good springs in Yao Ming's shoes.

Mrs. Smith: It is an advertising strategy to attract buyers. Actually, the advertisers gave Yao millions of dollars for wearing the shoes.

John: Just a pair of shoes, mom, and my birthday is coming.

Mrs. Smith: I don't think you can spend that much for your basketball games. Basketball training and skills are important than just a pair of shoes.

Dialogue 2　Coupons

(Jenny and Kate are discussing ways of shopping with less money.)

Jenny: I saved 10 Yuan when I had McDonald this noon.

David: How on earth did you do that? You must order very simple food.

Jenny: On the contrary, I had a hero hamburger, two chicken wings, one ice-cream and a large Coca-Cola.

David: Hey, don't keep me waiting. How did you do it?

Jenny: I used the coupons from the newspaper I bought.

David: I know McDonald had coupons delivered in the newspapers and magazines, but I never have them.

Jenny: Actually, I have a file folder where I keep all my coupons and they are filed according to the type of products and services: food, shoes, clothes, hair-cutting etc.

David: How did you gather these coupons?

Jenny: You have to be well-informed. I get some of them from the newspapers and magazines. Some are delivered by promoters. Some are just downloaded and printed from the Internet.

David: From the Internet? That is interesting.

Jenny: Yeah. Take the Pizza Hut for example. There are always coupons available on the website of the restaurant. As long as you download them and have them printed, you'll save a lot.

David: Sending coupons is indeed a good way to advertise. If you have no coupons of a particular store, it is unlikely that you would visit the store.

Jenny: You are right. However, as a consumer, we need to be wise and selective. I use coupons to shop because I really want to buy things, not because I have the coupons.

Words and Expressions

worn	adj.	破损的	file	n.	文件夹
misleading	adj.	误导的	well-informed	adj.	信息灵通的
spring	n.	弹跳力	promoter	n.	推销的人
strategy	n.	策略	Pizza Hut		必胜客
coupon	n.	优惠券	hero hamburger		巨无霸

Part Two: Related Questions with Suggested Answers

1. What is an advertisement? How do you classify advertisements?

Advertisement is a notice or announcement in a public medium promoting a product, service, or event or publicizing a job. Advertisements are designed to persuade customers to buy more products or service. People see advertisements on TV or newspaper and are attracted by the description about the products in advertisement. Then they buy the products no matter whether they need them or not. Therefore, advertisements can create more buyers and persuade the potential customers to buy the products. There are several types of advertising. The most typical one is advertising through commercial advertising media such as wall painting, billboard, and street furniture components and so on. The second one is covert advertising. It means an advertisement is made when a brand or a product is shown in entertainment and media. The third one is TV commercial. It is a kind of long visual advertisement. The last one is infomercial.

2. What are some of the roles of advertisement?

In the first place, advertisement tells people where and when they can buy the products they need. People can learn all the information about one product through advertisement without going to the market. It can help people to save a lot of time. In addition, it can guide people how to spend their money. People can be informed of the latest styles by advertisement. Secondly, it is beneficial to the merchants. Advertisers spend a large sum of money on advertising in order to increase sales. Most advertisements are so attractive that consumers can not resist their desire to buy the products. Almost every one has the experience that they buy a product that they actually do not need due to the advertisements.

3. Why can advertisements be harmful?

There are as many disadvantages as its advantages about advertisement. Advertisement adds the cost of the products. Advertisers spend a lot of money on advertising. They will add the money on the products. Therefore, when we buy one product we also pay for the advertisement. Advertisement also makes us spend more money. Most advertisements are so attractive that people often buy some products that they do not need. Besides, many advertisements are not true. The description about products in advertisement is not reliable. When people get or use the product, they find that it is not as good as the advertisement says.

4. Do you like to be interrupted by commercials on TV when you watch TV programs? Why or why not?

I hate commercials in TV programs. The commercial appears every time the program reaches the critical point. I always feel angry when this happens. And then I will change to another channel and change back when the commercial ends. But I often change the channel at the wrong time and miss some parts of the program. This makes me dislike watching TV to some extent.

5. Is there any advertisement that attracts your particular attention? And how?

Once I was attracted by a charity advertisement. There are three characters in this advertisement: a little boy, his mother and his grandmother. At the beginning, the mother is washing the grandmother's feet. When the little boy sees this, he holds a large basin with water to his mother. He says to his mother: "Mum, let me help wash your feet." Every time I watch this advertisement, I am deeply moved. The little boy is so young and lovely. This advertisement tells us that the parents will set an example for their children. So parents should mind their behavior. If you are good, your children will be good.

6. How does advertising help you with shopping?

When I want to buy a particular product, I will first collect the information about that product. Then I will go to where I can buy this product. I will compare all the information to figure out which one is the best and cheapest one. But sometimes advertisements are misleading. When I use the best product said in the advertisement, I find that I am cheated. Advertisement also makes me spend more money. When I read an advertisement saying that one product is on sale, I will buy it even though I don't need it.

7. How do consumers and advertisers benefit from advertising?

Adverting is indeed useful for consumers. It makes consumers' shopping convenient. People can get all the useful information about products without going out. They can also compare different types of the same product before they decide which one to buy. Advertisers benefit more from advertising. Advertisements help them to attract more consumers. They often invite super stars to make advertisements for them. And then their brands will be more popular. In that way, they can make much more money.

8. What are some of the language features used in advertising?

With the development of economy, producers begin to realize the important role of advertisement. From the point of psychology, one could remember the product if the advertisement can give people a deep impression. Therefore, successful advertisements aim at impressing people, so that they can be remembered by consumers for a longer time. By applying the rules of psychology, advertisers appeal to consumers' memory. Advertising language must be short, vivid and easy to remember. Besides, advertising language should be rhythmic. People can remember them if they are euphonious.

9. Advertising is finding its way to campus. What do you think of it?

Students are a large group of consumers who are curious to know and quick to follow fashions. They are potential buyers. Many advertisers have directed their attention to this particular group. They put advertisements in schools. We can see advertisements on tables in schools' cafeteria, on trees and so on. Some advertisers give out brochures to students in classrooms or students' dorms. I think it is improper to do so. It will make campus untidy. Schools have to spend a lot of money in cleaning up the advertisements. In addition, advertisers interrupt students when they distribute brochures to the students who are studying. Advertisements in

schools also can affect students' consumption behavior. Some students follow the fashions blindly and buy products that they possibly don't need or buy things they can not afford.

10. People say globalization will not be successful without advertisements. What do you think of it?

I do not agree to this opinion. Advertisements are useful for the globalization for they transmit cultural values to the consumers with other cultural backgrounds. They help consumers understand other cultures when they buy and use the products made in other countries. Advertising helps quicken the process of globalization. However, globalization will be successful without advertisements. Globalization is the inevitable trend with the development of economy. Globalization does not depend on advertisements.

Words and Expressions

potential	adj.	潜在的	merchant	n.	商人
billboard	n.	广告牌	commercial	n.	商业广告
covert	adj.	隐蔽性的	euphonious	adj.	悦耳的，动听的
infomercial	adj.	专题广告片			

Part Three: Related Pictures with Suggested Descriptions

◀ Picture One   Advertising Media ▶

Advertisers can put advertisements everywhere such as wall paintings, billboards, street furniture components, printed flyers and rack cards, radio, cinema and television ads, web banners, mobile telephone screens, shopping carts, web popups, skywriting, bus stop benches, human directional, magazines, newspapers, town criers, sides of buses or airplanes, in-flight advertisements on seatback tray tables or overhead storage bins, taxicab doors, roof mounts and passenger screens, musical stage shows, subway platforms and trains, elastic bands on disposable diapers, stickers on apples in supermarkets, shopping cart handles, the opening section of streaming audio and video, posters, and the backs of event tickets and supermarket receipts.

Widely speaking, any place an advertiser pays to deliver their message through a medium is advertising. That is to say, people are wrapped by advertisements. Advertises use ad tracking to measure advertising effectiveness. This advertising research methodology measures shifts in target market perceptions about the brand and product or service. These shifts in perception are plotted against the consumers' levels of exposure to the company's advertisements and promotions. Advertisers use Ad Tracking in order to provide a measure of the combined effect of the media weight or spending level. The effectiveness of ads can be shown by this technology. According to the report provided by ad tracking, advertisers will change their strategies.

▶ Picture Two　I'll Get a Camera ◀

It is a joke about the influence of advertisement. It happened in a TV store. One day before the closing time, a man rushed into a TV store. He told the shop assistant that he wanted to buy a TV set. He said that in order to get TV set, he had saved money for several months. The friendly shop assistant was very pleased for he was waiting for the day's first  and 100th customer to reach his sales target. If he succeeded, he would get his bonus. So the shop assistant warmly greeted the man and showed him various models on display. He told the man that the image on the screen was sharp and colorful. At that moment, an advertisement appeared on the screen of the TV. It was introducing a popular brand of camera. It showed some beautiful pictures the camera had taken. The man was attracted by the camera and the pictures. He suddenly changed his mind. He told the shop assistant: "I want to buy a camera instead of a TV set now. Thank you for the advertisement. I will at once go to the camera store to buy a camera."

This joke is interesting. From this joke, we can see how the advertisement will influence people's decision.

▶ Picture Three　Coca-Cola ◀

As we all know, Coca-Cola and Pepsi are the largest cola companies. They have deeply connected with people's ordinary life. These two companies have both paid much attention to their advertisements. In 1995, Shaquille O'Neal, a popular basketball player, made a Pepsi advertisement. This ad begins with Shaq playing basketball and a little boy is watching him. The

boy is very excited and cries out the name of his hero. Shaq turns to the boy and sees that he has a Pepsi in his hand. Shaq walks to the boy and asks: "Can I have it?" To his surprise, the boy says: "Don't even think about it." This ad was very popular and had been showed on TV for three years. In 1970s, a football star named Joe Green made an ad for Coca-Cola. There is a little boy as well. After a game, when the football star is leaving the field, the boy gives his hero a bottle of Coca-Cola. Joe is pleased and in order to thank that boy, he throws his towel to him. The boy excitedly catches the gift.

All these advertisements are attractive. They are as popular as the cola. The language used in the advertisements is also popular and frequently quoted by people.

Words and Expressions

flyer	*n.*	（广告）传单	town crier		小商小贩
rack card		积分卡	disposable	*adj.*	可更换的
web banner		网幅广告；旗帜广告；横幅广告	diaper	*n.*	尿布
			track	*v.*	跟踪
web popup		网络弹出式广告	plot (against)	*v.*	密谋（反对）
skywriting	*n.*	空中文字广告	exposure	*n.*	曝光
directional	*n.*	指示物	bonus	*n.*	奖金

Part Four: Related Passages

1. Advertising in U. S. A

As we all know that advertising is used to promote commercial goods and services. It is called commercial advertising. It can be used to inform, educate and motivate the public as well. Then it is called non-commercial advertising or public service advertising. This kind of adverting is usually about issues, such as AIDS, political ideology, energy conservation, religious recruitment, and deforestation. Non-commercial advertising are also called Public service advertising, public interest advertising.

Non-commercial advertising is a powerful educational tool. It is capable of reaching and motivating large audiences. Some people even claim that public service advertising is more powerful than the commercial one. It is useful for the progress of the society. Many public service advertisements are attractive. They will give people a deep impression by their moving language and beautiful pictures. They tell people what is loftiness and encourage people to do the right.

In the United States, television and radio licenses are granted of by the FCC. If the station wants to get the license it has to broadcast a certain amount of public service advertising. To meet these requirements, many broadcast stations in America broadcast most of their required Public Service Announcements during the late night or early morning when the smallest percentage of viewers are watching, leaving more day and prime time commercial slots available for high-paying advertisers.

Public service advertising is becoming more and more important all over the world. We should not only focus on the individual interest but the social interest.

2. History—Advertising

Indian rock-art paintings in 4000 BCE are the earliest wall advertising. Few people could read in ancient towns. So signs on the street had no words. The sign was the shape of a boot, a suit, a hat, a clock, a diamond, a horse shoe, a candle or even a bag of flour. As education became widespread and reading as well printing developed, and in the 15th and 16th century, advertising began to include handbills. In the 17th century advertisements started to appear in weekly newspapers in England. These early print advertisements were used mainly to promote books and newspapers and medicines. As the economy expanded during the 19th century, advertising grew alongside. In the United States, the success of this advertising format eventually led to the growth of mail-order advertising.

In 1836, French newspaper called La Presse is the first to include paid advertising in its pages. This action enables it to lower its price and makes it the leader of among other presses. The formula is soon copied by all titles. Around the same time, in France, Charles-Louis Havas increased the services of his news agency. At first, agencies were brokers for advertisement space in newspapers. N. W. Ayer & Son was the first full-service agency to advertise for others.

At the turn of the century, women had few career choices in business. However, advertising was one of the few. Since women often do shopping in their household, they are keener and more suitable for advertising.

3. Specialized Advertising

In modern time, advertising has been specialized. In general, the social supply exceeds the demand. Different manufacturers of the same kind of product are forced to face great competition. They have to attract more customers to stand strong in the field. In order to remind the consumers of the name and quality of their product, they make advertisement. The manufactures advertise in the newspapers and on posters and other places they can think about. They make advertisements or pay for songs about their products in commercial radio programs. They invite movie stars to make advertisement for them. Of course, they have to pay a large sum of money for the stars. They often organize beauty or singing competitions and give prize to the winners. Some advertisers hold a small concert in the public square to give people a deep impression. In the past, advertisers advertise on the screen of local cinema. But now, we all have TVs. They put advertisements in the middle of the programs. It is annoying, but we cannot get rid of it.

Manufactures spend a lot of money on advertisements. It is said that some advertisers spend more money on advertising than the products themselves. When we buy a certain product, we pay for the product as well as the advertisement. Therefore, the most expensive one is not always the best one.

4. The Rise of Entertaining Advertising

Many new advertising methods appear with the development of the Internet such as Popup, Flash, banner, Popunder, advergaming, and email advertisements.

Since the rise of "entertaining" advertising, some people may like an advertisement enough to wish to watch it later or show a friend. In general, the advertising community has not yet made this easy, although some have used the Internet to widely distribute their ads to anyone willing to see or hear them.

Another trend of advertising in the future is the growing importance of targeted ads. With the help of internet, advertisers will have the ability to reach specific audiences. In the past, in order to deliver a message efficiently advertisers have to blanket as much market audience as possible. Now, usage tracking, customer profiles and social networking sites provide advertisers with audiences that are smaller but much better defined. Ads will go to the most relevant viewers and will be more effective. Among others, Comcast Spotlight is one such advertiser employing this method in their video on demand menus. These advertisements are targeted to a specific group and can be viewed by anyone wishing to find out more about a particular business or practice at any time, right from their home. This is convenient for the viewers and they may choose what they are viewing.

There are more and more embedded advertising or in-film ad placements than ever before. They are all new methods of advertising which are getting increasingly popular.

5. Advertising Regulation

People now are paying much attention to protect the public interest by regulating the content and the influence of advertising. Many countries have banned television tobacco advertising and the advertising to children under twelve.

People all over the world argue a lot about the regulation of TV advertising. In many countries such as New Zealand, South Africa, Canada, and many European countries—the advertising industry operates a system of self-regulation. Advertisers, advertising agencies and the media reach an agreement that they attempt to uphold. The main aim of such agreement is to ensure that any advertising is "legal, decent, honest and truthful".

In the UK most forms of outdoor advertising such as the display of billboards is regulated by the UK Town and County Planning system. If an advertisement dose not get consent from the Planning Authority, it is a criminal offense. All of the major outdoor billboard companies in the UK have convictions of this nature.

Of course, many advertisers dislike governmental regulation or even self-regulation. Therefore, they employ a wide-variety of linguistic devices to bypass regulatory laws. Different governments have different regulations about the controversial products such as cigarettes and condoms. For instance, the tobacco industry is required by law in most countries to display warnings about the health hazards of their products in their advertisements.

Topic Nine Women

Part One: Dialogues

Dialogue 1 What Is In?

(Lily and Susan are talking about the latest trend of clothes.)

Lily: Aren't your jeans awfully loose?

Susan: Sure. Everyone's wearing them this way.

Lily: Not anymore now. That was last year. This year they have to be tight.

Susan: Are you sure?

Lily: Yeah, look at the tight green jeans I bought yesterday.

Susan: The color is too bright for me.

Lily: Colorful jeans are in. This is fashion.

Susan: I guess they must have cost a fortune.

Lily: That's not the point. I enjoy choosing clothes that suit me.

Susan: Well, that doesn't mean they're fashions. And, that green color doesn't flatter your complexion at all. To me, what is in doesn't make sense.

Lily: So what? Green is my favorite color.

Susan: Well, I think it's better to choose clothes that look nice on me.

Lily: Adding fashionable items to my wardrobe makes me feel good and gives me self-confidence. Look at my bracelet. (Show her bracket of Bohemian style to Susan) Vogue magazine said it was one of the top 10 accessories of the year.

Susan: You know me, I'm just down-to-earth and we'll never see eye-to-eye.

Dialogue 2 Losing Weight

(Cathy is standing on a scale in her room and her friend is reading a piece of newspaper.)

Cathy: Wow! I've gained two pounds. I eat ice-cream sundae a lot recently. It's terrible.

Amy: These days you calculate calories of every serving of food you have and weigh on a scale more than 5 times a day. It's terrible, isn't it?

Cathy: I am on my diet.

Amy: Actually, you are by no means fat. You're just chubby.

Cathy: Losing 5 kilograms is my goal. I just want to have the perfect waist to wear bikini. Models, movie stars eat almost nothing to keep their figures. Some just rely on fruits to be alive.

Amy: And some even take medicine.

Cathy: Yeah, see. Being slim means a lot to women.

Amy: I could not agree with you. Look at the advertisements about keeping fit and loosing weight in the newspaper. You are the perfect target. I will not follow that trend.

Cathy: How could you reject being more pretty and more charming?

Amy: It's more important to be healthy than to be slim. Let's take having medicine as an example. One of my friends tried almost all lose-weight products and they did her more harm than good. She felt dizzy, weak and had severe diarrhea after having these medicines. These products cost her a lot of money and cause health-related problems, but she shed not even ounce of weight.

Cathy: It's scaring. I won't have medicine. But, you know, I have a sweet tooth. I think I have no hope of losing weight.

Amy: Don't blame the ice-cream. To do exercise more and eat balanced and nourishing meals are keys to keep fit. I am planning to do exercise to stretch my arms and legs. How about going for a sport together every afternoon after we finish our lessons?

Cathy: That's great! What exercise do you like best?

Amy: I hear that a Yoga training-program is posted in front of the building of University's PE Department. Let's go for details.

Amy: Sure!

Words and Expressions

jean	*n.*	牛仔裤		chubby	*adj.*	（婴儿样）圆圆胖胖的
flatter	*v.*	吹捧		bikini	*n.*	比基尼
complexion	*n.*	脸色；面容		slim	*adj.*	苗条的
bracelet	*n.*	手镯		trend	*n.*	趋势
Bohemian	*adj.*	波西米亚的		dizzy	*adj.*	头昏的
vogue	*n.*	时尚		diarrhea	*n.*	腹泻
accessory	*n.*	陪饰		ounce	*n.*	盎司
down-to-earth	*adj.*	实在的		nourishing	*adj.*	有营养的
sundae	*n.*	圣代		Yoga	*n.*	瑜伽
see eye-to-eye		（与某人）看法一致				

Part Two: Related Questions with Suggested Answers

1. What are the main differences between men and women?

In the first place, they are different in their bodies. Generally, men are stronger and taller than women. Men have more strength than women. They are more suitable for some laborious work. Secondly, they differ in their personalities. Men are assumed to be straightforward and women are more careful and reserved. Men are tough and they seldom cry. Thirdly, they differ in thinking. Men are more logical while women are more sensitive. Especially when they meet some urgent matters, men are more rational than women. Men can calm down quickly and think of solutions.

2. Compared with men, what are women's advantages and disadvantages?

Women are gentle and careful and they are good at taking care of their children and husbands. So it is usually their responsibility to take charge of the household so that men can be more devoted in their work. Women are suitable for civil service. They are more considerate than men. But women have many disadvantages due to their personalities. Sometimes they are too emotional. They deal with things sensitively but not logically. So some jobs that require much ration do not fit them. Women are weaker than men. They can only do some work that require less labor. Women need to take care of their children. So many employers do not want to hire women for they will have babies and must spend much time and energy attending to their children.

3. Are there any jobs that are more suitable for women than for men? Why?

Yes, there are. Generally speaking, women are weaker yet more careful and warm-hearted. So women are suitable for jobs that require less labor such as civil service and nursing. Most nurses in hospitals are women. Women are more patient so they can be better teachers. Women talk more and they tend to be very talkative and persuasive. Therefore, they can do some public service. In China, most waiters in restaurants and hotels are women. The free service phones are mostly answered by women.

4. Why is it more difficult for female graduates to find jobs than male graduates nowadays?

Recently, female students will meet more difficulties than male students when they try to find jobs. Many employers make it clear in their job advertisements that they do not need female employees. Some do not admit this but they will not give female students job opportunities. This is gender discrimination. Female students are as qualified as male students. But employers have their own reasons. The main reason is that females will have babies a few years after they get married. The employers have to give them holidays and also pay them. And the female employees will spend more time and energy taking care of their children. They can be distracted from their work and cannot focus on their work. Therefore the employers may not be happy about it.

5. Why do some people don't like the idea of women being engaged in sports such as boxing and weight lifting?

As we all know, people who are engaged in boxing and weight lifting are usually very strong and heavy. They have to eat much to get as much strength as possible. Most women want to be beautiful, attractive and slim. They don't like to put on more weight. Therefore, women themselves do not like to be engaged in boxing or weight lifting. Traditionally, people think that women should be gentle and delicate. They do not like those women who have more muscles than men. In addiction, boxing is supposed to be a violent sport not suitable for women.

6. What are some of the main discriminations against women in our society? Why?

Nowadays in our society there are discriminations against women. Women are considered weak and unqualified sex. Gender discrimination can arise in different contexts. For instance an employee may be discriminated against by being asked discriminatory questions during a job interview, or because an employer did not hire, promote or wrongfully terminated an employee based on her gender. In an educational setting, girls are more likely to be deprived of educational opportunities. Parents in the countryside would rather give their boys opportunities than girls for education. In terms of payment, women are generally underpaid because they often perform low-status jobs, compared to men.

7. Why do more school-age girls drop out of school in the countryside?

I come from the countryside. I know this situation. When I was in junior school, many of my girl classmates left school and went to other big cities to make money. When I went to high school I had fewer girl classmates. This is common in the countryside. People in the countryside are poor and there are usually two or three children in a family. Parents do not have enough money to send all their children to school. Because of their conventional ideas, parents prefer to send their sons to school and force their daughters to work. At present, this situation is improving because of the one-family-one-child policy. It is not allowed to have more than one child in a family. So most girls can go to school.

8. Who impressed you most as an outstanding woman in China?

Deng Yaping impressed me most as an outstanding woman in China. When I was young, she was very famous. She was not tall but played table tennis very skillfully. She has won four gold medals for Olympic Games. She has got 14 world championships. Some people said that she was a miracle. Her success resulted from her efforts, resolution and confidence. When she decided to play table tennis, many people did not think that was a good choice for her because she did not look like a good player. However, she made it. She once said that: "I am not cleverer than others, but I can try. If I make the decision, I will not give up." This is what we should learn from her.

9. What should women do if they are harassed by their bosses?

Women, especially beautiful ones, are often harassed by their bosses. In my opinion, women should not tolerate their bosses if they are bothered. Firstly, they can tell their bosses frankly that they dislike such behavior. If their bosses keep on doing like that, women can just warn them, saying they would sue them. If it still does not work, women can quit their jobs.

10. What is feminism?

Feminism is a political discourse aimed at equal rights and legal protection for women. Feminism is a diverse collection of social theories, political movements, and moral philosophies. Some versions are critical of past and present social relations. Many focus on analyzing what they believe to be social constructions of gender and sexuality. Many focus on studying gender inequality and promoting women's rights, interests, and issues.

Feminist theory deals with the nature of gender inequality and focuses on gender politics, power relations and sexuality. Feminism is also based on experiences of gender roles and relations. Feminist political activism commonly campaigns on issues such as maternity leave, equal pay, sexual harassment, discrimination, and sexual violence.

Words and Expressions

straightforward	adj.	直率的	miracle	n.	奇迹
reserved	adj.	含蓄的，矜持的	harass	v.	骚扰
rational	adj.	有理智的	feminism	n.	女性主义
civil service		公务员	discourse	n.	话语
considerate	adj.	体贴的	diverse	adj.	不同的
persuasive	adj.	有说服力的	version	n.	版本
distract from...		从……上分心	construction	n.	建立
delicate	adj.	微妙的	issue	n.	事物
discrimination	n.	歧视	activism	n.	激进主义，行动主义
terminate	v.	中断	campaign on...		以……为宗旨发起
be deprived of		被剥夺			运动
underpaid	adj.	报酬不高的	maternity leave		产假
conventional	adj.	世俗的			

Part Three: Related Pictures with Suggested Descriptions

Picture One Gender Roles

Men and women have different roles in work since the ancient time. In hunter-gatherer societies, women's job was to gather plant foods, small animal foods, fish, and learn to use dairy products. Meanwhile men had to hunt meat from large animals.

The gender roles of women have changed greatly with the development of the society. Middle-class women only had to take care of their children and did not enter paid employment. Poorer women were forced to make money outside. They were lower than the men worker and got less than them.

Women's situation got better with changes in the labor market for women. Women's availability of employment changed from only "dirty" to "cleaner" and more respectable office jobs where more education was demanded. It was reported that women's occupation in the U.S. labor force rose from 6% in 1900 to 23% in 1923. From then on, people have changed their attitudes of women at work.

In women's movements, they require equal right and treatment with men. In recent years, women in most countries now have got the same social status as men thanks to a series of women movements.

The gender gap in most countries has been reduced over the last 30 years. Younger women today are far more likely to have completed their education. In many countries, the number of women graduating from university-level programs is equal to or exceeds that of men.

Picture Two Betty Friedan

Betty Friedan was an American feminist and writer. She was the starter of the second wave of feminism. She was important for reshaping of American attitudes toward women's lives and rights. Betty Friedan was a founder of the national organization for women.

She was well known for her book *The Feminine Mystique*. It has influenced many individuals like authors, educators, writers, anthropologists, journalists, activists, organizations,

unions, and you everyday woman to take part in the feminist movement. It has inspired many people for her active role during the 1960s in the feminist movement to write books, be activist and join part in feminism. This great writing has been regarded as the most powerful work in America. Allan Wolf is an author who has been very much influenced by Friedan. She writes about Friedan's life and has studied *The Feminine Mystique* in great detail in this article *The Mystique of Betty Friedan*. Wolf says that "She helped to change not only the thinking but the lives of many American women, but recent books throw into question the intellectual and personal sources of her work." Although there have been some arguments on Friedan's work *The Feminine Mystique* her work truly has great influence for women all over the world.

Picture Three   Virginia Woolf

Recently women's writing came to exist as a separate branch of literature and in modern time, there is specialized study on women's writing. In the West, second-wave feminism made people to understand women's historical contributions. Some subjects such as women's history and women's writing developed in response to the movement. Much of this early period of feminist literary scholarship was given over to the texts written by women. Commensurate with the growth in scholarly interest, various presses began the task  of reissuing long-out-of-print texts. More recently, Broadview Press has begun to issue eighteenth- and nineteenth-century works, and University of Kentucky has a series of republications of early women's novels.

Virginia Woolf was an English novelist and essayist, regarded as one of the foremost modernist literary figures of the twentieth century. Woolf is considered one of the greatest innovators in the English language. In her works she experimented with stream-of-consciousness and the underlying psychological as well as emotional motives of characters. She had a bad time after World War II, but her glory was re-established with the surge of Feminist criticism in the 1970s. Researchers are interested in Woolf's insight into shell shock, war, class, and modern British society. Her best-known nonfiction work, *A Room of One's Own* (1929) shows the difficulties female writers faced in an era when men held legal and economic power and she holds that women have their own right in education and society. Recently, studies of Virginia Woolf have focused on feminist and lesbian themes in her work.

Words and Expressions

hunter-gatherer	n.	采猎者		essayist	n.	散文家
availability	n.	可得到的（机会）		innovator	n.	革新者
exceed	v.	超过		stream-of-		
reshape	v.	重新塑造		consciousness	n.	意识流
anthropologist	n.	人类学家		motive	n.	动机
union	n.	工会		surge	v.	涌出 涌现
commensurate with		于……相当		shell shock		炮弹休克；弹震症
long-out-of-print	adj.	长期未印刷的		lesbian	n.	（女）同性恋

Part Four: Related Passages

1. Sign and Names for Women

Both men and women have their own symbols. The sign for the female gender is the symbol for the planet Venus. It is a stylized representation of the goddess Venus's hand mirror or an abstract symbol for the goddess. The Venus symbol also represented femininity, and in ancient alchemy stood for copper.

There were three ages of woman historically known as "maiden, matron, and crone" and are sometimes quoted as "maiden, mother and crone". In the ancient time, a woman in the third part of her life was known as a crone, which was originally not a bad term. In modern English, there is no commonly-used word for a woman who is in the third stage. This could perhaps be called in modern English as "little girl", "woman of reproductive age" and "older lady".

There are a lot of words used to describe the quality of being a woman. The term "womanhood" merely means the state of being a woman; "femininity" is used to refer to a set of supposedly typical female qualities associated with a certain attitude to gender roles; "womanliness" is the same as "femininity", but is usually associated with a different view of gender roles; "femaleness" is a general term, but is often used as a shortening for "human femaleness"; "distaff" is derived from women's conventional role as a spinner; "muliebrity" is meant to provide a female counterpart of "virility", but used very loosely, sometimes to mean merely "womanhood", sometimes "femininity", and sometimes even as a collective term for women.

2. Men and Women Differ

Men and women have different life expectancy. Although fewer females than males are born, there are only 81 men aged 60 and 100 women of the same age due to a longer life expectancy. Among the oldest populations, there are only 53 men for every 100 women. Women typically have a longer life expectancy than men. There are several factors for this: the first one is genetics. Genes present on sex chromosomes in women are redundant and varied. The second one is sociology. In most countries women are not being expected to perform military service. The third one is health-impacting choices. Men use more cigarettes and alcohol than women.

To a large extent, women suffer from the same illnesses as men. However, there are some diseases that affect women first, such as lupus. Also, there are some sex-related illnesses that are found more frequently in women and some attack women only such as breast cancer, cervical cancer, or ovarian cancer. Women and men may have different symptoms of an illness and may also respond differently to medical treatment. This area of medical research is studied by gender-based medicine.

During early fetal development, embryos of both sexes appear no difference in gender; the physical appearance between male and female is changed by release of hormones. It is said that as in other cases without two sexes, the gender-neutral appearance is closer to female than to male.

3. Women Can Be Just as Aggressive and Violent as Men

People are different. Some people are smarter than others, some are taller, and some have certain desires. That is the Marxist accusation against capitalism that some people do better than others, regardless of their needs. What they do and how much money they get is determined by the free trade of the marketplace. People have some preconception about how people, or the sexes, must be the same. This will reduce the freedom not only of what they do but of what they are.

It is not impossible to say that men and women are different. It is truly accepted in every age and every place that they are in a certain respects different. There is little doubt that men are suited for war and women, mostly, are not. And men are suited for war because they are taller and stronger but also more aggressive and naturally violent. We should admit the former qualities but the latter qualities are merely the result of social conditioning. Women can be just as aggressive and violent if they had been taught and expected to be that way when they were young. And if aggressiveness and violence are the result of conditioning, then violent crime by males is the result of society conditioning. It is true that social norms have hatred of women. Women fought and are fighting for their freedom. They do not want to be the slavery of the forced power or the conventional idea.

4. Gender or Sex?

On some formal occasions, we use the word "gender" instead of "sex". This has become a habit and custom, by which speakers marked themselves through speech as having a proper feminist consciousness. However, these two words almost have no difference in meaning. Gender can simply replace all uses of the word "sex", except for direct references to sexual activities.

When the answers are "male" and "female", it indicates that the question is about the sex of the person, and if the answers are "masculine" and "feminine", it indicates that the question is about gender. "What gender are you?" where the answer is clearly expected to be "male" or "female" rather than "masculine" or "feminine". If this replacement becomes complete, however, then the original feminist distinction simply disappears, and the word "gender" can easily take on the whole original meaning of "sex", including all the differences, physical or otherwise, between the sexes.

Feminists are not sure about whether to rejoice in their transformation of ordinary language. They worry that such a transformation will not actually make any difference by obscuring the distinction they wanted to make. They may well wonder when Rush Limbaugh can say "gender" instead of "sex" without ideological difficulty.

5. Three Waves of Feminism

There are three waves of feminism movements. First-wave feminism refers to a period of feminist activity during the nineteenth century and early twentieth century in the United Kingdom and the United States. At first it focused on the equal contract and property rights for women. However, by the end of the nineteenth century, activism focused on gaining political power for the women.

Second-wave feminism began in the early 1960s and lasted through the late 1980s. Second-wave feminism has continued to exist since that time and coexists with what is termed third-wave feminism. The first wave focused on rights whereas the second wave was largely concerned with other issues of equality, such as ending discrimination.

Third-wave feminism began in the early 1990s. It arose as a response to perceived failures of the second wave and also as a response to the backlash against movements created by the second wave. Third-wave feminism seeks to challenge or avoid definitions of femininity used in second wave. It had over-emphasized the experiences of upper middle-class white women.

Third-wave feminism also contains internal debates between difference feminists such as the psychologist Carol Gilligan. She believes that there are important differences between the sexes. There are others who believe that there are no inherent differences between the sexes and hold that gender roles are due to social conditioning.

Topic Ten   Tourism

Part One: Dialogues

◆ Dialogue 1   Planning a Vacation

(Mr. and Mrs. Smith are talking with his two children Jenny and John about their travel plan before they leave Nanjing, China for America.)

Mr. Smith: Our budget is a little tight this year, kids. As we plan our vacation, let's keep it in mind.

Mrs. Smith: There are a lot of very interesting things to see that are close to Nanjing. Maybe we could consider something like camping and backpacking.

John: I know we've been to Shanghai before, but I'd really like to take a trip to the exciting city again.

Jenny: You're kidding, aren't you? I am tired of hustling and busting of big cities. I want to see the real side of China. Remember last time we went to Tibet. That is what a true trip is!

John: If you really like to be close to nature, I suggest going to Yellow Mountain.

Mrs. Smith: Do you know how far that is?

John: I've heard that it is six-hour train away. It's about 6 miles from the south rim to the north rim of the range.

Jenny: I don't know about you, John, but I've never tried walking that far.

John: We don't have to make it all in one day. We can hike down at the middle of the route the first day and spend the night at a camp site. And Mom and Dad may take the cable if the mountain route is steep.

Mr. Smith: I know there are many beautiful places in Yellow Mountain and we even may spend a day or two camping on the mountain and exploring the spot.

Mrs. Smith: I like your idea, John. Are there any other suggestions for our vacation?

John: No, not from me! This is a trip I have always wanted to take.

Jenny: I know the sceneries in Yellow Mountain are amazing. But the mountain route is a real challenge. I am going to run and strengthen my legs before we leave.

Mr. Smith: If Mom is in favor, I guess we'll plan for it. We need to start preparing the camping and backpacking equipment and someone will have to get the food.

Mrs. Smith: I'll be happy to plan the menus if the rest of you will take care of the equipment.

John: Great! This will be a wonderful vacation!

◆ Dialogue 2   A Wonderful Vacation

(Jenny is talking about her vacation in Hainan with her friend Cathy.)

Jenny: We had a wonderful vacation this year. My whole family enjoyed it.

Cathy: Tell me about it. What made it so good! Where did you go?

Jenny: We went to Hainan. Since the whole family enjoys water, we spend most of the time in Sanya where you can swim. My brother really enjoyed surfing and I enjoyed catching up on my reading while getting a suntan.

Cathy: Did you spend all of your time at the beach?

Jenny: No, not all. My Dad has a native friend at Sanya who took us sailing and deep sea fishing. We all enjoyed that. We also visited some other tourist attractions: Marine World, Diving World and of course Tropic Botanic Garden.

Cathy: How did you like Sanya Botanic Garden? I visited the Botanic Garden of our province last year with my brothers. What an amazing place! I got to know thousands of plants, flowers and trees. They varied in size and shape. As to cacti, there were more than 100 kinds of species.

Jenny: Yeah, our family got a real kick out of that. Those tropic plants were so diversified and even some extinct species of tropic plants were kept and grown in the Garden. The outlay of the garden was great and we were like strolling in a tropic forest while visiting.

Cathy: It sounds like you all enjoyed yourselves. Did your family start planning next year's vacation yet?

Jenny: Good heavens, no! Let me get rested from this one first.

Words and Expressions

camp	v.	野营	suntan	n.	日光浴
backpack	v.	（背背包）徒步旅行	marine world		海底世界
hustling and busting		熙熙攘攘	diving world		潜水世界
rim	n.	（山谷的）边缘	tropic botanic garden		热带植物园
hike	v.	徒步旅行	cacti	n.	仙人掌
cable	n.	缆车	get a real kick		玩得真开心
surf	v.	冲浪	extinct	v.	灭绝
catch up on		补时间	outlay	n.	布局

Part Two: Related Questions with Suggested Answers

1. Do you like traveling? Why or why not?

Definitely yes, I enjoy traveling for at least three reasons. Firstly, we can enjoy the beautiful scenery in different places. We can see many places read in books, and visit some famous cities and scenic spots. Secondly, we can meet people with different interests and see interesting things. We can get ideas of the conditions and customs of other people, taste different foods and local flavors if we like. In this way, we can understand how differently other people live. Finally, traveling not only helps us gain knowledge, but also helps us keep healthy and make us open-minded. Travel does benefit us both mentally and physically.

With all of these advantages of travel, it is no wonder that travel is becoming more and more popular.

2. What means of transportation do you like to use when you travel? Why?

Well, I'd travel by plane because it is more relaxing when you sit on a plane with beautiful airhostesses serving you food and drinks. The most important thing of air travel is that it is quicker. You can travel to Beijing from Shanghai only in one and a half hours. Once you sit in a plane with a refreshing cup of coffee or tea, some nice food and a small talk with a passenger nearby you find yourself in Beijing already. Furthermore, traveling by plane is very easy. Someone takes your luggage after you have checked in and all you have to do is to get on and sit down. Another point in favor of air travel is that it is now relatively cheaper, especially for long distance travel. You can enjoy discount tickets from time to time.

3. Is there any place that you traveled and also impressed you much? How did it impress you?

Yes. I went to Yellow Mountain last year. Its unique scenery impressed me most. Yellow Mountain is a marvel and it is characterized by the four wonders, namely, odd-shaped pines, craggy rocks, sea of clouds and crystal-clear hot springs. Yellow Mountain is celebrated for having all the significant features of mountain sceneries. Widely recognized as the NO.1 Mountain under heaven, it features numerous imposing peaks, forests of stone pillars and ever-green sturdy pines; other features include grotesquely-shaped rocks, waterfalls, pools and hot springs. Yellow Mountain was already declared a World Natural and Cultural Heritage by UNESCO Heritage Committee in 1990. Once you are in Yellow Mountain you will find you are in a wonder land.

4. Would you like to travel by yourself or by joining a package tour?

Well, I prefer to traveling on my own. I like traveling on my own not only because it costs much less but because it gives me more freedom. Traveling on my own, I'm my own boss; and I can decide when to start on my way, where to linger a little longer and which spots can be skipped over to save efforts or time for other more preferred ones. I can always adjust my plans. On the contrary, in a package tour you're deprived of the freedom. At the sound of the whistle, you have to jump up from a sound sleep and, with heavy-lidded eyes, hurry to gathering place where you are collected and counted to board a coach. At the sight of the little flag waving, you must immediately take yourself away from the scenes you are marveling at and follow the guide whose sole interest is to cover all the spots according to his strict schedule, regardless of the weather or your health condition.

5. Do you like the saying that "The only way to travel is on foot"? Why or why not?

Well, I don't like the saying. I think traveling in the 21st century should be easy and enjoyable. Traveling on foot takes you a lot of time though you are freer and more independent. Also, traveling a long distance on foot makes you exhausted. If you depend too much on your legs, you will harm them. There are a lot of modern means of transportation for you to choose. Planes, trains and cars will take you anywhere you want with less time and less efforts. With supersonic airplanes, modern trains and fast-moving cars you can travel faster, see more places and know more people. Save your legs and make machines work for you.

6. What do you think of the saying that "The best way to know the world is by traveling"?

I agree with the saying. First of all, traveling is just like visiting new places and meeting new people. Once you are in new places you will get to know a new life and new culture in which you can see how people with different cultural backgrounds behave and think. You can learn their customs and their values. Also visiting other places can improve your communication skills. For example, when you travel to an area where a group of minority nationalities live you can learn how to communicate with them with their customs and even with their rituals. Otherwise you appear awkward and clumsy. Finally, traveling gives you a chance to study new languages. It is a great fun if you can utter some words of their languages when you talk with natives.

7. How do we get better prepared for a trip?

Well, I think we can do the following things to get better prepared for a trip. Firstly, we need preparation several weeks before our departure. If we travel abroad, make sure our passport is in order and good for at least six months. Then obtain visas, as required, for the countries we'll be visiting. The second thing to worry about is the transportation. Once our destination is decided and our traveling time is fixed, the round-trip ticket should also be prepared in advance. Since our destination is very far away, airplane is a good choice. Now comes the most important part, scheduling. It is also a difficult part. However, we have a good assistant-internet. There are lots of traveling forums. We can read travelogues from other travelers and learn experience from them. After scheduling is done, the next thing is reserving hotels. Hotels should be close to the scenery spot we will visit. Which hotel is better? We can get the information by searching on Google. We can choose a cheaper one if only it is clean and safe. We can also choose a special one for it has a especial service, like bar or concert. We can book hotel by ourselves through telephone or email. We can also reserve from the local agents. So, careful preparation is essential for a perfect journey. Try to get better prepared for a trip.

8. Why do you think more and more travelers are coming to China these days?

Well, it is true that in recent years more and more travelers from foreign countries are coming to China. This is because, first of all, China is becoming stronger and stronger politically and economically. People's livelihood has been improved greatly. The great changes that have taken place in the ancient country of ours since the 1980's surprised the world. Foreigners keep wondering how all that could have happened. They are curious to know and eager to see things in China. So they come.

Also, China has a long history of five thousand years. It is the only continuous ancient civilization. Other ancient civilizations have changed, discontinued, withered or perished. Why is it so enduring? Why is it so coherent, sticking to itself, remaining undivided? Why is it so dynamic, always able to revive, regenerate and revitalize itself? These are questions that puzzle most outsiders. They come to know and to learn.

Moreover, China is an ancient, mysterious and beautiful land always appealing to adventurous foreign visitors. As the third largest country in the world China occupies an area of 9,600,000 sq km. To most Europeans, this huge land is more like a continent than a country. A wide variety of terrain and climate shape its numerous natural attractions. Abundant in a variety of resources, plants, animals, and minerals, the land has nurtured countless generations of Chinese people.

9. What suggestions would you like to give to the government to develop the country's tourism? Why?

Well, in the past ten years, tourism in China has witnessed a rapid development. It has generated numerous job opportunities and it has made a great contribution to the development of Chinese economy. In order to sustain such a development, I think the government should do the following things. Firstly, the government should upgrade its facilities to give travelers more convenience and more comfort. Secondly, the government should train hotel managers, tourist guides, interpreters and make them more professional. Thirdly, China should develop its tourism by using Internet. Experts say that compared with other tourism nations, China's online tourism is still quite small. There is huge potential for developing tourism websites.

10. Is it necessary for us to protect our environment in developing our tourism? Why or why not?

Of course it is necessary. I think sound environmental policies and practices are prerequisites for a successful and sustainable tourism industry. Firstly, if you want to attract tourists, it has to be a place with easy access. So transportation is very important for tourists. Transportation should be easily available, fast and safe. Secondly there should be a clean environment for tourists to enjoy with amenities like toilets, food establishments nearby. If the locations can provide these, tourists will go. Thirdly, pollution should be reduced and controlled. Nowadays, many of the more popular tourism destinations, especially in coastal areas, experience degraded marine and terrestrial systems because of pollutants emanating from tourism. That should be improved. Finally, natural areas and parks should be established in order to have more places for tourists to see.

Words and Expressions

airhostess	*n.*	空姐	forum	*n.*	论坛
refreshing	*adj.*	提神的	travelogue	*n.*	旅游日志
marvel	*n.*	令人惊喜的事	reserve	*v.*	预定
craggy rock		怪石	wither	*v.*	枯萎
crystal-clear	*adj.*	清澈的	coherent	*adj.*	连贯的
imposing	*adj.*	给人留下深刻印象的	dynamic	*adj.*	有活力的；有动感的
pillar	*n.*	柱子	regenerate	*v.*	产生
sturdy	*adj.*	粗壮的	revitalize	*v.*	（使）新生；（使）恢复生机
pine	*n.*	松树			
grotesquely-shaped		形状嶙峋怪异的	terrain	*n.*	地貌
heritage	*n.*	遗产	nurture	*v.*	养育
linger	*v.*	逗留	upgrade	*v.*	（使）升级
skip over		跳过，忽略	facility	*n.*	设备
package tour		跟团旅游	prerequisite	*n.*	必要因素
heavy-lidded	*adj.*	眼袋大的	amenity	*n.*	生活设施
supersonic	*adj.*	超音速的	destination	*n.*	目的地
ritual	*n.*	仪式	marine	*adj.*	海的，海上的
awkward	*adj.*	尴尬的	terrestrial	*adj.*	地球的；陆地的
utter	*v.*	说	emanate	*v.*	来自（某物）

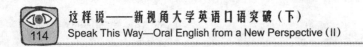
Part Three: Related Pictures with Suggested Descriptions

Picture One　Advantages and Disadvantages of Package Tours

Well, I think there are both advantages and disadvantages of package tours.

The advantages are apparent. Firstly, we don't need to think many things because the travel agency has already done the plan for us. Secondly, it is less expensive than traveling by our own because we can enjoy a good group rate. In addition to this, we can have a better consumption plan because the budget is known in advance. Thirdly, because tour guides are included in a package tour, we will have no language problems and will also have an efficient way to see all the "must-see" spots. Finally, we can have much fun, especially when we take part in a group activity during our tour because we have many travel companions.

There are also some disadvantages of package tours. The main disadvantages are that you have to strictly follow the package tour schedule and you don't have other choices to go. Also you have to pay in advance. What's worse, the tour guides will take us to go shopping and we won't have enough time to see scenery and take pictures on our own.

To sum up, every coin has two sides. What we can do is to compare the advantages and disadvantages before we travel, and then decide whether to take a package tour according to different times, different places, and different situations.

Picture Two　The Means of Traveling

What kind of means will you choose to travel? Plane, train, car or even bicycle? Well, as for me, I will choose air travel. I think air travel is very fast and enjoyable. A modern jet plane can take us to the other side of the world in a little more than ten hours. It seems the world is becoming a smaller place to live in and to get around. In the future, air travel will become more common and convenient. We will fly faster and in greater comfort.

However, air traffic is a mixed blessing. Though time-saving, it has created many challenging problems. Airplanes cost huge sums of money to build. Jet pollution is very harmful to health and property. Sonic boom is driving us mad. How many people wish the cursed bird would disappear from the sky! Shouldn't air traffic be developed under closer control?

I believe someday we'll have clean planes run on solar energy or a fuel that does not pollute. When this comes true, we will enjoy air travel even more.

Picture Three   Traveling

It is exciting to visit different places. As you travel, you will see beautiful sceneries typical of the region. Besides, you can meet and make friends with people of different colors and races. Finally, you can get to know the customs and living habits of the local people. Today people are so fond of traveling that tourism has become one of the faster growing industries in most countries.

The main reason why people travel is, perhaps, for pleasure. For example, having worked hard throughout the weekdays, people will find a widened trip to the nearby mountains or beaches a real relaxation. For another example, spending an annual holiday traveling abroad is an especially satisfying experience for those who do not have much of an opportunity to be away from their homelands. When people return from their travel, they will generally feel fresh and energetic, ready to work harder.

Traveling is also one of the best means for learning. You may have read or heard about something but you can never get an accurate picture of it until you see it for yourself. Seeing is believing. Furthermore, if you are a careful observer, you can learn much during your travel about the geography, biology, and history of the places you visit. No matter how well educated you are, there is always a lot for you to learn through traveling. The knowledge acquired from travel, as you will have found in your life, is no less valuable than that from any influential reference book.

Words and Expressions

jet plane		喷气式飞机	cursed	adj.	可恨的；讨厌的
a mixed blessing		好坏参半之事	widened trip		深度游
sonic boom		超音波爆声	energetic	adj.	精力充沛的

Part Four: Related Passages

1. "It Is Only 5:30 Now!"

This year during the Spring Festival, I went to Thailand to travel. We stayed at the First Hotel for five days. At the first day, we made a mistake, which was very funny.

On that morning, we got up very early, because our guide told us that we must get together at 7:25 and the restaurant was opened at half past six. But when we came into the restaurant at 6:40, there were few people and little food. Then we had breakfast and finished it at 6:50. Because there was almost no food for us, we just had congee. Then we waited for our guide. But until 7:30, he didn't appear. So we called him. We asked him why he didn't appear at 7:30. He heard that and laughed, and then he said, "It is only 5:30 now!"

We made a mistake about the time. We knew there was one hour's difference between Thailand and China. So we got up earlier about one hour. But in the fact the time in Thailand is later than the time in China! So that morning, we got up at four o'clock of the Thailand's time!

2. Air Travel Can Be Tiring

Air travel is such an everyday experience these days. But frequent long distance flying can be so tiring that the traveler begins to feel his brain is in one country, his digestion in another and his powers of concentration nowhere—in short, he hardly knows where he is.

The fatigue we normally experience after a long journey is accentuated when we fly from east to west or vice versa because we cross time zones. Air travel is so quick nowadays that we can leave London after breakfast and be in New York in eight hours. Yet what really disturbs us is that when we arrive it is only lunch time, but we have already had lunch on the plane and are expecting dinner.

Doctors say that since air travelers are in no condition to work after crossing a number of time zones, they should go straight to bed on arrival. Airline pilots, in fact, whose experience is so obviously relevant that it ought to serve as a guide, often live by their own watches, ignoring local time, and have breakfast at midnight if necessary. They have far less reason to worry about their health than others because they are used to flying and are physically fit.

3. A Tour Guide Does a Lot for Us

With the improvement of living standard, tourism has thrived increasingly over time. Many people have already concerned to travel several times per year. Although there are various ways to travel, joining a group led by a tour guide is the most prevailing and best way.

The guide in a tour group can provide many interesting tales or stories to complement our knowledge and offer a reasonable schedule. The guide regards as a tour expert in certain section, who knows everything about his or her job, such as the perpetuate history of the town or museum, or knowing which plot is perfect to shoot. No one is able to compete with a tour guide about this knowledge. Furthermore, a tour guide is able to schedule our trip reasonably in limited time.

Moreover, to associate with a tour group on vocation is an economical perspective. As all we know, anyone tends to budget their expenditure at any cost. A canny consumer will plan his or her vocation carefully because it costs not only time but money. This means choosing a good way to travel is a significant factor. Most people are likely to follow a tour group because they could save their money in many ways as booking hotel, having meal, the discount tickets and transportation fee. As a matter of fact, the immediate benefit is convenience to travelers who associate with the tour company, as they do not have to consider many trivial things on their own, such as to scheme particular travel routes.

To sum up, I believe travel in a group led by a tour guide is the best and favorite way. In regard to its advantages I mentioned above, people could not only enjoy their vocation but complement their knowledge and save their money.

4. The Advantages and Disadvantages of International Travel

International travel has become cheaper, more and more countries open their doors and more tourists go abroad for traveling.

With the tremendous thriving and growth of both economy and cultural diversity, international travel has already jumped onto the level of the leading industries. Many would argue that its advantages have already dispersed disadvantages, and many others negate this view.

The advantages from international travel are multifarious and prevalent. As we can see in many metropolises, people with different tongues and dialects are swarming from many different countries, and many of them may dwell in these strange cities for decades and deliver their own cultures and languages as well. Together with this communication brought by international traveling, people would get accommodated with many other life styles. For example, you now can find many French wines in nearly every corner in the world for travelers would ask for this beverage when they find they are available. But we can not neglect the disadvantages of this industry either. Many nationalities may be eliminated for this cultural expansion. They may try to learn something modern and finally lose their mother language, which may already be on the verge of extinction.

At the end of a day, we can list many other advantages and disadvantages in both culture and economy. But one thing we know for sure is that we can try our best to remove those disadvantages through hard work in cooperation and conciliation, we can also amplify our advantages after long years of persistence.

5. I Enjoy Traveling on My Own

With the general standard of living improving and the working week becoming shorter, more

and more people are able to make a holiday trip to places of interest. While many like to join package tours for convenience, I prefer to travel on my own.

I like traveling on my own not only because it costs much less but because it gives a great degree of independence and freedom. Traveling on my own, I'm my own boss; and can decide when to start on my way, where to linger a little longer and which spot can be skipped over to save energy or time for another spot. I can always adjust my plan. On the contrary, in a package tour you're deprived of as much freedom as in a military base. At the sound of the whistle, you have to jump up from a sound sleep and, with heavy-lidded eyes, hurry to the gathering place where you are collected and counted to board a coach. At the sight of the little flag waving, you must immediately to yourself away from the scenes you are marveling at and follow the guide whose sole interest is to cover all spots according to his strict schedule, regardless of the weather or your health condition.

True, you may encounter inconveniences if you travel individually, for instance, getting accommodations for the night and finding a place for meals. But nothing can be compared with the freedom which is vital to a person who takes a holiday trip mainly to escape from constraints of his routine life.

Topic Eleven Arts

Part One: Dialogues

 Dialogue 1 Chinese Traditional Painting and Western Oil Painting

(Wu, a Chinese teacher, is talking about Chinese Traditional Painting and Western Oil Painting with an American teacher, Susan.)

Wu: Look at the Chinese Traditional Painting by Daqian Zhang. It's fantastic, isn't it?

Susan: To be frank, I don't quite understand Chinese art. By the way, have you ever seen the oil painting "La Place Saint-Georges" by Renoir?

Wu: Yeah.

Susan: Do you remember the rich hues and shades of color that resulted from the morning rays? The sun's rays warm the chestnut trees. You can almost feel the warmth. It's incredible.

Wu: I was very much impressed, too. Actually, Western Oil Painting and Chinese Traditional Painting are very different with their own principles. When you're used to one style, you really need to understand the other style in a new perspective.

Susan: I've noticed there are differences between the two types, but I don't really understand them. Could you help me out here, Xiao Wu?

Wu: Well, to western painters, light and perspective are two major concerns. So, western oil paintings are defined by colors and shadows.

Susan: That's right.

Wu: Chinese Traditional Paintings are governed by lines and strokes, like our calligraphy. So, Chinese painters don't deliberately mirror the world, instead they use their paintbrushes to give a general "description" on rice-paper. For example, a few strokes may stand for a mountain in the distance; and a few lines may represent the drifting clouds in the sky. Several dots may represent a flower.

Susan: It sounds quite abstract.

Wu: Chinese painting and western painting are all complex works of art. What I know is just a tip of the iceberg.

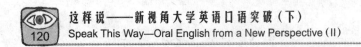
◆ Dialogue 2   Audrey Hepburn

(Linda and Nancy are on their way from cinema. They just watched the movie *Holidays in Roman*.)

Linda: I really enjoyed the movie.

Nancy: So did I. It's great!

Linda: Though the plot is somewhat simple, the brilliant acting of Audrey Hepburn and Gregory Peck has made it a timeless piece.

Nancy: I agree. You know, I'm not much of a moviegoer, but it is the third time I've seen this movie.

Linda: Me too. It has never lost its hold on me. Every time I watch it I seem to discover something new.

Nancy: Hepburn is really one of the all-time actresses.

Linda: You know, the critics say she was the Queen of Hollywood, with dazzling smiles, refined manners and great spirit.

Nancy: Well, that is exactly what she was.

Linda: She won the 1953 Oscar for Best Actress, and after that she starred in many box-office hits.

Nancy: Life must have been fantastic for such a celebrity.

Linda: Well, she struggled for a life of simplicity in spite of her fame. You know she was also devoted to humanitarian work.

Nancy: I heard she worked tirelessly as a good-will ambassador for UNICEF, raising funds for children in poverty-stricken areas.

Words and Expressions

hue	*n.*	颜色；色彩	refined manner		优雅的举止
shade	*n.*	较阴暗的部分	star	*v.*	出演
perspective	*n.*	视角	box-office hits		高票房卖座影片
incredible	*adj.*	不可思议的	celebrity	*n.*	名人
deliberate	*adj.*	特意的	humanitarian	*adj.*	人道主义
calligraphy	*n.*	书法	goodwill ambassador		亲善大使
paintbrush	*n.*	毛笔	UNICEF		联合国儿童基金会
iceberg	*n.*	冰山	fund	*n.*	资金
dazzling smile		迷人的微笑	poverty-stricken	*adj.*	穷困潦倒的

Part Two: Related Questions with Suggested Answers

1. Why do you think universities attach importance to arts education now?

Well, I think arts are essential to university education. Similar to English, math, science and other core subjects, arts, such as dance, music, theater and so on, are challenging subjects with rigorous content and can benefit students in their intellectual, personal, and social development. From another aspect, arts give students foundation skills needed for employment, as well as for life. The skills include imagination, reasoning, making decisions, solving problems, which are all important for the education of students.

2. What kind of music is most popular with young people in your country? Why?

En, I think pop music is popular with young people in my country. Young people like to listen to pop music for several reasons. Firstly, pop music is something of a fashion. Young people want to follow fashions. Secondly, pop music is easy to understand because of its simple rhythm. You can easily get the point the singer wishes to tell you. Finally, most pop songs are about young people's lives, and can make them excited when they are frustrated both in their work and in their life. To sum up, I think pop music has more universal appeal to young people in my country.

3. Music can be entertaining and informative. Why?

Music can be entertaining because when you listen to music you are emotionally affected with the melody, harmony and rhythm you hear. It is generally found that the intensity of the emotional effect of music is proportional to its musicalness, which suggests that the brain calculates musicalness first, and then uses that calculated information to alter its emotional response accordingly. So the direct result of enjoying music is pleasure. In having enjoyable things you get entertained.

Music can also be informative because music gives you information. It is agreed that all music is a message from the people in the time and place in which it was written. Information communicated through musical sound carries with it an emotional content that reveals the impact of a person's or society's experience. For instance, one hears, within the righteous tunes and ballads of Celtic music, the breadth of the culture's history. There is Celtic music that sonically upholds a valiant fight for freedom, and lilting ballads that speak passionately about human rights. The haunting melodies of some Celtic songs express the universal longing for love, life, and happiness. All music speaks of the human experience.

4. Who is your favorite singer? Why?

My favorite singer is Jay Chou. Jay Chou is a popular Taiwanese musician and singer specializing in R&B (Rhythm and Blues) and rap. Also known as the King of Chinese music, he is known for combining both Chinese and Western musical styles to produce a fresh sound that is quite unlike what is produced in mainstream Taiwanese pop. He is also noted for his unique lyrics which touch on various issues. For example, in "Dad I am Back", we know domestic violence. In "Rice Fields" we get the idea of eco-awareness. In "Wounds of War", we understand his idea of the destructiveness of war. Jay's music is popular throughout Asia, most notably in Taiwan. I listen to his music a lot. I am his fan.

5. Why do you think countries have their national songs?

Well, in my opinion, national songs or national anthems are the symbols of countries. National anthems have strongly symbolic political or social meanings. They are the representatives of national identities, often expressing the nation's patriotic sensitivity. They are used in a wide array of contexts. They are played on national holidays and festivals, and have also come to be closely connected with sporting events. During sporting competitions, such as the Olympic Games, the national anthem of the gold medal winner is played at each medal ceremony. In some countries, the national anthem is played to students each day at the start of school as an exercise in patriotism. In other countries, the anthem may be played in a theatre before a play or in a cinema before a movie. Many radio and television stations have adopted this and play the national anthem when they sign on in the morning and again when they sign off at night.

National songs can make the people feel proud of their nationalities, and thus can bring people together in time of sadness and happiness.

6. How has technology affected the kinds of music popular with young people?

I think technology has greatly affected the music popular with young people. Pop music, for example, is so popular with young people nowadays because of the rhythm played with different electrical equipments, such as acoustics equipment, disk, earphone and so on. In addition, young people can easily have access to the music through CD, MP3. Internet technology also makes music enjoyed more by young people. It is much easier nowadays to download the music young people like instead of going to the store and buying CDs.

7. What kinds of skills do we need for painting?

If you want to improve your drawing skills, first of all, you need practice, practice and practice. Draw every day. Keep a sketchbook and use it. Set up a studio space you use only for creating art. Paint every day. Paint from life. Secondly, study art experts. You need to read art books. Visit art galleries. Copy an old master work for study. Explore art movements in history. Read biographies of other artists. Thirdly, dig deeper. Observe your subject and really "see" the details. Paint what you know. Research your subject. Fourthly, nurture your inner artist. Watch a sunset. Appreciate beauty. Visit local galleries and museums wherever you are. Travel for new discoveries and perspectives. Buy a new color of paint just because you like it. Fifthly, improve your artistic technique. Change colors every inch. Use economy of brush strokes. Add interesting shadows. Leave some white paper for sparkle. Observe light and shadow. Finally, start a critique group with other artists. Organize a show just for yourself or for your painting group—it's a wonderful motivation to keep painting.

8. Do you think Beijing Opera is popular with young people? Why or why not?

I don't think Beijing Opera is popular with us young people. I myself seldom listen to and watch Beijing Opera. One reason is that it is difficult to understand what actors and actresses say and sing. Without understanding the meaning of their performance you may lose your interest in it. Secondly, the tempo of music style of Beijing Opera is slow compared with the popular music that young people like. Young people are not patient enough to sit there for hours. Thirdly, Beijing Opera is too elaborate for it involves singing, acting, gesture, stagecraft, gymnastics and makeup. So it is difficult for young people to learn to sing. Yet it is an exciting and satisfying form of theatre. It is full of Chinese culture and history. If it is lost, it will be a shame not just for China but also for the rest of the world.

9. How do you understand the saying that art is a human activity?

I think art, like science that requires knowledge, is a human activity because art belongs to the areas of human endeavor that require skill. Skill is a person's ability to work well with a part of his or her body. Skill is talent and technique. An artist is someone who does something well or makes something well using hands and tools. Art is also skilled production. The baker who makes tasty, attractive bread, cakes, and pies is an artist. The person who arranges items for sale in a store is an artist. The composer of music is an artist. So art does something good for human beings. A beautiful thing is enjoyed, felt and experienced. All artists contribute to a better life for everyone.

10. What are some of the main differences between Chinese Traditional Painting and Western Modern Painting?

Chinese Traditional Paintings usually integrated poetry or Chinese calligraphy. Traditional Chinese painters mainly painted figures, landscapes, flowers, birds and other animals with their focus on the sentiments. On the whole, Chinese Traditional Painting emphasizes lines instead of color and occupies an important position in the world of art.

Western Paintings began with the cubist paintings based on Cézanne's idea that all the depictions of nature can be reduced to three solids: cube, sphere and cone. Other modern painters experimented with freedom of expression through color. Still others did their paintings with exaggerated perspectives. They mostly painted people with their distorted vision.

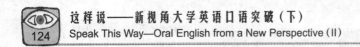
Words and Expressions

rigorous	adj.	严格的；精密的
intellectual	adj.	智力的
rhythm	n.	节奏
universal appeal		在全世界有吸引力
melody	n.	旋律
proportional to		于……成比例
musicalness	n.	音乐性
righteous	adj.	正直的
ballad	n.	歌谣
Celtic	adj.	凯尔特（人）的
valiant	adj.	勇敢的；顽强的
lilting	adj.	（音调）抑扬顿挫的
haunting	adj.	萦绕于心头的
Rhythm and Blues		（黑人热门音乐）强烈节奏蓝调
lyric	n.	歌词
eco-awareness	n.	环保意识
anthem	n.	国歌
patriotic	adj.	爱国的
array	n.	一系列
sign on		开始广播
sign off		结束广播

acoustics	n.	声学
sketchbook	n.	素描本
studio	n.	工作室
gallery	n.	画廊
perspective	n.	视角
sparkle	n.	灵感
critique	n.	评论
integrate	v.	结合；综合
Cézanne		塞尚，后期印象画派的代表人物，印象派到立体主义派之间的重要画家
cube	n.	立方体
sphere	n.	球体
cone	n.	圆锥体
exaggerate	adj.	夸张的
distort	v.	扭曲；歪曲
stagecraft	n.	舞台艺术
gymnastics	n.	体操
endeavor	n.	努力
baker	n.	面包师傅

Part Three: Related Pictures with Suggested Descriptions

Picture One   Peking Opera

Well, Beijing opera or Peking opera is a kind of Chinese opera which arose in the mid-19th century and was extremely popular in the Qing Dynasty court. It is widely regarded as one of the cultural treasures of China.

Beijing and Tianjin are respected as the base cities of Peking opera in the north while Shanghai is the base in the south.

Although it is called Beijing opera, its origins are in the Chinese provinces of Anhui and Hubei.

Beijing opera's two main melodies: Xipi and Erhuang originated from Anhui and Hubei operas. Much dialogue is also carried out in an archaic dialect originating partially from those regions. It also absorbed music and arises from other operas and musical arts such as the historic Qinqiang as well as being very strongly influenced by Kunqu, the form that preceded it as court art. It is regarded that Beijing opera was born when the Four Great Anhui Troupes came to Beijing in 1790. Beijing opera was originally staged for the court and came into the public later. In 1828, some famous Hubei troupes came to Beijing. They often jointly performed in the stage with Anhui troupes. The combination gradually formed Beijing opera's main melodies.

◄ Picture Two　Pop Music ►

Pop music (or "pop") is a sub genre of contemporary popular music that typically has a dance-along and happy rhythm or beat, simple melodies and a repeating structure. Pop song lyrics are often emotional, commonly relating to love, loss, emotion, or dancing. Pop music is distinguished from classical and from folk music.

Many people don't like pop music. In these people's eyes pop music is always in sharp contrast to "lofty music". The latter refers to symphonies and operas of the European countries. They show great concern for the fact that many people prefer pop music to symphonies, because for them pop music should be excluded from the holy palace of music.

By contrast, many people have an ardor for pop music. They argue that people who want us to listen to symphonies are advocating a kind of "elite culture". This notion is unacceptable to pop music fans, for they don't believe that symphonies are loftier than pop music. The difference only lies in the interests of different people.

In conclusion, my idea is that just as there are no distinction between high culture and low culture, so it is inappropriate to say pop music belongs to the "lower" people whereas symphonies in a higher, loftier form of music.

Picture Three   Chinese Painting

Chinese Painting has a long history, and it can be traced back to six or seven thousand years ago. Since similar tools and lines were used for the earliest painting and writing, painting is said to have the same origin as Chinese calligraphy. Thus, Chinese paintings usually integrate poetry or Chinese calligraphy with themes that include figures, landscapes, flowers, birds and other animals.

Traditional Chinese painting remains a highly valued genre, often on exhibit in China as well as other countries. The contemporary art world in China is also very active. Some Chinese artists have been adept at Western-style painting, both oil and watercolor. Many Chinese painters have created works that combine traditional Chinese painting techniques with those of the West, enhancing both forms. The China Art Gallery and other art galleries hold individual or joint art exhibitions year in year out. Art expositions are held each year in Beijing, Guangzhou and shanghai.

Chinese characters evolved from pictures and signs, and the Chinese art of calligraphy developed naturally from its unique writing system. Through the ages, great calligraphers developed representative calligraphic styles of their times. The love of calligraphy is deeply ingrained in Chinese scholars, and has been handed down to the present day.

Words and Expressions

Xipi	n.	西皮	ardor	n.	热情
Erhuang	n.	二黄	advocate	v.	宣传
archaic	adj.	古老的	elite culture		精华文化
dialect	n.	方言	high culture		高雅文化
Qinqiang	n.	秦腔	low culture		低俗文化
Kunqu	n.	昆曲	inappropriate	v.	不对称
troupe	n.	演出班子	genre	n.	种属
sub genre		子类型	adept at...		熟练于……
lofty music		高尚音乐	exposition	n.	博览会
symphony	n.	交响乐	ingrain	v.	植根于

Part Four: Related Passages

1. The University Arts Festival Should Be Better Organized

The University Arts Festival is supposed to provide the students a platform on which they can not only show off their talents of arts, their capabilities and intelligences in organization and cooperation, but also can have a chance to know each other better, thus enhance their friendships. To make the arts festival more lively and colorful, there are several aspects we should pay attention to.

First, the arts festival should be widely ranged according to the various interests of students, such as singing, dancing, instrument playing, and drama performing, chess playing and so on, so that every student may be able to find something that he is interested in and participate in.

Second, the arts festival should be organized in various forms, such as performance, lectures and shows. Students can compare and see the good points and bad points of themselves and other fellow students. They can also share their ideas with each other and thus improve their communicative skills.

In other words, university arts festival should not only give the students a chance to appreciate different arts, but also provide them a platform to learn, to communicate and to entertain. The essence of arts festival is to enhance the college life and to benefit university students spiritually.

2. Chinese Pottery and Porcelain

The origins of Chinese pottery and porcelain go back to distant antiquity, and from the masterful excellence of Chinese ceramics. Painted on the surfaces of these Ming and Ch'ing period pieces are delicate flowers, grasses, birds, and beasts that make one sigh and wonder how such fine work was ever produced.

The key to why ceramic art has been able to develop to such a high level in China lies in the spirit of Chinese craftsmen to strive for excellence. Ceramic and porcelain pieces dating back to various historical periods have demonstrated again and again how Chinese artisans overcame the shortcomings of the materials they used, and how craftsmanship can conquer the difficulties encountered in working with clay.

Pottery and porcelain artisans of today have full access to modern technological knowledge, and can freely choose their equipment. But they all still carry on in the traditional belief that man can indeed conquer nature. Some imitate ancient designs, others produce avant-garde pieces. With their minds, their hands, and clay and fire, these potters express the artist's perception of beauty, his professional experience, his sensitivity, and his level of artistic cultivation.

3. Jazz

The music that we call jazz was born around the year 1895 in New Orleans. It brought together the elements of Ragtime, marching band music, and the Blues. What made Jazz different from the other earlier forms of music was the use of improvisation. Jazz represented a break from traditional music where a composer wrote an entire piece of music on paper, leaving the musicians to break their backs playing exactly what was written on the score. In a Jazz piece, however, the song is simply a starting point, or sort of being played may have been popular and well-known that the musicians themselves didn't compose, but once they had finished, the Jazz musicians had more or less written a new piece of music that bore little resemblance to the original piece. Actually, many of these early musicians were bad sight readers and some couldn't even read music at all. Regardless, their superb playing amazed audiences and the upbeat music they played was a different but well-liked escape from the traditional music of that time.

The first Jazz is thought to have been played by African American and Creole musicians in New Orleans.

A young cornet player by the name of Louis Armstrong was discovered by Joe Oliver in New Orleans. He soon became one of the greatest and most successful musicians of all time, and later one of the biggest stars in the world. The impact of Armstrong and other early Jazz musicians changed the way we look at music, and their work will forever be studied and admired.

4. The Art of Living

The art of living is to know when to hold fast and when to let go. For life is a paradox: it enjoins us to cling to its many gifts even while it ordains their eventual relinquishment. The rabbis of old put it this way: "A man comes to this world with his fist clenched, but when he dies, his hand is open."

Surely we ought to hold fast to life, for it is wondrous, and full of a beauty that breaks through every pore of God's own earth. We know that this is so, but all too often we recognize this truth only in our backward glance when we remember what was and then suddenly realize that it is no more.

We remember a beauty that faded, a love that waned. But we remember with far greater pain that we did not see that beauty when it flowered, that we failed to respond with love when it was tendered.

Hold fast to life, but not so fast that you cannot let go. This is the second side of life's coin, the opposite pole of its paradox: we must accept our losses, and learn how to let go.

This is not an easy lesson to learn, especially when we are young and think that the world is ours to command, that whatever we desire with the full force of our passionate being can, nay, will, be ours. But then life moves along to confront us with realities, and slowly but surely this truth dawns upon us.

5. Arts and Science and Technology

It's undeniable and inevitable that science and technology has developed quite fast nowadays. Despite the immense development, musicians, painters, singers and so on are still highly respected. It's widely acknowledged that arts can't be replaced by science and technology.

Not like S&T which will be replaced by the newly coming ones, arts reflects times and won't be strictly restricted by times. Just like Marks said, "Developing concept can't be abstractly understood in the normal way, S&T would be washed out while arts can be eternal." As we all know, many arts have lasted for thousand of years, and people are still charmed with its beauty and fantasticality. It's immoral.

Further more, arts is abstract. It combines artist's soul, wisdom, imagination, creativity, and understanding for life, society, and appreciation of aesthetics. Some of the elements are inherent that can't be imitated. As life, life is unique and arts are unparalleled. Hence we can understand the phenomenon that after the death of some artists, their works can become invaluable.

All in all, S&T is material, and they might be the carrier of arts while they are definitely not the replacement of arts. S&T can make our life more convenient and comfortable, but arts can make our life more colorful and versatile, and arts can benefit people's mental edification.

To sum up, both S&T and arts are important. Only with S&T and arts as well, can people's life be abundant.

Topic Twelve   Social Problems

Part One: Dialogues

◆ Dialogue 1   Granny Is a Problem

(Linda and Julian are chatting in their dorm after class.)

Linda: What happens? Why don't we talk the whole afternoon?

Julian: I got a letter from my father this morning and knew that my old aunt passed away one week ago.

Linda: I feel so sorry to hear this.

Julian: She was paralyzed after a stroke three years ago and she had to lie on the bed being taken care by others. She used to be a happy old lady, but her temper changed a lot because of illness. And she also suffered from loss of memory in her last years. She even could not recognize me when I visited her last time.

Linda: In that case your old aunt finally got relieved. Don't be sad about it.

Julian: Yeah, she got relieved after many years' tormenting, but what I feel sad about is that her children did not take good care of her in her last years.

Linda: You mean that she becomes a problem? Is that so?

Julian: Yeah, it is very sad that parents give so much of their lives to bringing up their children and then when they become old and sick, they are regarded as a problem.

Linda: Senior citizens are now becoming a problem in our country. In China, family members used to live together and take care of each other. With the development of our society, more and more young people prefer living in their nuclear families and therefore leave their old parents alone.

Julian: Yeah, as long as people are able to look after themselves, the system works quite well. But when they need care and attention, the situation becomes very difficult indeed. Taking my old aunt as an example, when she was able to help her children to take care of the grandchildren and give a hand with the housework, everything worked well. After she suffered from stroke, the old granny suddenly became a problem and none of her children was willing to live with her.

Linda: It is terrible to hear about it, but a solution to this problem is to have the old in nursing homes.

Julian: Yes, but it's not as simple as that. Most public nursing homes are crowded and poor-conditioned. There are private nursing homes, but the cost is way out of reach of the average family.

Linda: As young people, we need to try our best to take good care of the old generation and do what we can do to make them happy.

Julian: Yeah, loving and caring the young and the old is our tradition. Furthermore, we need to set up a good example for our children. After all, one day we'll become old.

◆ Dialogue 2   I Got Mugged

(Jack is supposed to have dinner at 7:00 with his friend George. It's 7:30 when Jack arrives with a big bruise on his face.)

George: What happened to you?

Jack: I got mugged.

George: What?

Jack: I got mugged. Two men came up behind me in the street, pushed me up against a wall, put a knife up to my throat and took my wallet, my watch and MP3.

George: How did you get the bruise?

Jack: When they asked for my money I told them I wouldn't give it to them. So the tall guy punched me in the face.

George: You fool! A man's holding a knife to your throat and you told him you would not give him the money you had with you! You're really lucky! Robbers just punched you instead of stabbing you.

Jack: I suppose you're right, but I got angry.

George: I think that the wisest thing to do in that situation is to give them what they ask for. Are you OK now?

Jack: Yeah, I'm OK.

George: Jack, what were you thinking about on your way home?

Jack: Well, I'd just come out from the lab. I was really tired and walking very slowly and thinking about whether I'd made a big mistake in my experiment procedures this afternoon.

George: You did make a big mistake.

Jack: What do you mean?

George: Your big mistake was to think about your experiment on the way home. That makes you an easy target.

Jack: Yes. I've learned my lesson. From now on I would be more careful.

George: Good. Now how about dinner? I guess you must be starving.

Words and Expressions

paralyze	v.	瘫痪	bruise	n.	伤痕
relieve	v.	解脱	mug	v.	抢劫
tormenting	adj.	折磨人的	punch	v.	揍；用拳打
stroke	n.	中风	stab	v.	戳；刺伤；用刀捅
nursing home		养老院	target	n.	目标；对象

Part Two: Related Questions with Suggested Answers

1. Have you or your friends had anything stolen? Would you please tell us something about it?

Yes, unfortunately. Almost every person that I know has had something stolen, money, bike, cell-phone and laptop, to name just a few. And people often lose their belongings in public places as well as money in their homes. So it seems that nowhere is completely safe. I myself have similar experience, which left me terrible memory. It happened just on my 18th birthday. On that day, I planned to treat my friends in a restaurant for a celebration of my birthday. On our way to the restaurant, we got on an overcrowded bus. We were in such a high mood, chatting and laughing, that nobody paid attention to others that around us. We were just getting off the bus when I suddenly found my bag open and my wallet missing. Alas! Someone just stole my money on the bus and it became useless for me to run after that bus. What a terrible birthday! Things like that happen almost everywhere. Bicycles are the commonest item that gets stolen on campus. Houses sometimes are broken into and money and bankbooks get lost. Cell-phones are increasingly becoming the target of thieves in public places like shopping malls. Thus people can never be too cautious of their properties to prevent them from being stolen.

2. Are there any crimes on campus these days? What are some of the causes of campus crimes?

Yes, there are. It is more and more common that a credit card, a bicycle or a laptop is stolen on campus or in the dormitory. Sometimes students gather to engage in an affray and end up with someone spending months in hospital. Moreover, some students abuse animals like stray cats and dogs and cruelly torture them to death. Some even murder his or her roommates in a small quarrel. It is noticed that campus crimes are on the rise nowadays, which can be attributed to various causes. With the implement of one child policy, children grow up under the care of indulgent parents and grandparents. The spoiled younger ones become self-centered and indifferent to other lives, lacking love and care for others. Once they are irritated by others they tend to resort to violence, taking revenge immediately. Another cause of campus crime is the deficiency of examination-oriented education system. Under the high stress from intensified competition among peers, students' nerves are so tightened that they cannot afford any failure. Once young people could not live up to the high expectations of their parents and teachers, they would easily get frustrated and crazy, hence the juvenile delinquency. In addition, the mass media must also be to blame. With the modern media the young people are exposed to all kinds of cruel and bloody murders and violence, which further makes the youngsters follow suit when they're offended by others. All in all, these factors all contribute to the rise of the campus crimes.

3. Would you like to stop a pickpocket stealing a purse from a passenger on the bus? Why or why not?

Yes, I would. I think that it is everyone's responsibility to do so, because a pickpocket stealing in a public place, such as a bus, is a threat to the property security of all. Even if I were not the target, who knows I wouldn't be the next? Besides, stealing, though less serious than a murder, is definitely a crime, which needs preventing before committed. This helps not only the victim but also the pickpocket as well. By stopping a pickpocket stealing, we can, to some extent, give a lesson to the thief, warning him that giving up is always the right decision. Further, sitting around, doing nothing when a stealing takes place is the same as holding a candle to the devil. The pickpocket would succeed and escape the due punishment. Let's not assist criminals with our silence. Instead, we should work together and stop the crime so as to make the world a safer place.

4. We often heard reports on school violence on American campuses. What are some of the causes?

The number of extremely violent crimes occurring on American campuses has been increasing over the past years. The crimes in and around schools are threatening the well-being of students, as well as of the staff and the surrounding communities. When looking at the urgent problem of school violence one must take into account several factors including the characteristics of the offender, the causes of the violence occurring. Parenting failure has been found to be the number one cause for the violence occurring on campus. Students who lack parental supervision or who have been abused, neglected and received little support from a caring adult are extremely likely to show their frustrations with violence. The home life problems of students definitely contribute to school violence. Another factor that contributes to school violence is peer pressure. Peers of violent offenders believe that some offenders do not think about the repercussions. Drugs and alcohol are also two key factors that lead to the violent crimes on American campus. When investigated, prevention groups found no variation in the convenience for students to access drugs and alcohol. American students with different family incomes, locations, and different ethnic backgrounds have the same access. It is estimated that in the last two years the consumption of alcohol during a school violence has increased thirty-nine percent. With all the school violence going on in the United States little has been done to prevent it from occurring.

5. Do you think television is partially responsible for the violence done in the society? Why or why not?

Yes. Most people think that violence on television increases aggression in children and adolescents. Violence in the media helps promote and encourage children and adolescents to freely express their abusive behavior. Violence is a major part of today's television shows and movies that are targeted towards our youth. Through much exposure to television, children encounter many violent shows that are not suited for them. This can affect a child in many ways. Children, especially young, are not ready to distinguish right from wrong. When their favorite action hero is beating up a bad guy, kids think that it is all right. At a young age, a kid will envy a character on television and will have a preconceived idea that whatever the character does is acceptable. Children will also take what they see on television and try to do the same in their everyday life. Kids could think it is OK with fighting to settle their disputes. Violence on television can be harmful in many ways. On the one hand, young people will imitate what they watch. They could also very easily brainwashed. Youth may get a false impression of what the world is really like. Violence could also make the youth angry at the world, certain types of people, and specific groups. Contemporary television creates a seemingly insatiable appetite for all kinds of amusement without social or moral considerations.

6. Why is AIDS on the rise these days? How do we prevent them?

There are many factors that contribute to the rise of AIDS. One is people's misconception that HIV, the virus that leads to AIDS, can infect only homosexual men and drug users. In fact, everyone can catch HIV. Another factor is people's insecure sexual behavior without condom. As sex intercourse is the commonest way for HIV to spread, people, especially the youth who don't take secure measures, are of the high risk group.

There are many ways to prevent the transmission and spread of AIDS. One way to prevent infection is not to engage in the act of sexual intercourse with anyone who is or might be infected. If someone has to do it, he or she should at least use a latex condom. As to drug users, they should seek professional help to stop drug taking. They should never share hypodermic needles, syringes, or other injection equipment. Also, azidothymidine, commonly known as AZT, may reduce the risk of an infected woman transmitting it to her fetus or baby. Besides, infected women should not breast feed their infants, since HIV can be present in the breast milk of an infected woman.

7. Why are some people addicted to gambling?

People are getting addicted to gambling for many different reasons. Some indulge themselves in casinos to learn the skills needed to play the games, hoping that they will win lots of money. Some gambling addicts are for the entertainment because for them playing the game is an enjoyable experience and the lure of winning money adds to their excitement, such as slot machines. Some players enjoy the adrenaline rush and experience a high that accompanies the thrill when they risk their money on the games. For some, this feeling can be seductive and alluring and some players succumb to the darker side of gambling addiction. Some others are addicted to some highly risky gambles, for example, the sport betting and even the stock market. These people are those who believe they have control of their own destiny, take risks, and feel they have the skill to win in whatever they do. Addiction is a compulsive need. When the thrill of the game outweighs everything else, the player has crossed over the line from player to addict. Gambling, like all addictions, can be devastating for the person and his family.

8. Why are some people addicted to drugs?

Many people do not understand why individuals become addicted to drugs or how drugs change the brain to foster compulsive drug abuse. They mistakenly view drug abuse and addiction as strictly a social problem and may characterize those who take drugs as morally weak. One very common belief is that drug addicts should be able to stop taking drugs if they are truly willing to change their behavior. However, what people often underestimate is the complexity of drug addiction—that it is a disease that impacts the brain and because of that, stopping drug abuse is not simply a matter of willpower. Drug addiction is a brain disease because the abuse of the drugs leads to changes in the structure and function of the brain. Although it is true that for most, people the initial decision to take drugs is voluntary, over time the changes in the brain caused by repeated drug abuse can affect a person's self control and ability to make sound decisions, and at the same time send intense impulses to take drugs. Once you touch drugs, your body and brain will both become addicted to drugs, thus making it even harder for you to quit.

9. Why is the suicide rate rising nowadays?

The number of people committing suicide over the recent decades has been on the rise in China. The reasons for the increasing suicide rate fall down to many issues, social or personal. Someone may commit suicide because he is dumped by his girlfriend; some kids may end their lives just because of the pressure from study and parents who expect them too much. A large amount of people kill themselves because life is extremely difficult.

In recent years, prices keep rising with some doubled or even tripled while pay hasn't been remarkably raised. People cannot afford many things. With the gap between the rich and the poor further enlarging, life is harder and tougher for the people who live under poverty line.

Besides, owning to the only child policy, the first generation of that policy are in their thirties and don't have any brother or sister to share their obligation of supporting their parents. Thus, almost every couple needs to support five persons, namely, their own child and parents of

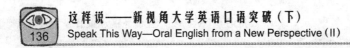

the couple. This adds to the already heavy burden on the bread-earners of the family. Under these circumstances, many poverty-stricken grown-ups tend to commit suicide to end their poor life.

Another reason is the house loan that crushes the people who are busy working day and night just to pay it off. Some of them cannot pay off the loan until ten or twenty years later. Therefore, the bread-earners are undergoing an impoverished life which leads them to ending their lives.

10. Is capital punishment one of the ways to stop crimes? Why or why not?

I guess capital punishment is not an effective way to stop crimes. You can imagine that a professional killer who wouldn't think twice about using his cosh or crowbar to batter some harmless old lady to death in order to rob her of her meager life-savings. So, capital punishment does not deter anyway. In the United States, the country with one of the highest execution rates in the world has one of the highest crime rates. So crime remains a major problem in the United States. By contrast, Canada, located right next door, has no death penalty and yet has one of the lowest crime rates in the world. It is an absolutely example to show that capital punishment couldn't be a major deterrent to crimes.

Words and Expressions

mall	n.	大型购物中心	abusive	adj.	侮辱性的
affray	n.	在公共场所闹事	exposure	n.	此处指接触
abuse	v.	虐待	preconceive	adj.	（思想，观念）事先形成的
stray	adj.	迷路的			
indulgent	adj.	放纵的	dispute	n.	争端
spoiled	adj.	宠坏的	brainwash	v.	洗脑
indifferent	adj.	漠不关心的	insatiable	adj.	不可满足的
irritated	adj.	激怒的；愤怒的	HIV		艾滋病病毒
resort to		诉诸……	condom	n.	避孕套
revenge	n.	报复	transmission	n.	传播
deficiency	n.	缺乏	hypodermic	adj.	皮下的
peer	n.	同龄的人	syringe	n.	注射器
pickpocket	n.	扒手	azidothymidine	n.	抗艾滋病药物
victim	n.	受害者	fetus	n.	胎儿；胚胎
offender	n.	犯人；犯罪的人	indulge	v.	放纵
repercussion	n.	（间接）影响；不良后果	casino	n.	赌场
			adrenaline rush		肾上腺素
access	v.	接触	high	n.	快感
adolescent	n.	青少年	thrill	n,.	刺激

seductive	*adj.*	引诱性的	fall down to		归于
alluring	*adj.*	诱惑人的	dump	*v.*	丢弃
succumb to	*v.*	受……诱惑	bread-earner	*n.*	挣钱养家的人
compulsive	*adj.*	上瘾的	crush	*v.*	压倒
outweigh	*v.*	比……重要	impoverish	*adj.*	穷困潦倒的
devastating	*adj.*	毁灭性的	cosh	*n.*	短棍
foster	*v.*	养成	crowbar	*n.*	铁锹
drug abuse		吸毒	batter	*v.*	接连猛击(某人 / 某物)
voluntary	*adj.*	主动的；自愿的	execution	*n.*	处以死刑
impulse	*n.*	冲动	deterrent	*n.*	起制止作用的事物

Part Three: Related Pictures with Suggested Descriptions

Picture One   Abortion

Abortion is one of the most controversial issues in today's society. This issue has caused a great deal of turmoil in the world. Let's first take a look at some of the circumstances in which people may decide to abort a child. Today's technology enables us to see at a very early stage of the pregnancy if the baby is in good health. If tests show that something is wrong and that the baby will never be able to survive or will only grow to be a

certain age, parents often have a very difficult decision to make. In these cases, I think that parents definitely have the right to opt for abortion. Unwanted pregnancies remain the main reason to opt for abortion. But the matter is very complex and there isn't a solution that is valid in every situation. If the pregnancy is the result of rape or sexual abuse, there should be no discussion. The victim has the right to choose for abortion. Mostly, unwanted pregnancies are the result of unsafe sex. In these cases, I feel that the mother has the right to decide what she is going to do with the baby, as young men often don't want to take the responsibility for their actions. If they do, then the couple should decide together. An important aspect of the decision is financial security. If you decide to have the child, you have to be certain that you will be able provide clothes and food for it. If not, I think that abortion is an acceptable solution. Hopefully, these young people will have learnt a valuable lesson from this predicament. I don't think, however, that abortion should be seen as some kind of safety valve. People confronted with unwanted pregnancies shouldn't think that they can have sex without contraceptives and if they get pregnant, they'll just have the fetus aborted. That's a totally wrong and regrettable mentality that among young people nowadays. If you are not sure that you will be able to provide a secure future for the child or if the pregnancy is a result of sexual abuse, there are sufficient grounds for abortion. But most important of all is to protect yourself from unsafe pregnancy.

Picture Two   Teenagers' Problems

Today in the modern society, there are a lot of problems, especially problems related with teenagers. A lot of factors contribute to the situation. For example some teenagers felt lack of love from their parents. Another factor is the lack of education because of poverty. In most cases there are problems with drugs, alcohol, prostitution, teen pregnancy, depression, etc. Drugs between teenagers are the most serious problems, because it causes a change in the behavior of any person and a physical change too. Most of the teenagers use them as an escape from their problems or sometimes they use them because of their friend's instigation. Poor children use it too, to forget their cold and hunger. Alcoholism is a society's sickness that affects all people, from teenagers to older ones. It is considered as a modern way to have fun and if you drink alcohol you are accepted among your friends. People who drink alcohol think that they can forget their problems and get out from reality if they do that. I think it is very bad to drink alcohol because it can turn in an addiction. Another problem is the prostitution. Most drug addicts have to do this because they don't find a good job and they need money. For this reason, they can become sick with Aids and other diseases. Another consequence can be teenage pregnancy because they don't have a good education and they don't know how to take care of themselves. The most devastating aspect of a teenage pregnancy is the little thought is given to the responsibilities required of the mother to support her new child. Consequently the likelihood is high that the next generation will not receive what it needs to become happy and healthy individuals. All these teenager's problems need to be resolved by the whole society.

Picture Three   Addictions

Physical and psychological addictions are very alike and very different at the same time.

Addiction means that the person addicted thrives on the substance or action. Physical addictions like alcoholism and heroin are sometimes very noticeable. But psychological addictions like gambling are very hard to diagnose.

The similarities between the two types of addictions are the stages that lead up to a full addiction. Addictions go through many stages before reaching the pinnacle of an addiction. For example, a gambler will first start off betting a dollar, then two, then ten, then a hundred until finally the gambler is broke. An example for a physical addiction would be the stages that lead to becoming a true alcoholic. It will start with one beer, then Jell-O shooters, then a margarita, then just drinking liquor straight up out of the bottle, then who knows what the drinker will turn to next. After going through all of these stages the term used for the addiction is usually disease because the addiction is going to slowly kill the person addicted.

Though the term addiction is usually thought of as someone on drugs or drinking, many people are addicted to the one thing that everyone has a little of everyday, caffeine. Caffeine is one of North America's leading addictions prevalent amongst teenagers. Caffeine is found in chocolate, soda, coffee, and tea. In conclusion, this shows that many things can become addictive. If more people would realize this there would be less of an addiction crisis than there is today.

Words and Expressions

controversial	*adj.*	有争议的	thrive on		依赖……发展
turmoil	*n.*	骚动；混乱	heroin	*n.*	海洛因
opt for		选择	diagnose	*v.*	诊断
predicament	*n.*	困境	pinnacle	*n.*	顶点；顶峰
valve	*n.*	阀门	broke	*adj.*	破产的
contraceptives	*n.*	避孕措施	Jell-O shooter		用酒制成的果冻
instigation	*n.*	怂恿；教唆	margarita	*n.*	大麻
alcoholism	*n.*	酗酒	caffeine	*n.*	咖啡因

Part Four: Related Passages

1. AIDS Stigma

With the appearance of AIDS in the late seventies and early eighties, the disease has had attached to it a significant social stigma. This AIDS related stigma has manifested itself in the form of discrimination, avoidance and fear of people living with AIDS (PLWAs). As a result, the social implications of the disease have been extended from those of other life threatening conditions to the point at which PLWAs are not only faced with a terminal illness but also social isolation and constant discrimination throughout society.

Various explanations have been suggested as to the underlying causes of this stigmatization. Many studies point to the relationship the disease has with deviant behavior. Others suggest that fear of contagion is the actual culprit. Examining the existing literature and putting it into societal context leads one to believe that there is no one cause. Instead, there would appear to be a collection of associated factors that influence society's attitudes towards AIDS and PLWAs. As the number of people infected with HIV increases, social workers are and will be increasingly called upon to deal with and serve PLWAs. Although not all social workers choose to work with PLWAs, the escalating incidence of HIV infection is creating a situation in which sera positive people are and will be showing up more often in almost all areas of social work practice. Many people express negative attitudes towards PLWAs regardless of how the virus was contracted or the person's background. The fact that there is no known cure for AIDS and as of yet the disease always ends in death validates this fear for many. As people are becoming more aware of how the virus is transmitted, they seem to be become less fearful of PLWAs. The effects of stigma for PLWAs are many. They suffer discrimination from the general public in a variety of settings, including work, school and within the health care environment. Many PLWAs also experience extreme social isolation due to their illness; because of the negative reactions of friends and family members, the seropositive person is often rejected by many members of their social entourage.

There are a variety of reasons for why this stigma exists and it is necessary to have some understanding of them in order to combat discrimination and the negative attitudes that surround AIDS. With the knowledge of how the stigma has been formed, it is possible to try and counter its effects and to educate the public in order to possibly lower the levels of present stigma. Before social workers can be truly effective, however, it is necessary that education and training practices are modified to sensitize present and future social workers to the issues surrounding AIDS. With the proper tools, social workers can facilitate changes in society and fight AIDS related stigma.

2. Media Violence Affects Children

Nowadays, most of the parents are working around the clock to meet the demands of life. Parents seldom have the time to care for their children. Therefore, children are often left alone in the house and spend their time watching television. The television shows whether it is a movie or a cartoon program poses a lot of treat to them. The children are likely to find themselves being influenced by media violence, without knowing it. They learn their behavior from the television instead of parents. Sometimes, watching a single violent program can increase aggressiveness.

They think that it is "cool" being aggressive just because the television says so. In other words, they do not have the power to distinguish what is good or bad for them. Children, who view cartoon shows, in which violence is very realistic, are more likely to imitate what they see. This is the belief that the media have almost magical powers to alter the ideas and behavior of their audience and the minds of individuals who are powerless to resist. Gradually, they will accept violence as a way to solve problems because he or she views shows whereby problems are settled through violence. In some of the shows of violence, the good always defeat the evil by means of killing each other. However, extensive viewing of television violence by people may have a long lasting effect on a person's mind. The impact of television violence may surface years later because people's mind has the ability to absorb information. The question is, what is it that large communities absorb over long periods of time? Young people can be affected even though the family atmosphere shows no tendency towards violence. As a conclusion, media violence that causes people to indulge in violence by means of internet, comics and television are capable of sustaining long term side effects, which in turn, threatens the society. The majority of people should therefore extend their precautions and practice self-censorship whenever possible to reduce the impact of media violence.

3. Who Was Responsible for the Children's Shocking Behavior?

The shocking headlines out of Waycross, Georgia—3rd-graders plotted to attack teacher, brought knife, handcuffs—lowered the bar on school violence and raised the alarm among parents, teachers, psychologists and just about anyone with an opinion about the country's future.

The third grade plotters—nine students between the ages of 8 and 10—were allegedly readying a revenge assault against a teacher who had given one of the children a time-out for standing on a chair. Tipped off by a student, police seized the kids' menacing arsenal at school, including a steak knife, duct tape, handcuffs, and a heavy paperweight. The teacher specialized in learning disabilities, including attention deficit disorder and hyperactivity, though it's not known if any of the plotters had those diagnoses. The sophistication of the plan—with kid-assigned jobs of covering classroom windows and cleaning up after the attack—stunned even the police. "We did not hear anybody say they intended to kill her," the police chief said, "but could they have accidentally killed her? Absolutely."

The big question—who or what was responsible for the children's shocking behavior—was debated across the U.S. on message boards and Main Street. The culprits ranged from peer pressure to parenting, with violent video games and television getting much of the blame. "Kids naturally think now that the solution to everything is to shoot someone like they see on TV," one comment read. "I weep for the future of America."

For the present, local authorities are uncertain exactly how to proceed. In Georgia, children under 13 can't be charged with a crime. Being declared "delinquent" by a judge may be the only legal penalty, but the state doesn't have detention facilities for third-graders.

4. Fear or Lack of Example?

If a picture is worth a thousand words, how many are needed to describe the video of a man being struck by a hit-and-run driver and left to bleed unaided in the road, while numerous motorists and pedestrians casually maneuver around him and continue on their way? What's to blame for such a horrible and inhuman tragedy? The answer may be fear and lack of example.

Did this happen because people today are fearful of getting involved, unsure of what the consequences will be if they take a role in such a situation? "Could I catch something if I help this person? Will I get in trouble if I don't give the right kind of help? Will the police think I was the perpetrator if I help this person? Will I get hurt if I step into the street, too, what if the other cars don't stop? Will other people get mad at me if I stop traffic?" Could it be similar to the fear one feels when passing by a homeless person begging at the roadside? "Maybe if I ignore this, I can pretend it doesn't exist and I can't be hurt by it" —mistrusting the truth of their need or not thinking about the feelings and person behind that sign.

Or, did this happen because we have a lack of examples to teach us what we could/should do in such an event? We have plentiful exposure to images in media and the movies about professional responders—police, fireman, medical personnel—or of people rushing to the aid of people they know, but perhaps not enough exposure to basic scenarios that help us view ourselves as capable enough to be first responders. It seems we need more "what would you do if…" discussions—over coffee, at church, around the dinner table, in the conference room, wherever. Hopefully that would at least result in the consensus that one should stop traffic and at least communicate with the injured person to reassure him help is on the way. Of course, it was a shocking trauma that occurred. It is easy to second guess the actions that happened there that day, but alas I was not there. I hope that in a similar situation I would be able to keep my wits about me and do the right thing.

5. What Do You Do if You've Found the Thief Who Stole Your Belongings?

What would you do if you've found the thief who stole your belongings? Would you catch him/her in person? Florida newspaper reporter observed just an extra-judicial bartering session between a victim and a thief at the scene of the crime, which, ironically, was a Tampa courtroom.

The victim—whom the reporter referred to as "Pinstripe Suit"—was 52 and in court for a case involving her son. She briefly stepped out of the courtroom, leaving her keys and cell phone behind. When she returned, the keys and phone were gone, and Pinstripe's seat had been taken by a 25 year-old woman wearing a red velour sweatshirt.

"Red Velour Sweatshirt", as the reporter dubbed her, denied having seen Pinstripe's possessions. So Pinstripe walked to the back of the court room, borrowed a cell phone, dialed her own number, and followed the sound of her buzzing phone—in Sweatshirt's pocket. Pinstripe plucked the phone out of Sweatshirt's pocket. Two sheriff's deputies watched but did nothing.

According to the reporter, Pinstripe then leaned over Sweatshirt and whispered, "I am going to have you arrested if you don't give me my keys." Sweatshirt replied, "I don't have them." Pinstripe then parked herself on the seat next to Sweatshirt and waited until finally Sweatshirt pulled a gold Lexus keychain from her other pocket. She dropped it into Pinstripe's lap and said, "I have enough problems already." Noticing that Sweatshirt had started to cry, Pinstripe hugged her and said, "Everything will be all right. Bless your heart."

Afterwards, Pinstripe told the reporter she didn't turn Sweatshirt in because she didn't want her to go to jail. Sweatshirt already had one arrest for theft, at age 16. Now at 25, she was in court fighting her second arrest, a child abuse charge.

A stranger steals your personal property. Instead of reporting the theft to authorities, you confront the suspect yourself. Your possessions are returned. You bypass the inconvenience of a police investigation and court appearances, and the offender goes without punishment.

But did you also bypass a responsibility to work within the justice system?

Topic Thirteen Economy

Part One: Dialogues

◆ Dialogue 1 Stock Exchange

(Jack and George are both majors of economics. They are talking about stock exchange.)

Jack: Hi, George, I'm going to be rich! By the end of the year, I'll be the proud owner of a fancy black BMW just like the one outside there.

George: Are you nuts? How are you going to do that? You're still in college.

Jack: My stocks doubled just this week!

George: Wow! I read that a lot of stockholders are back on their feet after setbacks in the bear market last year, and are earning a bundle in this year.

Jack: Right! To tell you the truth, I had a feeling that we were heading for the first real bull market in years.

George: So tell me, how can you afford to buy stocks?

Jack: With my pocket money and credit cards.

George: Weren't you scared if you'd lose it all?

Jack: No. Have you heard of Xiao Song, the guy from Sichuan University? According to a CCTV report, he earned 300,000 yuan by selling the stocks he'd bought with pocket money over the last three years. I hope I could win that much.

George: Get real. Stocks always involve speculation. It's really very risky to play the market with credit cards. If you lose the money and can't pay it back, your reputation and credibility will be damaged. That kind of thing could haunt you for years.

Jack: We're young and carefree. That's our advantage over other market players.

George: We might be intelligent, but students are only small shareholders. They never have a seat on the board or any control over the market. Either you strike it rich overnight, or all the money you just borrowed is gone. You'd better invest wisely.

Jack: So do you mean I should put some of my money in securities?

George: Well, I know mutual funds aren't the most glamorous investments, but they're safer. Chill, man. You'll get your Audi sooner or later.

Jack: But we can get hands-on experience in the stock market right now. Theoretical knowledge just doesn't interest me anymore.

George: Remember what Professor Wang said? If we really want to know how to invest, we need to do some research on failures as well as successes. And then, look before you leap.

◆ Dialogue 2   What Do You Think of the Economy of Our Country?

(Prof. Smith, an economic expert from Business College, is being interviewed by Amy, a journalist of campus newspaper.)

Amy: What do you think of the economy of our country, Mr. Smith?

Smith: Well, judging form the statistics I've recently seen, I think our economy is doing very well. Production is growing steadily, and the income of the majority of the people is rising.

Amy: Do you think the economy will continue to grow for the next two quarters?

Smith: As I see it, we are heading for an economic boom, and there's no reason why it shouldn't.

Amy: But what about the unemployment rate? Isn't it on the rise too?

Smith: I'm glad you raised that question. It's true that unemployment rate has risen in certain sectors of our country because of the financial crisis of America.

Amy: It's said that new graduates have been affected by the financial downturn in America.

Smith: Yeah, some multinational companies have cut back their graduate recruitment this year. Microsoft, for example, recruited over 300 graduates in China last year, but it has only 200 positions available this year. But the point is a great many new jobs have also been created and the overall market still needs labors.

Amy: Then will our application to American's universities be affected? It is reported that recently two major US student loan leaders—Citibank and JP Morgan Chase—announced they were leaving the student-loan industry altogether.

Smith: Yeah, applicants may find it difficult to get financial aid from American universities. Some universities may cut their aid because their donors experience financial difficulties. And at the same time banks currently have a deficiency of credit. They are reluctant to offer students low-interest loans and college students need to find new ways to pay their tuition fees and accommodations.

Amy: That's really depressing to Chinese applicants.

Smith: It's hard to say. If the crisis continues and the US economy worsens, dollars may become cheaper against the Chinese Yuan. This means applicants will spend less on tuition and living in the US.

Amy: Are savings of common citizens being affected?

Smith: I don't think so. First, Chinese banks have a small investment in the US financial sector. Second, Chinese banks profit from the interest rate gap between loans and deposits. This is a safe way to make money. China also requires foreign banks to operate separately from their domestic branch. This helps to protect Chinese citizens' savings even if foreign banks' domestic branch suffers.

Amy: That's to say we don't need to feel panic in the financial crisis.

Smith: That's right! People in our country may feel some of the effects, but, generally, we are safe.

Words and Expressions

stock exchange		股票交易	boom	n.	上升
BMW		宝马汽车	downturn	n.	低迷时期
stockholder	n.	股票持有者	recruit	v.	招收（新员工）
setback	n.	挫折	Citibank		花旗银行
bear market		（股市的）熊市	JP Morgan Chase		摩根大通公司
bull market		（股市的）牛市	deficiency of credit		信用缺失
speculation	n.	投机	accommodation	n.	膳宿
securities	n.	证券	tuition	n.	学费
glamorous	adj.	豪华的	loan	n.	贷款
hands-on experience		亲身的经历	deposit	n.	存款
statistics	n.	数据	panic	n.	恐慌

Part Two: Related Questions with Suggested Answers

1. What is the market economy? What is the planned economy?

A market economy is an economic system in which the production and distribution of goods and services takes place through the mechanism of free markets guided by a free price system rather than by the state in a planned economy. It is also called a free market economy or free enterprise economy. Market economies are contrasted with mixed economy where the price system is not entirely free but under some government control that is not extensive enough to constitute a planned economy.

A planned economy, is an economic system in which the state or government controls the factors of production and makes all decisions about their use and about the distribution of income.

It is also known as command economy and centrally planned economy. The planners decide what should be produced and direct enterprises to produce those goods.

2. Why does the Chinese government give priority to the market economy?

In the past three decades, China has established a market economy and the market has replaced the government to play a decisive role in resource allocation and social development. China has gradually assimilated into the global mainstream during the decades of reform and opening up. The market economy and democracy have proven to be the most successful institutional creations in human civilization up to the present day. In its reforms and opening up, China has learned the merits of these creations, and voluntarily observed the common rules for the development of human society so as to overcome the flaws of traditional Chinese concepts of rules and to promote augmentation of national welfare and restore wealth and power for the country.

The social market economy aims at maintaining a balance between a high rate of economic growth, low inflation, and low levels of unemployment, good working conditions, social welfare, and public services, by using state intervention. It is appropriate for the Chinese government to give priority to the market economy.

3. What are some of the fruits of reform and opening up, the policy taken by the Chinese government to develop its economy?

The decision to begin reform and opening up was made at the Third Plenary Session of the 11th Central Committee of the Communist Party of China (CPC) in December 1978. This policy has helped the Chinese people navigate through hard times and toward prosperity and rejuvenation in the past three decades. During the course, the Chinese people have attained distinguished achievements and learned many lessons.

One outstanding achievement is that China's economic and comprehensive national strengths have been continuously enhanced and the living standards and welfare of the people have been further improved. Another important change has taken place in the mindset of the people. Opening up has brought a new vitality to the people's tedious and uniform lifestyle and way of thinking. The people's spiritual and cultural life has been enriched to promote diversified thinking. Because of reform and opening up, the Chinese people are freer, more self-reliant and more independent. A review of China's history shows that the nation has been open, strong and prosperous, thanks to the reform and opening up.

4. What is holiday economy? How do holidays in China promote the national economy?

Holiday economy is accompanied by China's first "Golden Week" to arise. During the 7-day golden week holiday, traveling has already become an indispensable part of people's relaxation activities. The lengthy holidays have caused unexpected great travel craze and brisk economic activities. Holiday spending, however, adds fuel to the Chinese economy, which in turn leads to the creation of a new term "holiday economy" and it sparks a hot debate about it. There are several advantages of the holiday economy. To begin with, the holiday economy can prompt the consumption. During the tour, tourists spend money on playing, living, eating and shopping, all of which are the impetus to the development of society. In addition, it also brings profit to the transportation because of large demand of traveling by plane, ship and coach. In one way or another, the national economy of China is promoted by holidays.

5. How do businessmen use holidays to make more money?

Holidays are usually a profitable session for many industries, being the travel agency, the shopping mall, the transportation departments and other retailers. After a long tedious period of working or studying, people choose to travel to some scenic spots at home or abroad in order to get relaxed. Travel agencies usually get busy promoting some sound travel routes, especially by cutting down the fee to attract clients weeks ahead or even months ahead. Apart from package tours, some people may visit their relatives or friends in another city. So the transportation departments, the airlines in particular, offer discounted tickets to get their flights full so as to make money. To some extent, holidays mean shopping. In order to attract as many customers as possible, department stores provide discounts, lower than other time of the year, lottery drawing and so on. In one way or another, businessmen try to reap profits from customers in holidays.

6. Why do we have to spend more on food these days?

I think there are three major reasons for Chinese people spending more money on food: the soaring food price, the improvement of food and the improvement of people's living standard. As the Chinese old saying goes, "To the common people, food is as important as heaven." Chinese people pay much attention to food, which can be justified by the various kinds of dishes and local cuisines in different parts of China. As to the soaring food prices, a key factor is growing demand, not just from increasing population but also because people in big cities are becoming richer and can afford more expensive food. Nowadays, with the quality of food improved and a lot of foreign food imported, the prices of food are increasingly raised. But the Chinese people don't hesitate to try different food, especially those quality food and foreign cuisines, which were rare before. Besides, with the fast development of economy, Chinese people are becoming richer and can afford more fine food. Thus despite high food prices, people still pursue fine food, thinking that the food is helpful to their health and it also presents their lifestyle and status. All in all, Chinese people are spending more on food.

7. Is it reasonable for college students to pay their tuition? Why or why not?

Tuition system has become one of the hottest topics in China since it was put into effect. Different people have different opinions on it. I think it is reasonable for college students to pay their tuition. As China is a developing country with the largest population in the world the government is unable to allocate enough funds to pay for various teaching facilities and expenses. Many universities in China lack enough funds to develop themselves. One of the ways to solve the problem is to let students pay their own tuition. The money raised in this way can be used to improve the conditions for running schools so that more students can be enrolled to receive higher education.

However, others are opposed to the tuition system. They argue that the living standard of the Chinese people, especially of those in the poor rural areas, is still low, compared with that in the Western World. The university tuition will certainly add to the already heavy burden of the parents, who live on their salaries or wages. Moreover, tuition may become an obstacle to the development of China's higher education. This is because it hinders some talented people from entering the university just on account of their poverty.

8. What do you think of some students nowadays being busy buying and selling stocks?

Well, you know practice with study can bring some positive effects for a student. However, dealing in stocks isn't suitable for students. Obviously, its negative effects overweight its benefits for the following reasons. Students have limited spare time and stock dealing costs their energy and a lot of their time. By taking the lack of related knowledge into account, it is suggested that students should leave stock market. What's more, buying and selling stocks mean taking great economic risks. If they lose much money in stock market, perhaps they cannot adjust their mind and afford the loss. The last but not least, the main task for students is to study and prepare for their better future. Most students have no stable income other than allowances from their parents. So dealing in stocks is likely to add burdens to their parents. Above all, students should not deal in stocks.

9. Is money everything? Why or why not?

Money is considered by some people as the most important thing in their life. They think that the majority of the material things in our daily life have to be bought with money and that if they have a lot of money, they can make themselves very comfortable by having a fine house to live in, beautiful clothes to put on, and delicious food to eat.

But money is not everything. Take time and life for example. No matter what we do or how much money we are willing to pay, we cannot make the day last longer than 24 hours. Suppose there is a millionaire who possesses everything except good health. By the time he is suffering from a fatal illness, what he wants most is life. Though money can help him get first-rate doctors and the best medical care, money cannot buy him a longer life.

Indeed, money can buy a lot of things we need. But there are many, many wonderful things in the world that cannot be bought with money. For example, knowledge cannot be bought with money. There are still many other things that cannot be bought with money: health, happiness,

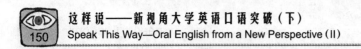

friendship, love and so on. Just imagine is the money everything without all of these?

10. What do you think of the saying "Take care of the pence and the pounds will take care of themselves"?

I think this saying is to call for everyone to make good use of money rather than squander. It could also mean something else. It could mean that you should start from the very beginning and even tiny things before you achieve any accomplishment. This is rather important attitude towards study or life career. One can end up in nothing by just dreaming of becoming success without any hard work, effort or labor. If one wants to master a foreign language, he or she needs to first learn that language, than bear anything related in mind. He or she has to learn a lot of things before mastering a foreign language. Apart from knowledge accumulating, practice of the language is also critical. Speaking, listening, reading, writing and translation are the basic skills in language learning. Learn to practice. Practice makes perfect. Only in this way is it possible for him or her to master a language. It is the same as becoming a champion of a swimming contest, getting promoted to the CEO of a company and making a medical breakthrough, etc.

Words and Expressions

distribution	*n.*	分配	craze	*n.*	时髦；时尚
mechanism	*n.*	机制	brisk	*adj.*	（生意）兴隆的
constitute	*v.*	包括	spark	*v.*	激发
assimilate	*v.*	溶入；加入	impetus	*n.*	推动力
mainstream	*n.*	主流	discounted	*adj.*	打折的
merit	*n.*	优点	lottery drawing		抽奖
flaw	*n.*	缺点；缺陷	soaring	*adj.*	高得惊人的
augmentation	*n.*	提高；增大	cuisines	*n.*	菜肴
welfare	*n.*	福利	allocate	*v.*	分配
inflation	*n.*	膨胀	hinder	*v.*	阻碍
intervention	*n.*	干预；介入	on account of		因为；由于
navigate	*v.*	导航；指引方向	overweight	*v.*	（前者）比（后者）
rejuvenation	*n.*	恢复活力；变得年轻			重要
comprehensive	*adj.*	综合的	millionaire	*n.*	百万富翁
vitality	*n.*	生命力；活力	fatal	*adj.*	致命的
tedious	*adj.*	枯燥的	squander	*v.*	挥霍
diversified	*adj.*	多样化的	CEO (Chief		
Golden Week		黄金周	Executive Officer)		首席执行官

Part Three: Related Pictures with Suggested Descriptions

Picture One　Motivators for Working

The majority of us gets up each morning and goes to work in order to earn money. But what are the true motivators for working? How do wage rates and other forms of compensation affect the quantity of labor supplied to the market? This will point out how labor affects the economy. Each person working plays a role in society and production output. These are areas that need to be addressed when the supply of labor is being discussed. The motivation to work arises from a variety of social, psychological and economic forces. People need income to pay their bills, feel that they have a role in society and also feel a sense of achievement. Although there is always a choice, that is not working and not getting paid. People choose between labor and leisure according to the perceived rewards of each.

Possibly attracted by the abundance of jobs or forced by economic necessity, there are more people working. Not everyone works for money. A large percentage of workers say they would continue to work even if they had enough money to live comfortably without working. Apparently, each hour of work yields more satisfaction. Another aspect of happiness from labor is the non-monetary incentives. That is the working environment. People prefer to work in a safe, well lit, pleasantly colorful environment.

In conclusion, there are many different reasons why we work every day. But, there will always be more to purchase, more bills to pay and a certain need to feel a part of society. To realize what needs to be improved to induce workers to choose work is still being studied. Realizing what our true needs are can either motivate us to become more productive or do the opposite and cause us to work less.

Picture Two　Disparity Between the Rich and the Poor

In recent years, the Chinese people feel stronger about the unfair disparity between the rich

and the poor than people in other countries, as much of the disparity is attributed to monopolies and privilege in China. The government has failed to effectively protect the legitimate rights and interests of the laborers, who as a result can't share the fruits of the national economic growth. At the initial stage of reform and opening up, China was short of capital but abundant in labor, and as a result, attracting foreign investment became an important task of local governments at all levels, as well as a standard to assess the performance and administrative achievements of officials. The rights and interests of workers, on the contrary, were neglected, and they don't have the rights to collectively negotiate over payment, not to mention all kinds of social rights such as welfare and insurance that are common in developed countries.

China remains a low-income developing country despite the huge achievements it has made over the past 30 years. The basic knowledge, strategic plotting and policies drafted related to reform and opening up in the future should be based on the basic national condition that China remains a developing country in the primary stage of socialism, so that confronting emerging problems in reform and development can be understood. In the reform and opening-up drive in the coming years, the Chinese Government should adhere to its primary experience and fundamental policies of the past 30 years, continue to focus on economic development, promote the role of the market in resource distribution, and seek correct solutions of contradictions and problems that accrue in the process of socio-economic development.

Picture Three WTO: the Rich Get Richer and the Poor Get Poorer

The stated aim of the WTO is to promote free trade and stimulate economic growth. Some people argue that free trade leads to a divergence instead of convergence of income levels within rich and poor countries. The rich get richer and the poor get poorer. It is argued by some experts that the WTO does not manage the global economy impartially, but in its operation has a systematic bias toward rich countries and multinational corporations, harming smaller countries which have less negotiation power.

Developing countries have not benefited from the WTO Agreements because, among other reasons, market access in industry has not improved; these countries have no gains yet from the phasing out of textiles quotas; non-tariff barriers such as anti-dumping measures have increased; and domestic support and export subsidies for agricultural products in the rich countries remain high. Whereas, someone asserts that there is greater tariff protection on manufacturers in the poor countries, which are also overtaking the rich nations in the number of anti-dumping filings.

Other critics claim that the issues of labor relations and environment are steadfastly ignored. Some believe that the WTO should begin to address the link between trade and labor and environmental concerns. Further, labor unions condemn the labor rights record of developing countries, arguing that to the extent the WTO succeeds in promoting globalization, and then in equal measure do the environment and labor rights suffer. On the other side, if environment and labor were to enter the WTO system it would be conceptually difficult to argue why other social and cultural issues should also not enter.

Other critics have characterized the decision making in the WTO as complicated, ineffective, unrepresentative and non-inclusive, and they have proposed the establishment of a small, informal steering committee that can be delegated responsibility for developing consensus on trade issues among the member countries. Many world organizations argue that democratic participation in the WTO could be enhanced through the creation of a parliamentary assembly, although other analysts have characterized this proposal as ineffective.

Words and Expressions

motivator	n.	动机	quota	n.	定额；定量
abundance	n.	丰富	tariff	n.	关税
yield	v.	产生	anti-dumping	n.	反倾销
incentive	n.	刺激；鼓励	assert	v.	宣称
disparity	n.	不同；差异	overtake	v.	（发展）快于……
monopoly	n.	垄断；专营	filing	n.	档案
legitimate	adj.	合法的	conceptual	adj.	概念上的；观念上的
plot	v.	密谋			
draft	v.	起草	non-inclusive	adj.	不包括……的
accrue	v.	形成	steering committee		程序委员会
divergence	n.	偏离	delegate	v.	委托；委派
convergence	n.	融合；聚合	consensus	n.	一致意见
impartial	adj.	公正的；不偏不倚的	parliamentary	adj.	议会的；国会的
bias	n.	偏见	assembly	n.	议会；立法机构
access	n.	渠道			

Part Four: Related Passages

1. The Real Victims of the Financial Crisis

The financial crisis that erupted in Asia in mid-1997 has led to sharp declines in the currencies, stock markets, and other asset prices of many Asian countries. It is hard to understand what these declines will actually affect the world market. This decline is expected to halve the rate of world growth in 1998 from the four percent that was projected pre-crisis to an estimated outcome of about 2 percent. The countries that are included in the East Asian crisis are Hong Kong, South Korea, Singapore, and Taiwan, known as "Asia Four Little Dragons", and Indonesia, Malaysia, the Philippines, and Thailand.

For these countries to participate effectively in the exchange of goods, services, and assets, an international monetary system is needed to facilitate economic transactions. This monetary system most importantly requires an efficient balance of payments adjustment mechanism so that deficits and surpluses are not prolonged but are eliminated with relative ease in a reasonably short time period. The Asian crisis falls into this category of inefficient balance of payments facilitated by depreciation of its currency. Thus to some extent, Asia was exporting its deflation, its overcapacity and its lack of growth to the West. No other group of countries in the world had produced more rapid economic growth and dramatic reduction in poverty than East Asia. Korea, Malaysia, and Thailand have virtually eliminated absolute poverty, and Indonesia is within reach of that goal. Nevertheless, this financial crisis has exposed weaknesses in Asian economies that must be addressed if the region is to return to its high growth of those years.

Despite the great cries of anguish we hear from bankers and corporations, the real victims of the collapse of "globalization" in Asia, are the same people who were the victims of the "miracle". Millions of casual construction workers were idle across the region. And hundreds of thousands of public sector employees and finance sector workers were being sacked as the IMF enforced government budget cuts, bank and finance company closures. Later, to support East Asian governments the World Bank focused on carrying out several principal objectives. There emerged visible help with the social costs of reform, particularly protection for the unemployed; the financial and corporate sectors were then better regulated, more transparent, and adequately capitalized to regain the confidence of investors, both foreign and domestic.

2. Economic Growth—Some Lessons to Learn

The last three decades have witnessed China's remarkable accomplishment after the reform and opening up. The root factor behind all these achievements is that China has followed the path of building socialism with Chinese characteristics and has formed a theoretical system of socialism with Chinese characteristics. Knowledge of China's basic national condition—the fact that China is at the primary stage of socialism and will remain so for a long time to come—is pertinent to understanding the essence of this theory. To recognize this fact indicates that China has eventually embarked on the road of seeking truth from facts and respecting objective laws.

Besides its achievements and experience, mistakes have also been made and there are lessons to be learned from these.

First, economic growth was achieved at cost of environmental destruction and excessive consumption of resources. If it is safe to say that the economic achievements China has attained in the past 30 years would have taken a Western country a century to do, then it is equally safe to claim that the environmental destruction China has suffered during the period would take any Western country a century to encounter. China's sustainable development is endangered if no changes are made to its developmental model.

Second, the gap between the rich and the poor is widening. In China, the overall national income, despite increases in the past 30 years, is still lagging behind many countries. This is primarily because labor enjoys no preference in the nation's income allocation pattern, though China's huge population is another reason. The wealth created by the people has been transferred into capital and fiscal revenue, in the form of profit and tax, including those to importers in Western countries through granting exporters export subsidies. This imbalanced allocation has worsened the rich-poor gap in China.

3. China's Central and Western Regions Are more Affected by the Global Economic Crisis

At present, the whole world is undergoing hardship brought about by the global economic crisis. As to China, compared with coastal regions, China's less-developed central and western parts are likely to suffer more in the unfolding global economic slowdown.

Contrary to conventional thinking that coastal regions in East China will be worst hurt by global financial woes which had already brought many of its export-oriented manufacturers to closure, it is believed by the expert that the financial crisis will have a deeper impact on less-developed central and western regions in a longer term, though it is not yet visible. There are three reasons to backup this judgment.

Firstly, economies in central and western China, which are largely small in scale and are resource intensive, will be slow to adapt to the changes brought along by the financial crisis.

Secondly, as many of the manufacturers in those regions depends on exporting raw materials, their business will be badly hurt as the prices of raw materials keep on dropping in the international market.

Finally, the weaker economy in central and western regions will not be able to provide enough job opportunities for migrant workers returned from bankrupt manufacturing factories in East China, and then social conflicts will arise. The central and the western regions are China's major labor exporters.

It is believed by some officials from the Chinese government that to make the central and western regions less vulnerable to the global financial turmoil, these regions should shake up their economy by benefiting from an industry transfer from East China. In addition, the central and western regions should take up a bigger share in the government's 4-trillion-yuan stimulus plan.

4. Inflation

In economics, inflation is a rise in the general level of prices of goods and services in an economy over a period of time. The term "inflation" once referred to increases in the money supply (monetary inflation); however, economic debates about the relationship between money supply and price levels have led to its primary use today in describing price inflation. Inflation can also be described as a decline in the real value of money—a loss of purchasing power in the medium of exchange which is also the monetary unit of account. When the general price level rises, each unit of currency buys fewer goods and services. A chief measure of price inflation is the inflation rate, which is the percentage change in a price index over time.

Inflation can cause adverse effects on the economy. For example, uncertainty about future inflation may discourage investment and saving. High inflation may lead to shortages of goods if consumers begin hoarding out of concern that prices will increase in the future.

Economists generally agree that high rates of inflation and hyperinflation are caused by an excessive growth of the money supply. Views on which factors determine low to moderate rates of inflation are more varied. Low or moderate inflation may be attributed to fluctuations in real demand for goods and services, or changes in available supplies such as during scarcities, as well as to growth in the money supply. However, the consensus view is that a long sustained period of inflation is caused when money supply increases faster than the rate of economic growth. Today, most economists favor a low steady rate of inflation. The task of keeping the rate of inflation low is usually given to monetary authorities who establish monetary policy. Generally, these monetary authorities are the central banks that control the size of the money supply through the setting of interest rates, through open market operations, and through the setting of banking reserve requirements.

5. The Global Financial Crisis of 2008-2009

The global financial crisis of 2008-2009 is an ongoing major financial crisis. It became prominently visible in September 2008 with the failure, merger or conservatorship of several large United States-based financial firms. The underlying causes leading to the crisis had been reported in business journals for many months before September, with commentary about the financial stability of leading U.S. and European investment banks, insurance firms and mortgage banks consequent to the subprime mortgage crisis.

Beginning with failures of large financial institutions in the United States, it rapidly evolved into a global credit crisis, deflation and sharp reductions in shipping resulting in a number of

European bank failures and declines in various stock indexes, and large reductions in the market value of stock and commodities worldwide. The credit crisis was exacerbated by Section 128 of the Emergency Economic Stabilization Act of 2008 which allowed the Federal Reserve System to pay interest on excess reserve requirement balances held on deposit from banks, removing the longstanding incentive for banks to extend credit instead of hoard cash on deposit with the Fed. The crisis led to a liquidity problem and the de-leveraging of financial institutions especially in the United States and Europe, which further accelerated the liquidity crisis, and a decrease in international shipping and commerce. World political leaders and national ministers of finance and central bank directors have coordinated their efforts to reduce fears but the crisis is ongoing and continues to change, evolving at the close of October into a currency crisis with investors transferring vast capital resources into stronger currencies such as the yen, the dollar and the Swiss franc, leading many emergent economies to seek aid from the International Monetary Fund. The crisis was triggered by the subprime mortgage crisis and is an acute phase of the financial crisis of 2007-2008.

Topic Fourteen　Information Technology

Part One: Dialogues

◆ Dialogue 1　Learn English via the Internet

(Wang is learning English on the computer in his room, and his friend Chen is sitting next to him reading some magazines.)

Chen: What are you listening to? You've done some listening on your computer for half an hour and giggled from time to time.

Wang: *The Adventure of Hackberry Finn.*

Chen: The novel by Mark Twain, the famous American writer?

Wang: Yeah, actually I am listening to the audio book on the Internet. It's a great fun.

Chen: Hey, the audio book, a novel thing? I finally know the reason why you are good at English. Tell me some of your knack for learning English.

Wang: (Smile and point out the computer) Just learning English via the Internet. There is a considerable resource we can use for English learning on the Internet.

Chen: What is this resource about?

Wang: For example, on the website I am surfing, besides audio books, there are news, essays, short stories, songs and even visual materials. They are live and entertaining. We are learning English while we have fun.

Chen: That's great! Now one big problem I have is that I want to improve my listening.

Wang: Well, there are some good news websites. Let's try one.

Chen: Their speaking is clear, but I just find reporters speaking too fast. I could not follow them. Could you recommend some news websites that fit beginners?

Wang: Then I suggest that you start with VOA special English. And I strongly recommend you a website dedicated to VOA special English programs. Let's try it now. (Wang types the VOA website on his computer and the VOA programs are reported slowly out of the loudspeaker of the computer.)

Chen: Wow, I can follow the reporter. It's amazing! But I have a question. Could we get the latest news of VOA on the website? As we know most of information on the website is out-of-date and sometimes is even misleading.

Wang: Runners of this website update news each day, and therefore listeners may get the latest news. Once you browse the website, you'll know that their services are very popular among English learners.

Chen: Wow, that's terrific.

Wang: Besides, you may have a vocabulary problem, I'm afraid. There are a lot of words that you might have not learned from textbooks.

Chen: What shall I do then?

Wang: Don't worry. The website also provides news script. You can look up the words that you don't understand in your dictionary.

Chen: That's a good idea! My last question, do we need to pay for listening to the news program?

Wang: No, you don't have to. Runners of the website are nice. They do these just for free.

Chen: I can't wait to browse it.

◆ Dialogue 2   Writing on Paper or Writing with Computer

(S2 is writing his essay on paper. S1, a computer geek, enters his dorm.)

S1: Hey, this is the 21st century. You are still writing on paper?

S2: What's wrong with that?

S1: Come on. It is e-time! You gotta go with the flow! Why don't you get a computer? Oh, wait a minute...are you broke?

S2: No, I can afford a computer. I just can't afford to waste my time.

S1: Don't trust some old-fashioned guys when they say about Internet being a waste of time. Actually, Internet gives you a lot of information if you know how to get them.

S2: What information?

S1: I have a friend who is a businesswoman and is quite non-technical. Last year, when she found out she could chat with friends all over the country through the Internet, she bought a portable computer. Now she's learned how to do business on the Internet.

S2: To do business?

S1: Yeah, internet is a powerful commercial medium and it connects hundreds of millions of customers home and abroad.

S2: This sounds too good to be true.

S1: So tell me, where do you find what you need without Internet?

S2: In libraries, of course. How do you get information on Internet?

S1: Have you ever heard of search engines like Baidu and Google? If you want information about China, Baidu is the place to go to. On the other hand, Google is a better choice for anything international. Let's go to the computer lab and give it a try.

S2: Great idea!

Words and Expressions

audio book		有声书籍	script	*n.*	（新闻听力的）原文
knack	*n.*	诀窍	runner	*n.*	（网站的）管理人员
surf	*v.*	（网上）冲浪	e-time	*n.*	e时代
dedicated	*adj.*	专用的	portable	*adj.*	便携的
browse	*v.*	浏览	search engine		搜索引擎

Part Two: Related Questions with Suggested Answers

1. How do computers help you in your studies?

How could I study without computers is really the question. For me, writing essay and doing research could not have been finished without using computer.

I used to go to the school library to borrow and read books. But now I don't have to go there. I can stay in my dorm and use my computer to see if books I want are in stacks. I can also log into the school library's online system, reserve books for you and then you could go and find them in certain place. How easy and convenient it is. Even, if you like, some books have electronic editions, and you could just search and download them to your computer and read them at home.

You can also use computers to learn English. You can listen to English programs online. You can practice your spoken English online. You can use computers to solve your mathematical and engineering problems quickly. You can draw pictures with your computers. You can talk with your friends online. So computers make your study and your life much easier.

2. How do you like multi-media technology used in classroom teaching?

My mum, who is a teacher, is so obsessed with multi-media technology used in classroom teaching. It makes her class more lively and popular. I like multi-media technology too. In classroom teaching, usually we only have books. When we talk about history, music and wild life, it would be great if we could have something visible and audible, such as PPT and video clips. For example, if you are going to introduce the musical Cat to your students you don't have to tell them how marvelous the musical Cat is. You should show it in your classroom by showing them a video clip about the musical Cat. Multi-media technology gives us new possibility to know this world. Classroom teaching with multi-media technology makes instructions more informative, vivid and easy to get. For us students if we are supposed to give presentations don't forget that you can resort to multi-media technology to make your presentations interesting and well received.

3. How does internet help you with your English learning?

Before internet came to our life, English learning used to be different from now. Limited resource of English books and tapes could not meet the needs of English learners. We all remember when the first ICQ came out, it swept many countries. Some of us found it could be very helpful for finding friends to study and speak with. Learning English together can be very encouraging, especially when you speak with some English speaking people. Internet can help us find friends to speak English over the internet. Communicating with native people of English is very effective in English learning.

Not only chatting with friends, internet also brings us a lot of English videos and books. If you like, you could even learn English by using textbooks that are used by native speakers.

Use the Internet. The Internet is the most exciting, unlimited English resource that anyone could imagine and it is right at your fingertips.

4. What do you think of the increasing use of computers in our daily life?

Thanks to many advanced technology, computers are widely used nowadays in different fields and for various reasons. Take the Internet and the teaching for example.

The Internet has opened up many opportunities, such as finding out information, conducting communications globally, e.g. through e-mail, voice mail, skype, e-commerce or generally just having fun through online chats or instant messaging. One often wonders: How did people manage before the time of the Internet? How much harder was it for people to communicate and find out information they needed, quickly and easily? A PC connected to the Internet whether through a dialup connection, broadband or Wi-Fi has indeed made it a facile act for many people.

PC, Internet based ICT, is currently used within the English school curriculum. This kind of ICT (amongst others) is now seen as a core subject that is taught in some primary and secondary schools. The major advantage to this development is ICT has become a transferable subject. Computers or interactive whiteboards are now used across most school subjects as well as innovative schools using more technology like PDA's, Mobile phones and some games consoles. The interaction created by the use of this ICT makes lessons much more effective and allow children to learn in a way that they can enjoy.

5. Is it good for some students to spend too much time playing computer games? Why or why not?

I don't think it is good for students to stick to computer games rather than get involved in real life activities. The game manufactures made it clear that playing computer games may help people keep brain simple and sharp, but unfortunately the principle only functions when you play the right type of game for a right length of time. There are both psychological and physical harms for the students who play computer games over too long a time. That would take up students so much time and would affect students' inter-person skills. Moreover, the computer games with violence may extremely harm students. The games with violence would result in the anti-social behaviors. Another obvious problem is that it is bad for students' sight if one plays computer games too much.

6. How do you like chatting on the Internet?

You've probably heard about chatrooms from your friends who say it's the coolest things since toilet paper was invented. You know we can't live without toilet paper. Chatting on the internet is one of the coolest things among young people and it is part of my life now. For one thing, chatting on the internet could save you some money especially when you need to contact some friends or families abroad. You could also see them from the screen.

But it is not the main point that we like chatting on the internet. We like it because we could meet various people that you may never meet in your real life and it would be easier for us to tell secrets to strangers than to people around you so as to get rid of stress. Sometimes, it would be more difficult to talk to people face to face. We prefer to use keyboards and let the screen tell what we want to say. The internet chatting can also serve as an outlet for our depressed feelings and also for relaxation.

7. Why do some people still prefer letter writing to sending e-mails?

Some people still prefer letter writing to sending e-mails because they think that they can save some postal fee. I can say that they are right to a certain extent. I myself prefer letter writing not because I can save some postal fee. I do letter writing because I think it is more personal. If you write a letter to your mom with your own handwriting you put more of your feelings in paper. Your mom likes to see your handwriting because your handwriting could bring her more happy memory. She could see your smile and hear you're talking with the handwriting that is familiar to your mom even from your childhood.

I don't feel well if I write letters on computer. Every weekend I like to sit in my dorm and write letters to my parents and friends. In addition, I would like to collect packs of letters more than just save a box of emails that would be easily deleted from computers.

8. Do you like online shopping? Why or why not?

I have no idea who invented online shopping but I like online shopping very much.

With its advent in the early 1990s, online shopping has entered our life, linking consumers and sellers more closely. Online shopping helps us buy what we want at our convenient time and also helps us do virtual shopping online. In doing online shopping you can imagine yourselves buying, owning and using the commodities you like to buy. In doing online shopping you don't have to travel far to supermarkets and department stores. It saves you a lot of time. It also saves you some money because commodities sold online are cheaper than those sold in supermarkets and department stories. For some people, shopping online is becoming a fashion. If you can do shopping online it shows that you are different from ordinary people because you know how to do it technically and you trust the sellers as you pay money in advance.

9. Why have mobile phones made our life easier?

Between the 1980s and the 2000s, the mobile phone has gone from being an expensive item used by business elites to a pervasive, personal communication tool for the general public.

The main advantage of mobile phones is that people can use them anytime and anywhere, especially for an emergency. In addition, people can access the internet whenever they use the mobile phones, so business people can use them at work to get information from the internet more conveniently. Moreover, it is very easy to send messages to your friends. Mobile phones can make people keep informed in spite of long distance. Mobile phones are turning the world into a small village where we can communicate with each other easily and simply.

Our life would be much easier if we could use mobile phones properly. We don't want to get addicted to mobile phones like some people. Nowadays without mobile phones we would feel uncomfortable and our life would be more difficult.

10. Who is the master of our life now, computer or man? Why?

Who is the master of our life now, computer or man? It's really an interesting question. To answer this question, we'd better come up with another one. Who is the master of computer? It is true that we human beings depend heavily on computers, either for work or for entertainment. But we human beings are masters of computers because we make computers, we design computer software and we push the buttons to get computers working for us. We are the masters of computers. There are still lots of things we human beings can do while computers could not do. We can climb mountains on weekends. We can cook delicious food. We can play guitar, piano or any other musical instrument. There are so many things we can do to make our life happy and meaningful, and we don't need computers at all when we are doing those things. Of course, if you work in an office or if you are a student, computers will be very necessary in your career life or your study. But never forget that they are just tools, and the real master of our lives is always man.

Words and Expressions

reserve	v.	保留	dial up connection		拨号连接	
obsessed with		对……着迷	Wi-Fi (Wireless Fidelity)		无线电波联网	
video clip		视频片段			的技术	
resort to		求助于……	facile	adj.	肤浅的	
ICQ (I seek you)		是世界上最流	transferable	adj.	可替换的	
		行的聊天工具，	PDA (Personal		个人数码助	
		网上寻呼机	Digital Assistant)		理，一般是	
voice mail		语音邮件			指掌上电脑	
skype	n.	网络即时语音	outlet	n.	发泄口；出口	
		沟通工具	commodity	n.	商品	
instant messaging		即时消息	pervasive	adj.	极其普遍的	

Part Three: Related Pictures with Suggested Descriptions

Picture One   Newspaper and Information Technology

The advance of mass printing in the 16th century has once brought about magnificent influence to the world both socially and politically. A piece of newspaper in hand, one could be informed of what was happening around the world even without having to get out of his armchair.

Nowadays, however, the role of newspaper is being seriously challenged by the booming IT (Information Technology) industry or World Wide Web, satellites, optic-cables, to name just a few. As a matter of fact, in today's world where nearly everything starts with an "e", newspaper will be replaced by other computer based means.

First of all, newspaper can never match internet in its speed. Actually, information of any kind can be transported digitally at up to 300,000,000 meters per second. In a world of efficiency, newspaper can be defeated for this reason solely.

Besides, with internet, information can be transmitted 3 dimensional, which consists of sound, live show and even interaction. But in paper, only words and photographs can be presented in news stories. Therefore, the former has been made more vivid and descriptive.

Last but not least, computerizing the process of information dissemination provides us with a more objective point of view. Through internet, we can obtain every detail we might want to know, which was sometimes unrevealed by newspapers for this or that reason. Obviously, the more accurate the facts are, the more easily an objective opinion can be formed.

In conclusion, though newspaper is still regarded as indispensable for our daily routines, it cannot match internet in many aspects. After all, one can read news on the web of some press, but he can never surf the internet through just a piece of newspaper.

▶ Picture Two　Internet Today ◀

Before we know it, technology is going to pass us by. With the invention of the computer and the Internet, the possibilities are endless. Society is changing by leaps and bounds, with no chance of a stopping point in the near future. All this change is dealing with computers and the effects that it will have on the way we live tomorrow.

The Internet affects us in every way, most importantly with our social lives, our jobs, and our entertainment. Our social lives are not just communicating with telephones and mail anymore. Going "online" is the new way we like to communicate with people. Chatrooms on the Internet are open for people to talk with other people who may live on the other side of the world. E-Mail is also another popular way to correspond with others. Two seconds to send e-mail to someone on the other side of the world is much quicker than a week or more through the ordinary mail.

The Internet can also affect our jobs. Computers can calculate and figure out things much quicker than the average person. This process cannot only save time, but money too. Stock trading is now on the Internet, along with banking and any other type of business you could imagine. The world wants thing to be quick and easy. The best answer to that is to have a computer do it for you. In the future, hundreds of millions of jobs will be taken away from honest hard-working employees and will be given to computers.

Computers and the Internet are definitely affecting the way we entertain ourselves. On the

Internet, you can play chess and card games, gamble with online casinos, place bets on a horse race, and watch movies and TV series. People can do all of these activities at home. No gas money is wasted or time spent driving around to find entertainment. So people are happy. The inevitable outcome of this magnificent invention is changing the world. Society is happy about the way things are changing. Cheaper is better, less time consuming is better. With the choice of having a computer and being online, there is almost nothing you cannot do. This remarkable idea of the Internet is going to revolutionize the way we live in the future.

Picture Three   Internet and Online Commerce

The Internet has become the largest single form of communication worldwide. With a large number of online individuals, the Internet's boundaries can only be imagined. Often described as "the information superhighway", the internet offers to users a wide variety of services. Any form of communication via the internet is cheaper and rather faster than any service from other facilities. The "internet phone", which is slowly but surely replacing the regular phone, enables anyone to make free long distance calls, through the computer. With the appearance of "streaming" technologies, broadcasting companies and radio stations are transmitting regularly over the internet, which makes them accessible anywhere on the globe.

One of the recent innovations the internet made available is online commerce, which includes online shopping, online banking, online trading and many more. Consumers can effectively dive into an immense range and selection of merchandise, effortlessly compare prices and quickly shop from remote locations. As to online banking, people can, anytime and anywhere, access their bank accounts, pay their bills, transfer their money and even trade their stocks.

The internet is, beyond doubt, the most efficient and economic tool of this era. But, the dark side of the internet reveals some serious drawbacks. First, it was not designed with tight security in mind. This is demonstrated by so-called "crackers" who attack on internet credit card data and many other offenders. Secondly, the internet's structures do not only transport data, but it also transports computer viruses. These artificial clever beasts that destroy data have existed since the very first birth of personal computers. With the growth of the internet, virus authors have been faced up to nothing but a widespread gate to the information superhighway, efficiently supplied with new viruses.

The "information superhighway", as any other invention, has its strengths residing in its popular aspects like the World Wide Web, online commerce. The internet has also its weaknesses, some of which can be very damaging. I believe, however, that these drawbacks will be overcome in time as technology advances.

Words and Expressions

digital	*adj.*	电子		boundary	*n.*	边界
dimensional	*adj.*	维度的		streaming technology		流媒体技术
dissemination	*n.*	传播		accessible	*adj.*	可得到的；可
indispensable	*adj.*	不可缺少的				接触到的
routine	*n.*	惯例；常规		merchandise	*n.*	商品
leaps and bounds		迅速地；突飞		cracker	*n.*	黑客
		猛进地		drawback	*n.*	缺点；弊端
correspond with...		与……联络				
revolutionize	*v.*	（使）发生革命				
		性的（变化）				

Part Four: Related Passages

1. Information Technology and Knowledge Economy

The knowledge society will be a highly competitive one, for organizations and individuals alike. Information technology, although only one of many new features of the next society, is already having one hugely important effect: it is allowing knowledge to spread near-instantly, and making it accessible to everyone. Given the ease and speed at which information travels, every institution in the knowledge society—not only businesses, but also schools, universities, hospitals and increasingly government agencies too—has to be globally competitive, even though most organizations will continue to be local in their activities and in their markets. This is because the Internet will keep customers everywhere informed on what is available anywhere in the world, and at what price.

This new knowledge economy will rely heavily on knowledge workers. At present, this term is widely used to describe people with considerable theoretical knowledge and learning: doctors, lawyers, teachers, accountants, chemical engineers. But the most striking growth will be in "knowledge technologists": computer technicians, software designers, analysts in clinical labs, manufacturing technologists, paralegals. These people are as much manual workers and they are knowledge workers; in fact, they usually spend far more time working with their hands than with their brains, but their manual work is based on a substantial amount of theoretical knowledge which can be acquired only through formal education, not through an apprenticeship. They are not, as a rule, much better paid than traditional skilled workers, but they see themselves as "professionals", just as unskilled manual workers in manufacturing were the dominant social and political force in the 21st century, knowledge technologists are likely to become the dominant social—and perhaps also political—force over the next decades.

2. Internet—A Mixed Blessing

The Internet is a wonderful place of entertainment and education. But like all places used by millions of people, it has some murky corners people would prefer children not to explore. In the physical world, society as a whole wants to protect children, but there are no social or physical constraints to Internet surfing. The Internet Censorship Bill of 1995, also known as the Exon/Coats Communications Decency Act, has been introduced in the U.S. Congress. It would make it a criminal offense to make available to children anything that is indecent, or to send anything indecent with intent to annoy, abuse, threaten, or harass. The goal of this bill is to try to make all public discourse on the Internet suitable for young children.

The Internet was originally a place for people to freely express their ideas worldwide. Ordinary people use the Net for communication, expressing their opinions, or obtaining up-to-date information from the World Wide Web (WWW). Internet users can broadcast or express anything they want. The fact that the Net has no single authority figure sets forth a problem about what kind of materials could be available on the Net.

Another crucial Internet crime is the theft of credit card numbers. Companies do business on the Net, and credit card numbers are stored on their servers; everyone with the necessary computer knowledge could hack in and obtain such databases for illegal purposes. To cite an instance, the most infamous computer terrorist, Kevin Mitnick, charged with computer fraud and illegal use of a telephone access device.

The issue of whether is it necessary to have censorship on the Internet is being argued all over the world. It is true that we need to control the internet. But can censorship get rid of the harms of internet without violating people's freedom to speech? After all, the freedom of idea expression is what makes the Internet important and enjoyable, and it should not be waived for any reason.

3. E-commence Just Starts in China

The idea that only younger generations can profit from the Internet is baseless.

Xu Qixin was 60 when he retired from a State-owned company five years ago. He then opened his own glass fibre business and increased its value from US$165,000 to US$2.3 million. Perhaps the most remarkable thing is that he did it all online.

The Yangzhou resident barely knows how to use a computer, however.

Everyday an employee prints out online business inquiries from Alibaba.com, China's largest B2B portal, so Xu can type them out.

"I don't know how to use computers, but I do know how e-commerce can help my business," says Xu, who now has long-term partners in nine countries.

Hundreds of such online businessmen earlier this month gathered at the China Internet Summit, hosted by Alibaba on September 10 in Hangzhou, capital of East China's Zhejiang Province. Their success stories show that e-commence is big business in China, not just a passing trend. The significance of expanding e-commerce can contribute to improved efficiency and enlarge economies, because business opportunities abound on the Internet.

There are now 20 million e-commerce businesses in China, according to sources with the China Electronic Commerce Association (CECA).

Song Ling, head of the association, says people engaged in e-commerce in China range from chief executive officers (CEOs) with sales in the millions (of dollars) to individuals operating online stores that may only conduct one or two sales in a year.

Internet users in China, comparatively speaking, are very young. They are now university students or recent graduates, so within three to five years they will become affluent consumers. Patience is the way to make money here.

The domestic Internet market is still young, so we need to invest our money in developing it. The Chinese e-commerce company currently has about 200,000 customers in Europe, with a large portion of those located in the United Kingdom. Thus the future of e-commence in China is rather bright.

4. The Online Media Should Protect People's Legitimate Rights

The online media has the advantage of enabling the free flow of information at high speed and at low cost. Websites and bloggers in China are using this to expand their influence and reap profits. Yet in their fierce competition to grab the attention of Web browsers, they seem to have ignored the fact that there should be a limit to the kind of information they put out and spread online.

A recent case has shown that websites do not bother to ask themselves if the information they put online should be made public in the first place. On Nov 16, a thread titled "All you need to know about the 50 beauties at Nanchang University" was posted on the internet, one of China's biggest interactive entertainment portals. It provided names, photographs, ages, subjects of study, addresses, phone numbers and online chatroom IDs of the girls at the university.

Within two days, the thread appeared on the front pages of major websites and stayed there for quite some time. It gained more than 100,000 hits the first day it was posted on Tianya, a major Chinese online forum. It also ranked No.3 as the most searched for topic on the Baidu search engine this week.

The consequence, however, has resulted in nothing but harassment for the girls. They have been bombarded with phone calls, text messages, emails and visits to their dorms since their personal information was disclosed on the Web. They have unwittingly become public figures. They are the latest victims of the online media striving to increase website traffic by hook or by crook. They have increased their hits at the expense of these girls.

Invasion of privacy has become a prevailing problem on the Web. The Nanchang University girls are a case in point.

The online media has been criticized for spreading information that infringes upon a person's legal right to privacy. It is true that the Internet's strength lies in sharing of information. Yet what kind of information should be shared and how much of that information should be revealed remains the question. The protection of people's privacy as an important part of personal rights should be extended to the virtual world. A law is urgently needed to lay down the legal foundation to track down and punish violators and protect people's legitimate rights.

5. Weblogs

For the last two years or so, so-called Weblogs have slowly built a following among Internet users who like to dash off a few random thoughts, post them on a Web site and read similar musings by others. In the last two months, the universe of Weblogs has grown more quickly, with mainstream media analysts praising "blogs", as the sites are known, for bringing a new type of expression to the Internet.

The technology behind Weblogs makes it easier to post a few lines of text at a time, so instead of feeling obligated to compose a tome, before going through the sometimes arduous task of updating a Web site built with conventional home page software, bloggers can fire off thoughts on a whim, click a button and quickly have them appear on a site.

The result is that Weblogs frequently look like online diaries, with brief musings about the days' events, and perhaps a link or two of interest. Some bloggers include daily notes from novels in progress; others rant about the president or the television networks, to whoever might be listening.

Web logs differ from old-fashioned personal home pages in their emphasis on regular updates with brief entries. The most ambitious Web logs provide a view of the Web and the world through the eyes of a curious and avid surfer, offered up for anyone who might share the same tastes and interests. When these Web loggers come across an interesting article or a particularly beautiful, funny or obscure site, they link to it, adding their own comments.

Web logs are elaborately cross-linked, with Web loggers reading and commenting upon one another's sites, creating a kind of fragmented conversation. But a personal Web log is, in the end, a private playground, a place for self-expression without the criticism and hostility that can flame up in online forums.

Create a Web page. Update it regularly with brief personal reflections or witty commentary, sprinkled with links to other pages. Put new entries at the top of the page, pushing older ones down. You've got yourself a Web log.

Topic Fifteen   Culture

Part One: Dialogues

◆ Dialogue 1   Establishment of New Holidays

(Anne enters Li's room, while Li is packaging for the weekend holiday.)

Anne: You are leaving? Where are you heading for?

Li: I'm going back home. This year I finally get a chance to go back to join my family's tomb-sweeping.

Anne: Are you going to sweep your ancestral tombs?

Li: Yeah. This is our Chinese tradition. Around Qing Ming Festival, every family is supposed to show their respect for their departed family members.

Anne: Oh, I see a lot of chrysanthemum sold in flower shops recently.

Li: We used to bring cracks, food, wine and paper money to tombs. Now for the sake of environmental protection, we begin to use flowers to express our feelings.

Anne: Does every Chinese family observe the tradition?

Li: It's hard to say; but it's a tradition in most part of China. Besides, it is bright in late spring and the air is fresh. The grass has turned green and peach trees, plum trees and pear trees are in blossom. People feel comfortable when they go outing in the countryside.

Anne: Indeed.

Li: Before the new calendar of holidays, we were not off on Qing Ming Festival.

Anne: They say that in June we will have another holiday called Dragon Boat Festival. Could you tell me what particular tradition is related to this holiday?

Li: You mean the Double Fifth Festival? The festival was originally held to the memory of the ancient patriotic poet called *Qu Yuan*. When his country was defeated in a war by the neighboring country, he drowned himself in despair on the fifth day of the fifth lunar month. So when the people of his country knew the news, they rushed from all over, rowing dragon boats on the river in an attempt to find his remains. Meanwhile, people throw *Zongzi* into the river to feed fish to keep *Qu Yuan's* remains from being bitten by fish.

Anne: What a beautiful tale!

Li: Did you taste *Zongzi*, the rice wrapped up with weed leaves?

Anne: Not yet.

Li: My mom makes Zongzi every year. And in my county, we have a dragon race. I want to invite you to come to my hometown to experience a real Chinese dragon boat festival if you are interested in it.

Anne: Oh, you mean it? It's so nice of you to have invited me. I can't wait!

◆ Dialogue 2　Culture Shock

(Winter vacation is coming. Li plans to go back to her hometown to celebrate the Spring Festival with her family)

Li: I am looking forward to going back to my hometown. Do you want to go along with me and have a real Spring Festival?

Anne: I'd love to, but …

Li: What's that?

Anne: I haven't lived in any Chinese family before. I am afraid that I could probably be in for a cultural shock. I would make myself a scene in your family.

Li: But you don't have to worry about that. People in different countries have different customs. You'll get used to ours soon.

Anne: I studied Chinese culture before I came to China. I know that in China, before entering their houses, guests must take off their shoes.

Li: Well, you might be right. It is true in some parts of China. China is a big country and has different customs in different regions. Take taking off shoes as an example. In my hometown we rarely take off our shoes before entering our friends' and relatives' houses.

Anne: I know that when they have a drink in a Chinese family, guests should leave a little in their glass to show that their have had enough. However, in my country we always finish it or eat up food to show that we have enjoyed it.

Li: If you finish everything in your bowl hosts will give you more no matter whether you're full or not. Aha aha, that is because our Chinese are very hospitable and hosts are afraid that their guests haven't enjoyed the drink and the food to their hearts' content.

Anne: Oh, I see.

Li: Actually, there is a difference between Chinese and Western concepts of personal privacy.

Anne: What do you mean?

Li: Until recent years our Chinese had only a vague idea of personal privacy. For some Chinese, a person's age, income or marital status is no secret at all. On the contrary, in some small cities, these are topics to start a conversation between strangers.

Anne: How weird! Why do Chinese people treat their personal privacy like this?

Li: Maybe this is because Chinese people are used to communal life and big families, where everything is shared and nothing is private. So if you are asked about your age, income or marital status, don't get offended. People are just trying to be concerned about you.

Anne: Thank you for telling me so much. I'll try to be a good guest when I visit your family.

Words and Expressions

tomb-sweeping	*n.*	扫墓	make a scene		出洋相
chrysanthemum	*n.*	菊花	hospitable	*adj.*	好客的
in blossom		盛开	do sth. to one's hearts' content		
Dragon Boat Festival		端午节			尽情地做某事
weed leave		棕叶	marital status		婚姻状况
be in for		将要遭遇（不愉快的事）	get offended		感到受冒犯
			communal	*adj.*	公共的；公用的
cultural shock		文化撞击；文化休克			

Part Two: Related Questions with Suggested Answers

1. What are some of the main characteristics of western culture?

Well, I think there are so many characteristics of the western culture. In general, the main characteristics of the western culture can be known from some core ideals and values. They include individualism, happiness, rights, capitalism.

Individualism means emphasis on the individual person. Westerners embrace individualism because they believe that the individual has the ability to reason. A group of people does not have the ability to reason, strictly speaking. Only the individuals comprising the group do because all perception and thought takes place within the individual mind.

Another characteristic is happiness. To westerners, happiness is a fundamental and lasting sense of joy that results from achieving personally meaningful and rational values. To pursuit one's own happiness is to pursue one's own interests, one's own success and one's own well-being.

Next, westerners value rights which might include right to liberty, property and the pursuit of happiness.

Furthermore, western culture values capitalism. Capitalism is characterized by capital accumulation, exchange and money, the profit motive, the freedoms of economic competition and economic inequality, the price system, economic progress.

2. What are some of the main characteristics of Chinese culture?

Well, firstly, Chinese culture is based on collectivism. People in a collectivistic culture place country and family above their ownself. Secondly, Chinese culture is based on humanism and people. The Chinese government gives its primary consideration to the ordinary people, thinking about their well-being and interests. Thirdly, to resolve the relationship between man and nature, Chinese culture values the unity of man and "heaven" as one. Fourthly, to resolve human relationship, Chinese people value ethics and tolerance. Fifthly, Chinese culture focuses on "mean". "Mean" in Chinese culture refers to "middle way". One doesn't have to go to extreme. Peace and harmony are always honored.

3. What is individualism?

Well, individualism is the moral stance, political philosophy, ideology, or social outlook that stresses independence and self-reliance. Individualism holds that the individual is the primary unit of reality and the ultimate standard of value. Individualism emphasizes privacy, competition, individual interest and so on. Individualists promote the exercise of one's goals and desires, while opposing most external interference upon one's choices, whether by society, or any other group or institution. Individualism is opposed to collectivism, which stresses that communal, community, group, societal, or national goals should take priority over individual goals.

4. What is collectivism?

Well, collectivism is the opposite concept of individualism. Collectivism holds that the group—the nation, the community, the race, etc.—is the primary unit of reality and the ultimate standard of value. This view does not deny the reality of the individual, but ultimately holds that one's identity is determined by the groups one interacts with, that one's identity is constituted essentially by relationships with others. Collectivism emphasizes interdependence, intimacy, harmony, group interest and so on. And collectivism is a main character of eastern cultures.

5. What is a stereotype? How do we avoid it in intercultural communication?

Well, stereotype is a categorization that mentally organizes our experiences and guides our behavior toward a particular group of people. Stereotyping is a means of organizing our images into fixed and simple categories that we use to stand for the entire collection of people. When we say women are "homemakers" and "Jews are shrewd" we are producing stereotypes. Stereotyping is found in nearly every intercultural situation, and sometimes, it deeply hampers intercultural communication. So in intercultural communication, we should try our best to avoid it. We should specify individual characteristics in stead of assuming that all members of a group have exactly the same traits. We should not over-simplify, over-generalize, or exaggerate some characters of a certain culture.

6. What are some of the differences in the food that westerners and Chinese people have?

Well, in China, we prefer noodles, rice, jiaozi as the main course. We like cooking a lot of delicious dishes. Then we set up tables and put dishes on the tables. And then we sit together and taste the dishes we have made together. We don't eat with individual plates. While eating, we like chatting and laughing, and we think it's a great fun to eat this way.

In western countries, people like having hamburgers, chips, pizza, and pasta as their main course. They eat them with vegetable, salad and also with drinks (wine, juice or water). They eat with separate plates. After they finish meals, they will still have desserts.

7. Why do English teachers attach more importance to culture learning in teaching English?

Well, English teachers attach more importance to culture learning in teaching English because culture learning can help students learn English more effectively. As we all know, language is closely related to culture. Language expresses and embodies cultural reality. If we are in different countries, we must know their cultures. Then, we can use the language freely. On the other hand, language, as a product of culture, helps perpetuate the culture, and the changes in language uses reflect the culture changes in return.

8. What are some of the Chinese traditional values?

Well, I think Chinese traditional values are mostly specified in orthodox version of Confucianism. These traditional values include tolerance of others, harmony with others, solidarity with others, non-competitiveness, trustworthiness, contentedness, modesty, filial piety, chastity in women, intimate friendship and so on.

9. Why should we respect cultural diversity in intercultural communication?

Now we are living in a modern world. Our world has some 6,000 communities and as many distinct languages. Such difference naturally leads to diversity of vision, values, beliefs, practice and expression, which all deserve equal respect and dignity.

Cultural diversity is our everyday reality. The international migration rate is growing fast every year. Immigrants move to other countries for different reasons. They might be economic or political or out of personal choice. But one thing is sure that we now live in an increasingly heterogeneous society.

Cultural diversity reflects the respect of fundamental rights. Culture encompasses, in addition to art and literature, lifestyles, ways of living together, values systems, traditions and

beliefs. Respecting and safeguarding culture is a matter of human rights. Cultural diversity presupposes respect of fundamental freedoms, namely freedom of thought, conscience and religion, freedom of opinion and expression, and freedom to participate in the cultural life of one's choice.

Cultural diversity is our collective strength. It is about plurality of knowledge, wisdom and energy which all contribute to improving and moving the world forward.

10. How do we work more effectively with the staff with foreign cultural backgrounds?

Now there are more and more multinational companies in China. In these companies we have staff from different cultural backgrounds. In order to work more effectively with them, first of all, we should develop an intercultural awareness. We should understand social values, social customs, social norms, and social systems. Secondly develop behavioral flexibility. Learn to select an appropriate behavior in different contexts and situations. Perform different behavioral strategies in order to achieve communication goals. Thirdly communicate with the staff with different cultural backgrounds as much as possible. Feel comfortable while interacting with them.

Words and Expressions

individualism	n.	个人主义	exaggerate	v.	夸大
embrace	v.	接受；采纳	hamburger	n.	汉堡包
comprise	v.	包括；包含	pasta	n.	意大利面食
capital accumulation		资金积累	dessert	n.	甜点
collectivism	n.	集体主义	perpetuate	v.	（使）长存；（使）
mean	n.	中间			永恒
stance	n.	姿态	orthodox version		正统版本
ultimate	adj.	最终的	Confucianism	n.	儒家思想
primary	adj.	主要的	solidarity	n.	团结；一致
priority	n.	优先考虑的事情	contentedness	n.	心满意足
intimacy	n.	亲密	filial piety		孝顺
stereotype	n.	老一套；模式化	chastity	n.	贞洁
		的思想	heterogeneous	adj.	不同的；多元的
categorization	n.	概括	encompass	v.	包括
category	n.	范畴；种属	presuppose	v.	意味着
hamper	v.	阻碍	conscience	n.	良心
trait	n.	特性；品质	plurality	n.	大量
over-generalize	v.	过度概括	appropriate	adj.	合适的；适宜的

Part Three: Related Pictures with Suggested Descriptions

Picture One   Chinese Knots

Well, this is a traditional Chinese decorative knot, also known as Chinese knot. It is a distinctive and traditional Chinese folk handicraft woven separately from onc piece of thread and named according to its shape and meaning.

Chinese knot is a symbol of traditional Chinese culture. In China, "knot" means everything can be connected together, so it represents reunion, friendliness, peace, warmth, marriage, love and so on. Chinese knots are often used to express good wishes, including happiness, prosperity, love and the absence of evil. Chinese people have known how to tie knots using cords thousands of years ago, and as civilization advanced, Chinese knots has come in many forms. The endless variations and elegant patterns of the Chinese knot, as well as different materials that can be used, have expanded the functions and widened the applications of the Chinese knot. Jewelry, clothes, gift-wrapping and furniture can be accentuated with unique Chinese knot creations. Large Chinese knot wall hangings have the same decorative value as fine paintings or photographs, and are perfectly suitable for decorating a living-room or study.

The Chinese knot, with its classic elegance and ever-changing variations, is both practical and ornamental, fully reflecting the grace and depth of Chinese culture.

Picture Two   Christianity and Western Culture

Well, to some extent, Christianity is the religion that includes the largest number of the people in the world. It is originated from the East while lots of people think it is just a big part of western culture. Every phase of man's life is touched by this religion, and it has become part and parcel of western culture. This is no doubt that Christianity influences western culture more than any other culture. It says that if people don't know about Christianity, they wouldn't know western culture.

Christianity has been a major influence in forming western culture during the last millennium. Christianity has fostered education, art, literature, law and science. There are many Christian festivals in the western world, and Christmas is the biggest festival in most western countries. So it is reasonable to argue that the West would not achieve its ascendancy without this support. The universities that emerged during the late Middle Ages were originally religious institutions. Their primary purpose was to train clergy, but while doing so they became centers for the development of literacy and intellectual enquiry. These great learning institutions would not have been possible without the financial resources of the Church to support them.

In the development of western culture, the Church didn't always plant the seed, but it did plow the paddock.

Picture Three   Intercultural Communication

Well, intercultural communication usually refers to the communication of two cultures or two languages across the political boundaries of a nation—one culture—one language, and on the national boundaries. But intercultural communication may also refer to communication between people from different ethnic, social, gendered cultures within the boundaries of the same national language. For example, whether negotiating a

major contract with the American, discussing a joint venture with a German company, being supervised by someone of a different gender, counseling, a young student from another city, working alongside someone who doesn't speak English, or interviewing a member of a co-culture for a new position, we all encounter people with cultural backgrounds different from our own. These are all called intercultural communications.

Intercultural communication, well, as you might suspect, is not new. Wandering nomads, religious missionaries, and conquering warriors have encountered people different from themselves since the beginning of time. Those meetings were frequently confusing and quite often hostile. In ancient times, the recognition of alien differences lacked accompanying cultural knowledge and often elicited the human propensity to respond malevolently to those differences. Today's intercultural encounters are more common and differ from earlier meetings. They are more abundant and, because of the interconnectedness of the world, more significant. We can now board a plane and fly anywhere in the world in a matter of hours, and the reality of a global economy makes today's contacts far more commonplace than in any other period of the world's history.

Words and Expressions

decorative	*adj.*	装饰性的	literacy	*adj.*	文化的
cord	*n.*	粗绳	paddock	*n.*	小牧场
wrap	*v.*	包裹	gendered	*adj.*	分性别的
accentuate	*v.*	强调；着重指出	venture	*n.*	企业；公司
elegance	*n.*	优雅	counseling	*n.*	辅导
ornamental	*adj.*	装饰性的	interview	*v.*	面试
Christianity	*n.*	基督教	wander	*v.*	漫游；游荡
part and parcel		是……不可缺的一部分	nomad	*n.*	游牧部落的成员
			warrior	*n.*	武士；士兵
millennium	*n.*	一千年	hostile	*adj.*	敌意的
foster	*v.*	养育	elicit	*v.*	引发
ascendancy	*n.*	上升	malevolently	*adv.*	恶毒地
clergy	*n.*	牧师			

Part Four: Related Passages

1. Cultural Shock

The term, culture shock, was introduced for the first time in 1958 to describe the anxiety produced when a person moves to a completely new environment. This term expresses the lack of direction, the feeling of not knowing what to do or how to do things in a new environment, and not knowing what is appropriate or inappropriate. The feeling of culture shock generally sets in after the first few weeks of coming to a new place.

We can describe culture shock as the physical and emotional discomfort one suffers when coming to live in another country or a place different from the place of origin. Often, the way that we lived before is not accepted as or considered as normal in the new place. Everything is different, for example, not speaking the language, not knowing how to use banking machines, not knowing how to use the telephone and so forth.

The symptoms of cultural shock can appear at different times. Although, one can experience real pain from culture shock; it is also an opportunity for redefining one's life objectives. It is a great opportunity for learning and acquiring new perspectives. Culture shock can make one develop a better understanding of oneself and stimulate personal creativity.

Culture shock has many stages. In the first stage, the new arrival may feel pleased by all of the new things encountered. This time is called the "honeymoon" stage. Afterwards, the second stage presents itself. In this stage, there may be feelings of discontent, impatience, anger, sadness and feeling incompetence. This happens when a person is trying to adapt to a new culture that is very different from the culture of origin. The third stage is characterized by gaining some understanding of the new culture. In the fourth stage, the person realizes that the new culture has good and bad things to offer. The fifth stage is the stage called the "re-entry shock". This occurs when a return to the country of origin is made. One may find that things are no longer the same. These stages are present at different times and each person has their own way of reacting in the stages of culture shock.

2. Understanding Culture

Culture is an essential part of conflict and conflict resolution. Cultures are like underground rivers that run through our lives and relationships, giving us messages that shape our perceptions, attributions, judgments, and ideas of self and other. Though cultures are powerful, they are often unconscious, influencing conflict and attempts to resolve conflict in imperceptible ways.

Cultures are more than language, dress, and food customs. Cultural groups may share race, ethnicity, or nationality, but they also arise from cleavages of generation, socioeconomic class, sexual orientation, ability and disability, political and religious affiliation, language, and gender— to name only a few.

Two things are essential to remember about cultures: they are always changing, and they relate to the symbolic dimension of life. The symbolic dimension is the place where we are constantly making meaning and enacting our identities. Cultural messages from the groups we belong to give us information about what is meaningful or important, and who we are in the world and in relation to others—our identities.

Cultural messages, simply, are what everyone in a group knows that outsiders do not know. They are the water fish swim in, unaware of its effect on their vision. They are a series of lenses that shape what we see and don't see, how we perceive and interpret, and where we draw boundaries. In shaping our values, cultures contain starting points and currencies. Starting points are those places it is natural to begin, whether with individual or group concerns, with the big picture or particularities. Currencies are those things we care about that influence and shape our interactions with others.

3. Smile Is Not Always Good

With the increase of contact and communication across cultures, people are more and more aware of cultural differences and the importance of understanding these differences. However, we tend to neglect some aspects of communication such as facial expressions. Smiling, for example, is taken for granted to be similar because "the whole world smiles". This failure to recognize the cultural differences of smiling often leads to unexpected cultural conflicts. The following true story is about how a mistaken perception of a smile made an awkward situation worse.

Peter was the general manager of an American company in China. Jun Chen, one of the Chinese managers, has made a serious mistake at work. He was very upset about what had happened and came to Peter's office to make a formal apology. Jun Chen told Peter how sorry he was with a smile he had been wearing since he walked into the office. But Peter refused to accept the apology because Jun Chen didn't look sorry at all. Seeing Peter getting angry, Jun Chen was desperate to make him understood. With a smile even broader than before, he said, "Peter, trust me, no one can feel any sorrier than I do about it." Peter was almost furious, "If you're that sorry, how can you still smile?"

This story shows that people from Eastern and Western countries may interpret a smile in quite different ways. Though the act of smiling is a universal facial expression, it is cultural-specific in that the amount of smiling and the stimulus that triggers the smile often vary from culture to culture.

4. Some English Wedding Traditions

The English have a great many wedding traditions, and some can be dated back to pagan times. An old rhyme was recited to assist couples who were planning their big day: Monday for wealth, Tuesday for health, Wednesday the best day of all, Thursday for losses, Friday for crosses, Saturday for no luck at all.

In spite of access to divorce and the gradual social acceptance of living together outside wedlock, marriage remains highly valued in England. In fact, numerous traditions surrounding the wedding ceremony are still observed to this day. One of the most popular traditions is: under no circumstances should a bride be seen by the groom in her wedding dress before the ceremony takes place.

According to a popular Victorian rhyme, it is considered good luck for the bride to wear "something old, something borrowed and something blue" on her big day.

It is customary for the groom to carry his bride over the threshold when they enter their home as a married couple for the first time.

5. Some Muslim Wedding Traditions

A Muslim marriage and subsequently a Muslim wedding is a weaving together of families, of two souls, and of two destinies. It's considered as a big and very auspicious occasion in all cultures of the world. Different cultures have different wedding traditions and ceremonies, and every culture has its own treasure of wedding ceremonies, wedding customs and rituals.

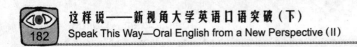

Weddings in various Muslim countries follow their respective cultural traditions. Some are more Islamic while others have adopted norms that are in the values of various cultures. Various cultures have introduced more ceremonies in the Muslim marriage and matrimonial process.

Brides are decorated and beautified in various ways for weddings. For example, in the Indian subcontinent (India, Pakistan and Bangladesh) traditions, Mehndi or Henna as it is called has a great significance. The brides are decorated both on the bride's hands and feet. In some Middle Eastern countries such as Morocco, it has a ceremonial bath a few days before the wedding and is decorated with henna and jewelry. Other countries vary in their celebrations of weddings.

Most weddings in Islamic and Arab cultures could become very expensive affairs. Hundreds and sometimes thousands of guests are not unheard of. Large spaces or hotels are rented to accommodate such a large gathering of guests. The bride is also decorated with very expensive jewelry. 22K gold is quite common that includes bracelets, ear rings, and jewelry for the head (worn over the wedding shawl).

Families that are more conservative Islamic usually avoid such lavish weddings as it is considered an unnecessary expense. More prefer instead to pay the amount to the bride and the groom to help them start their family.